F Nagorski, Andrew
N Last Stop to Vienna

DATE DUE

Also by Andrew Nagorski

The Birth of Freedom:
Shaping Lives and Societies in the
New Eastern Europe

Reluctant Farewell:
An American Reporter's Candid Look
Inside the Soviet Union

Last Stop Vienna

A Novel

ANDREW NAGORSKI

Simon & Schuster

New York London Toronto Sydney Singapore

SIMON & SCHUSTER
Rockefeller Center
1230 Avenue of the Americas
New York, NY 10020

This book is a work of fiction. Names, characters, places, and incidents
either are products of the author's imagination or are used fictitiously.

For information about special discounts for bulk purchases,
please contact Simon & Schuster Special Sales:
1-800-456-6798 or business@simonandschuster.com

Manufactured in the United States of America

1   3   5   7   9   10   8   6   4   2

Library of Congress Cataloging-in-Publication Data
Andrew Nagorski.
Last stop Vienna : a novel / Andrew Nagorski.
p. cm.
1. Germany—History—1918–1933—Fiction. 2. Hitler, Adolf, 1889–1945—Fiction.
3. Raubal, Geli, 1908–1931—Fiction. 4. Vienna (Austria)—Fiction. I. Title.
PS3614.A48 L37 2003
813'.54—dc21   2002030214
ISBN 0-7432-3750-1

ACKNOWLEDGMENTS

I owe many people thanks for helping me with advice or information at various stages of writing this novel. I want to mention in particular Claire Gerus, Janusz Glowacki, David Satter, Agatha Dominik, Agnieszka Holland, Susan Szeliga and Robby Lantz. My apologies to those whom I left out for brevity's sake.

It is customary to thank agents and editors, but there is nothing routine about the debt of gratitude I owe to Marshall Klein, my agent, and Alice Mayhew, my editor. Marshall's enthusiasm for this project was infectious when I needed it the most. I, of course, knew about Alice's legendary reputation as an editor, but I wasn't prepared for her to easily surpass my expectations, which she did from day one. I also want to thank her associate, Anja Schmidt, who performs the astonishing feat of keeping up with her.

My editors at *Newsweek,* especially the late Maynard Parker, made it possible for me to spend several years living and reporting from Germany, which allowed me to embark on the research for this book. *Danke.*

And then there's my family. They lived with my earliest ruminations about the premise for the book, and everyone contributed ideas, suggestions and, most of all, unfailing support. That includes my parents, Marie and Zygmunt; my children, Eva, Sonia, Adam and Alexander; and my wife, Christina. In Berlin and back in New York, Christina—or Krysia, as she is known—was not only my in-house editor and critic but also, as always, the person who made me feel that everything was possible. With her remarkable gifts, it is. Eva took over the job of first reader, first morale booster, first promoter. When we were on opposite sides of the Atlantic, I sometimes felt that her e-mail responses were flashing back even before my latest draft of a chapter could have reached her. I couldn't have done this book without her constant input, humor and love.

For my daughter Eva

Last Stop Vienna

Preface

No one would have noticed anything unusual about the young man on the tram that morning in late September. He sat straight in his seat, looking intently out the smudged window, watching for his stop as the tram clattered its way from Vienna's ring road past the Belvedere Palace and the factories and shops on the city's outskirts.

He was wearing rumpled dark pants, a white shirt, a thin tie and a worn poplin jacket. When he took off his hat, there was something about his face—hazel eyes, straight, narrow nose and full lips—that caught the eye of several young women who got on and off during his ride. His chin displayed a day's worth of still boyish stubble, and his curly brown hair was tousled.

Not that the young man noticed. When the long, high brick wall of the Central Cemetery came into view, he rose abruptly and asked something of an old woman who was clutching a bunch of fading tulips. He remained standing until the next stop, where he got off, carrying a small bag.

The young man stood for a moment in front of the imposing gate flanked by two large pillars. As he stepped onto the cemetery grounds, he gazed at the administration building. A breeze stirred the cool morning air, and he drew his light jacket around him. He went inside for a couple of minutes and then quickly made for the cemetery chapel a few hundred yards away.

A thin, balding priest emerged from the chapel and headed for the main gate. The young man intercepted him, doffed his hat and spoke briefly. The priest pointed to the right of the entrance and continued on his way.

The young man stood still, then turned in the direction the priest had indicated and walked briskly down a path deeper into the cemetery, passing rows of old graves before reaching an area with several new ones. He stopped in front of one with a freshly carved headstone set on packed earth.

He dropped to one knee, his head bent. His lips moved. He lowered his other knee to the ground. At the same moment, there was a commotion at the main gate. An important person seemed to be arriving, with a bodyguard on either side. They set off on the same path the young man had traveled.

He stood up and saw them approaching. They were still far off and hadn't noticed him. He moved away, placing himself between the fresh and old graves, keeping his head down as he circled around the three men. He crouched behind a large headstone close to the path. His eyes were locked on the men as he reached into the bag he had placed at his feet. He drew out a gun, a Browning, and shoved it under his jacket, keeping a grip on it.

The focus of his attention—so intense that it seemed almost certain one of the men would feel it—was the least imposing of the trio, leading the way. The man's short black hair was slicked back and parted on the right side. His eyes radiated unfocused energy from beneath equally dark eyebrows. A bushy, odd mustache appeared to prop up his nose, barely spreading wider than his nostrils. He wore a trench coat fastened off center with a belt that accentuated his modest but unmistakable middle-aged paunch. He, too, appeared lost in his thoughts.

Particularly when he reached the grave that the young man had just left. As his bodyguards paced, the man stood with his back to them, almost perfectly still. But once or twice his head jerked back and forth, and another time his shoulders twitched as if an electric current had jolted his body.

The bodyguards tensed as the man finally turned away from the grave. He took a few halting steps and stumbled slightly. One of the burly men rushed up to help, but the man shook him off and issued a command. What happened next was a blur. The bodyguard shot out his right arm in a salute and conferred briefly with his colleague, who ran back toward the main gate. The other one followed at a slower pace, clearing the path ahead of an approaching elderly couple. The man with the mustache trailed at a distance. He drew even with the young man behind the headstone. The young man stepped onto the path to face him, looking as determined as the other looked surprised. He raised the Browning and pointed it at the man's chest.

Chapter One

Why have I been writing it all down, keeping this journal? Tomorrow when I walk out of prison after serving seven of the ten years the Austrians sentenced me to, I'll take it with me, but I doubt I'll ever show it to anyone. If someone does eventually read it, it will probably be long after I'm gone. For now my only hope, if you can call it that, is to be left alone, to try to stop my deed from following me for the rest of my life. But even if I succeed, I will always be haunted by my memories of Geli.

I wrote simply because I had to write. Because during these seven years I could never stop thinking about her, seeing her, dreaming about her, longing for her. I couldn't stop wondering whether anything could have turned out differently, whether I made some horrible mistake. I don't know. I do know that even if I had managed to save Geli from him somehow, she probably wouldn't have wanted to stay with me. In this journal, at least, I have brought her back, and I have her all to myself. Some consolation, but better than none at all.

I can make a pretty good guess when it all began, when fate or whatever you want to call it began pushing me toward the path I took, toward the chain of events that would eventually lead me here to my small prison cell, where I have all the time in the world to remember and, presumably, reflect. I've never been very good at that, at reflection. But I have thought enough about what happened to know that I can't just start with Geli, with our first meeting. I have to go back further, much further. To November 9, 1918, to be exact.

I was only fifteen then, but it's a day that will always remain precisely etched in my memory.

The rumors that it was all over had been circulating around town for weeks. The Great War, the war we had all entered so cheerfully, thinking it'd be a short, triumphant adventure, was sputtering to an ignoble end. Four years of bloodshed, four years of death, millions of deaths, and what did we have to show for it? I wasn't yet ready to concede the obvious: that the answer was nothing. Or worse than nothing, since the war had destroyed more than those lives. It had spawned a sickness of the spirit.

As I crossed the Tiergarten early in the morning, with wet leaves clinging to my shoes and heavy moist air filling my nostrils, I was envisioning the returning troops marching with their heads held high, proud of their heroism. And I was seeing Gerhard marching with them, his mouth twisted in that odd half grin of his, one side curling up and the other pointing down, seemingly at odds. I had awoken with the feeling—no, the firm conviction—that this would be the day he'd finally come home. I knew he'd be coming. Before setting off, I had taken the roll my mother had given me for breakfast, smeared it with a precious bit of lard, wrapped it in a rag and jammed it into the pocket of my threadbare coat. Gerhard might be hungry.

We hadn't heard from my older brother since September, a month after he was called up. But in the confusion of those times, we didn't necessarily know what that meant. Or didn't want to know. It wasn't like my father, whose death had been reported two years earlier. By 1918 you couldn't count on much news.

No one knew for sure when the troops would enter the city, but the Tiergarten was already full of people streaming toward the Brandenburg Gate. Some of the women and little girls were carrying makeshift bouquets or a scraggly flower or two, although it was hard to imagine where they managed to get them. Scratching for food supplies had been hard enough. I hadn't seen milk or cheese for I don't know how long, and my mother and I had survived on turnips when the official rations of bread and meat—usually more gristle—ran out. The bread they gave us was often made from turnips. I had promised myself that when the war was over, I'd never touch a turnip again.

I should have waited for my mother that morning, but as so often lately, I hadn't given any thought to what she must have been feeling. I was angry and disappointed that I had been too young to follow my father and brother to the front; at the same time, I wouldn't admit how much I missed them both. Even my father, schoolteacher that he was, who had kept me at a distance and regularly scolded me, always making me feel that I failed to live up to his expectations. Every so often, after some transgression, he'd pull out a ruler and make me hold out my hand, just as he did with his pupils. The first time he delivered a stinging whack, my mother had come to the door. She said nothing when I cried out. Tears rolling down my cheeks, I looked beseechingly at her. She only dropped her eyes. At that moment I felt angrier with her than I did with my father. I couldn't understand why she hadn't defended me.

I soon learned to hold back the tears, fixing my face in a stony expression, even when my father dispensed with the ruler and slapped me hard across the face. My mother tried to comfort me afterward, but I turned my back on her.

When my father was going off to war, he solemnly instructed me on the need to obey Gerhard and my mother, to act more like a young man, but all I could think was that I'd be free of him for a while. When he appeared at home in full uniform, though, I couldn't believe my eyes. I knew him as a short, pudgy man who sported a handlebar mustache. I tried not to look at the top row of crooked brown teeth and kept as far away as I could from the sour smell of his breath. Now he seemed to stand taller and straighter, his gut no longer very noticeable, his face animated as he talked of certain victory. For the first time in my life, the thought crossed my mind that he was handsome. On the day we learned he had died in the first German assault on Verdun, I was torn by guilt and anger. Had I wished him dead? Was it my fault? Did he get himself killed just to punish me again?

It was then that I began frightening my mother by disappearing after school or skipping school altogether, taking off alone or with other boys from my class who had the same idea. She would come back from cleaning rich people's apartments in Charlottenburg and wait nervously for me to show up. Sometimes I'd return with a bit of stolen food as a peace offering, but that would alarm her more: "What's becoming of you?"

I told her about all the black-marketeers and rich folks who weren't suffering at all. Why, I demanded, should regular people be the only ones to suffer?

"If only your father were still alive, he'd straighten you out."

"You'd like that, wouldn't you? You'd like to watch him beat me."

"No."

"Yes, you would," I shouted. "You never stopped him."

Her voice dropped to a whisper. "You don't understand."

"Yes, I do."

"There was nothing I could do. Your father was a good man, but . . ."

"But what?"

She slumped down in her chair. "I won't, I can't." Her voice faltered. "He's dead, after all."

I briefly felt sorry for her but didn't show it. I kept that stony look I had perfected.

Today was different. Today Gerhard was coming home, and I was rushing to greet him. The sky was slate gray, and most people were wrapped up against the frequent gusts, but I was sweating as I ran through the Tiergarten. Approaching the Brandenburg Gate, I knew something was wrong even before I saw the soldiers marching through and then down Unter den Linden. No one was cheering, I realized, and instead of the sound of boots proudly pounding the road in unison, I could hear only a muffled shuffling.

I pushed my way forward. There wasn't a triumphant soldier to be seen, only exhausted men in torn, filthy uniforms, defeat written on their faces. When girls offered them flowers, they could barely summon the strength to thank them, much less smile. Their eyes had a hollowed-out look. As I cooled down, a shiver went through my body, and I felt hungry. I took out the roll and started nibbling on it, then pulled it away, horrified at what I had done. I had to keep it for Gerhard.

The soldiers' ranks began thinning out, with no sign of Gerhard. I shouted at the hunched figures: "Have you seen Private Gerhard Naumann?" They ignored me or just looked blank. One soldier patted me on the head. "Sorry."

I stood paralyzed for a moment and then raced after him, tugging on his sleeve. "You know him? You know what happened to him?" The soldier shook his head, without looking back. I latched on to his arm and tugged as hard as I could, refusing to let go. "Tell me."

With one swift motion, he sent me reeling, knocking me over on my side. I lay still for a moment, then jerked myself upright, realizing that my coat pocket with the roll was under me. Still in a sitting position, I cautiously reached in and pulled it out. It was a pathetic sight, partly eaten, partly squashed. I threw it into the bushes. I stood up shakily and, changing my mind, tried to retrieve it, growing more and more frantic when I couldn't find it. Pushing the bushes apart, I saw it on the ground, reached for it and stuffed it into my mouth, not pausing to wipe off the dirt that worked itself in between my teeth. Gerhard wasn't coming today, I told myself. I'll get a fresh one later. I tried to spit out the dirt. The aftertaste was all the more disgusting because I hated what I had done.

I was standing almost directly in front of the Adlon Hotel on the other side of the Brandenburg Gate, simultaneously angry and numb. Although I was now resigned to disappointment, I watched the stragglers until the last of them limped by. Just then I saw among the peasant women selling firewood and turnips an elegantly dressed older man in a top hat and morning coat, clutching a large wreath of wildflowers. The wreath fascinated me—where could he have gotten so many flowers? I hadn't seen a wreath like that since before the war. And even then only once, when my father had proudly taken me to a ceremony commemorating German unification.

A younger man approached the wreath bearer and took him gently by the arm, leading him to the hotel entrance. "That's Lorenz Adlon," a policeman sneered, and for the first time I realized that the hotel was named after a person, its owner. "He was waiting to congratulate the kaiser on his great victory. He didn't know he's abdicated and high-tailed it out of here."

"Rich people." Another man laughed. "They'll see what's coming to them."

A couple of weeks later, I came home to find my mother sitting on a stool in the kitchen, her face pale and her eyes red from crying.

I stood in the doorway.

"Yes, it's Gerhard. They say he died in the first battle of his unit." Her voice trailed off, but she summoned the strength to raise her arms to embrace me. I turned around and darted out of the apartment.

I kept running for a long time. I dropped out of school, roaming the streets and picking fights, often not returning home for several days at a stretch, sleeping in stairwells or semiabandoned buildings. I was hardly alone in deciding there wasn't any sense in obeying the rules anymore, in listening to anyone in authority. Berlin in defeat made the chaos of the war years look like a simpler, almost orderly time. Now there weren't just protests and starvation but armed revolts. Snipers perched on rooftops and shot people at random.

In the cafés and restaurants on Potsdamer Platz and in other fashionable quarters, life went on as usual, with most people seemingly oblivious to the anarchy all around them. At night, the cabarets, bars and whorehouses were in full swing. I remember the first time it began to dawn on me that the women and girls, many of them younger than I, were available for a few marks. I found myself gaping at a scraggly redhead, dressed incongruously in a dirndl that made a sumptuous display of her small breasts.

"Something the matter?" she asked, abruptly turning to meet my gaze. "Never seen a girl before?"

I felt my face flush. "No—I mean, yes, I have."

"Then scat."

When I remained frozen in place, she waved her arms: "Scat, scat, scat." This time I managed to propel myself away and afterward was quick to avert my eyes whenever I thought a girl was about to confront me.

On the Kurfürstendamm, which ran through the heart of the richer western part of the city, I was even more careful, not so much of the girls as the young boys with powdered faces who cruised the sidewalks hoping to snare customers.

An older man in a charcoal-gray suit and bowler hat asked me for directions to an elegant restaurant whose classic facade exuded wealth and promised meals I couldn't imagine. I pointed across the street. "It's right there."

He smiled and raised his hat. "Of course. Strange I didn't notice it. Would you care to join me for dinner?"

I was ravenous, but even on an empty stomach, I realized that dinner wouldn't come free. A wave of nausea came and quickly went. "No thanks," I muttered.

"Pity," the older man said. But I could see his eyes already surveying the area for other boys.

I kept wandering around the streets, but I felt out of place everywhere. I couldn't blend in, and I couldn't stay away. Not knowing what to do with myself, I took every political pamphlet that was thrust into my hands. The angrier their tone, the more I liked them.

I took a pamphlet from a group that had emerged right after the founding of the Weimar Republic. All I had heard about it was that it was supposed to be full of intellectuals and artists. "Dada," a bearded young man intoned as he handed the flyer to me. "Dada is the future."

I had no idea what he was talking about, but I liked what I read. "We shall blow Weimar sky-high," the pamphlet proclaimed. "Berlin is the place . . . da . . . da . . . Nobody and nothing will be spared. Turn out in masses!" It was signed: "The Dadaist headquarters of World Revolution." It announced a Dada International Exhibition. I stuffed it into my pocket, determined to check it out.

Two days later, on opening day, I was in a cavernous hall in the midst of a rambunctious crowd. There were a lot of young people dressed in loose, flowing clothes, with couples and even threesomes holding each other, hands draped around waists and sometimes casually dropping lower, in a way that fascinated and excited me. There were also more conventional-looking middle-aged men and women who, like me, edged uncertainly forward.

Suddenly, several of the young people laughed loudly and pointed upward. I followed the startled looks of the other spectators. A dummy dressed as a German general was hanging upside down from the ceiling. It took me a couple of seconds to register the fact that it had the head of a pig.

I froze. How could anyone make something that grotesque? This wasn't what Gerhard or Father had died for. I abruptly turned around and began shoving my way through the incoming visitors. A man grabbed me by the arm: "Hey, what do you think you're doing?" I punched him, catching the side of his face and knocking off his glasses. A woman next to him shrieked, and another man grabbed me by my shirt. I kicked him in the groin, and he doubled over. Before anyone could reach me, I was out the door, running. I heard shouts behind me, but I didn't look back.

It was this experience that first taught me a lot of so-called revolutionary intellectuals and artists were simply sick.

No, I wasn't going to go near anyone who might turn a general into a pig.

One afternoon as I was roaming the working-class streets of Neukölln, I ran into Jürgen, Peter and some other boys from school. I had always felt uneasy in their presence, envying their self-confidence and the way they joked among themselves, but I was happy to find company for a change. And even happier to feel accepted during the next several evenings.

But when they began hanging around the girls who were looking for clients, I held back as far as I could without making it obvious. I was convinced that I was the only one of the group who had never been with a woman, which made me all the more anxious to talk as tough as they did so they wouldn't find out.

Jürgen was always teasing the girls and egging us to do the same. They'd tell us to get lost—sometimes angrily, sometimes laughingly, depending on their mood. If they thought we were keeping potential customers away, they really got mad. They were not amused by our boasts that we'd show them "the time of their lives" if they'd only forget about the money.

On a dare from Jürgen, I sidled up to a blond girl with a thick layer of makeup that accentuated her young age; she couldn't have been more than thirteen or fourteen. I gave her a quick pat on the ass, not quite managing the squeeze that Jürgen had pushed for. She tossed me a look of utter contempt.

Jürgen laughed. "You didn't do it, Karl."

"Yes, I did," I insisted lamely.

"You know what I'd have her do to me?"

"The Ulrike treatment," I replied, alluding to his graphic description of how Ulrike, one of the girls in our class who had also dropped out, had allegedly warmed up for night work by "servicing" him. Since none of us had seen Ulrike for months, there was no one around to dispute his claims.

"What about you, Karl?" Peter demanded. "What would you do with that blonde we just saw?"

I paused. "The Erika treatment."

"Who the hell is that?"

"Oh, just someone I know," I said, trying to sound coy. "Someone I know very well." I made a pumping motion with my fist. "From the inside out, as it were."

"Yeah, right," Jürgen jumped in. "You're full of it."

"I mean it."

"Sure you do."

After that I was usually out on my own again. I wanted their company but feared their mockery, wishing there were some way I could be as sure of myself—and believable—as they were.

Late one of those evenings, I started to head home down a quiet side street. I heard a commotion behind me and a shout: "Stop, thief!" I wheeled around and saw a dark figure, his coat flying, running straight at me.

I pulled back, then, catching a glimpse of the uniformed figure chasing him, put out my foot to trip the thief. In a flash, though, he hurdled past me, and the cop and I collided, both of us crashing to the pavement.

Shakily, I stood up. "I'm sorry, I'm really sorry, I didn't mean to . . ."

Gathering himself up as well, brushing off his uniform and shaking his head, the cop looked toward where the guy had disappeared into the darkness. "Plain bad luck. I saw you try to get him. Another one of those damned pickpockets. Thanks—not many people try to help us these days."

The cop shook my hand and turned back. As I walked off, the thought flashed through my mind: Why had I tried to help him? But before I could find an answer, I heard a whisper from a doorway. "Psst, over here."

A young man in a long dark overcoat stepped partly out of the shadows, but I still couldn't see his face clearly. "I loved the way you nailed him. I owe you one."

"N-not at all," I stuttered.

"Don't be so modest, for Christ's sake." He paused and scanned the street. "The coast is clear. Come on, I owe you a drink."

"No, really . . ."

Before I knew it, he was steering me a short way to another small street and a doorway that led to a bar. Or, more accurately, a dingy room that smelled of beer, cigarettes and piss. The walls and ceiling were a muddy brown color, which failed to cover the large stains of moisture that formed a hodgepodge of creepy patterns. My companion looked totally at home and, spotting someone he knew, led me to his table.

"I'm Hans," he said, extending his hand. Pointing to the other man, he added: "And this is Konrad."

"Karl," I replied as he ordered a round of beers from a morose waiter with a filthy apron.

Hans turned toward Konrad. "Shit, you won't believe this kid. He sent that cop sprawling and made it look like he was trying to help him." He paused. "You got it, right?"

Konrad nodded, patting his pocket.

In the dim light, Hans examined my face. "Haven't I seen you someplace before?"

I saw that his face was familiar, but I wasn't sure from where. He was in his late teens, and he looked very pleased with himself.

He drew himself up. "I know—you're a friend of Jürgen's, aren't you?"

"Jürgen Majewski?"

He nodded. "I knew it. Jürgen's brother is in the same business. We work together sometimes. I remember seeing you."

We drank our beers, and I tried to sort out what this meant. It might come out all right, after all. Jürgen and Peter would be impressed with what I had done, or what Hans thought I had done.

The door swung open, bringing in a gust of cold, wet air and two girls, making almost all the heads in the male crowd turn. They were probably about nineteen or twenty. One was short and stocky, with long dark hair, brown eyes and a broad nose; the other was taller, with light brown hair, but so thin that you could see her bones poking out through her skin. Her angular face, framed by a boyishly short haircut, was attractive, but her expression was cold, a warning that she was definitely off duty. "Two beers over here, now," she ordered in a husky voice. I tried to pull my eyes away from her.

"Hey, Karl." Hans nudged me. "You like?"

"She's all right."

"Would you like to . . . you know?"

"Sure, but she's not the kind to just do it for free."

Hans took a swig of beer, wiped away the foam with the back of his hand and shot Konrad a look across the table. "We got enough for the two of them?"

"We could do them a few times over. It's a juicy wallet."

Before I could say anything, Hans was stepping over to the women. At first they looked irritated by the intrusion, but Hans kept talking. I couldn't hear what he was saying because of the other loud conversations, or mostly curses, around me; but the tall woman turned her head, and her eyes briefly held mine before focusing back on Hans. Although I had been drinking beer, my throat suddenly felt dry, and I wanted nothing more than to be out of there.

Hans came back triumphant. "Done deal, Karl. Let's go."

"Where?" My voice came out in a low whisper.

"You'll get the tall one all to yourself. The other one has agreed to take care of Konrad and me." He punched me lightly on the arm. "Relax, enjoy it. I said I owed you."

Before I could think of what to say, the five of us stumbled out of the bar and started walking down the street. "In here," the shorter woman said, pointing to the entrance of a building with a battered wooden door that creaked loudly as we pushed our way through. Once inside, she pulled out a key and opened the door to a ground-floor room. Turning to her friend, she said, "You take the pretty boy, and I'll go upstairs."

Pretty boy, I thought. No one had ever called me that.

"Come on," the tall woman told me. "This is it."

The room was tiny, with just enough space for a cot, a washbasin and a stool. A musty odor emanated from the walls, contributing to my sense of claustrophobia. The woman began unbuttoning her blouse and loosening her long skirt in quick, no-nonsense movements. I stood there, unsure where to look.

"What's your name?" I croaked.

She shrugged. "What do you want it to be?"

"Ulrike," I blurted out, surprising myself.

"So who's Ulrike? Your sweetheart?"

"No one, no one at all."

"It's all the same to me," she said, by now half undressed. As she leaned over to pull off her skirt the rest of the way, her blouse opened, and I caught a glimpse of dark nipples. She straightened up. "Yes, they're tits. Now, don't just stand there: You're pretty, like my friend said, but let's get on with it."

With that, she reached for my pants. Startled, I backed away.

"I haven't got all day, you know," she said and took a step forward that backed me against the wall. I felt her bony body against mine and reached up to tentatively cup my hands over her breasts. They were tiny but softer than I expected, and the nipples made my palms tingle. At the same moment, her hand plunged into my pants, grasping its target. I felt the surge.

"Wow," she scoffed, letting go of my already withering and soggy manhood. "That's it? What a hotshot! Sure makes my job easy."

I struggled to rebutton my clammy pants and pushed by her, heading right back out the door where I dumbly looked up and down the street.

"Hey, it's all right," she called after me, her voice dissolving into laughter mixed with a rasping cough. "Just think," she added, "you broke all the records."

Praying that Hans and Konrad were still busy upstairs, I fled. This time I wanted not just to flee but to disappear, evaporate, vaporize. At least from all the places in Berlin where I might be recognized, from anywhere I could be chased by the laughter of those who would quickly hear about my humiliation.

In the days and weeks that followed, I stayed well away from my usual haunts and ventured home to get something to eat or to change clothes only when I was sure my mother wasn't there. The last thing I wanted was to see the inevitable disappointment in her face, and I certainly didn't want to—or know how to—explain anything to her. I could wear the two shirts and loose overcoat Gerhard had left behind, which doubled my wardrobe. Clearly my mother knew I was dropping in, which accounted for whatever food she managed to put out on the table. But I never thanked her or even allowed her to catch sight of me. When I think about this today, I'm ashamed. But back then I was obsessed with another sense of shame. Hans would have told Jürgen's brother, I was convinced, and that meant that Jürgen, Peter and everybody else would know about what had happened. They might even know that I had asked the whore to call herself Ulrike.

I slept again in stairways and cellars, huddled up in both Gerhard's and my coats. During those days and evenings, I found myself drawn to the groups of Free Corps men, the returning soldiers who had no intention of laying down their arms. Their pamphlets promised to restore order, pride and might. They called for the support of everyone who believed that the sacrifices of so many Germans on the battlefield should not be in vain, and they vowed to destroy those who had betrayed their cause by accepting defeat.

I liked the way they still wore their army uniforms and now looked more defiant than defeated. In a group, they exuded a raw male strength and confidence that I envied. If only I could be like them, I thought. Probably that, more than their talk of defending German honor and traditions, accounted for my tagging behind them whenever I could.

The Free Corps had already proved its ability to fight. I could make little sense of the constant street battles and coups and counter-coups, but I did know that the army veterans' prime enemy were the Spartacists, as the communists called themselves. They were led by Karl Liebknecht and Rosa Luxemburg. Bloody Rosa, as her enemies called her. The Spartacists launched an uprising that was supposed to usher in the proletarian state, whatever that meant. The veterans in the Free Corps cursed the communist Jews, who they said were trying to destroy everything they had tried to protect. And it was thanks to their decision to fight alongside regular troops that the government was able to crush the big Spartacist revolt.

Tracked down in the Wilmersdorf section of the city, Liebknecht and Luxemburg were marched off by government troops to army head-quarters in the Eden Hotel. I heard later that they were tortured there, before they were ostensibly sent to Moabit Prison. Neither made it that far. Free Corps troops laughed about the fact that Liebknecht was found with a bullet in his head in the Tiergarten. Luxemburg, they added gleefully, had gone for a swim in one of the canals. Her bloated, disfigured body was fished out much later.

I had been a bystander, eagerly gobbling up whatever details I could of the confusing battles. But the deaths of Liebknecht and Luxemburg didn't put an immediate end to the Spartacist threat. As strikes kept breaking out, the killing continued.

One evening I was trailing along behind a cluster of Free Corps men when they stopped and pointed to three dark shapes on the pavement. It took me a moment to realize what they were: bodies, each one wearing the uniform of government troops and lying in a puddle of dark fluid. The Free Corps men turned them over and stepped back quickly. I could see that each of the soldiers had his throat cut. I felt giddy, nauseated, but couldn't tear my eyes away.

A couple of shots whizzed over the heads of the Free Corps men. "Over there," I shouted from behind, pointing to two men sprinting into the gate of a nearby building. They rushed into the courtyard after them, and I followed at a short distance. Within seconds, both of the Spartacists were sprawled on the ground, their guns kicked away and then pointed at them.

"Don't shoot," one of them pleaded.

I stood transfixed, my blood pumping so hard that it took all my strength just to stand still. In quick succession, both guns went off, and the heads of the men exploded in blood.

"Nice job," one of the executioners said, standing in front of me and holding his gun, which was still emitting a thin wisp of smoke. "It had to be done. Look at it this way: That's two less bastards in the world, two less enemies trying to destroy us and everything Germany stands for." He grinned. "I've seen you hanging around. So, you want to be one of us?"

"Yes," I managed to say. "I mean, if you'll have me."

"What do you think?" he asked the others. "Sure, why not? What's your name?"

"Karl Naumann."

"Hermann Hardtke." He put his arm around my shoulder. "You'll need some new clothes, but that can be arranged. A uniform. You're small, but so were some of our buddies who were killed by these bastards. By the way, you ever fired a gun before?"

"Not really."

"No matter, you'll learn. I bet you already know how to use your fists."

"Sure do," I said, finding my trembling gone.

"Good, you'll need them."

Hermann took me under his wing. It was rare for the Free Corps to accept someone who hadn't served in the war, but he saw to it that no one bothered me. He found me the basic gear: army shirt, pants and boots that were a fairly decent if loose fit, although I had to pull my belt tight to keep my pants from falling off and to stuff paper into the toes of my boots to fill them out. I suppose I looked a bit comical, a boy trying hard to be a man, and I suspect many of Hermann's friends saw me as a mascot. But at the time I wasn't aware of that. I knew only that the men I had so admired had accepted me, that I was wearing the same uniform, that Hermann was teaching me how to fight with my fists or a knife and how to shoot a gun. Puffed up with a sense of belonging, I wasn't about to question their mission or why such methods were necessary. Whatever they said I took as gospel.

The credo they espoused focused mainly on saving the country from the reds, the Bolsheviks. And, as they kept repeating, many of those Bolsheviks were Jews like Bloody Rosa.

The whole country was in constant revolt. There had been revolts in Munich, Stuttgart, Frankfurt am Main and almost everywhere else. The government of weaklings, led by the Social Democrat Ebert, was desperately trying to save itself. He was certainly afraid of us, but he needed us to help him put down the Spartacists, who didn't give up easily. When the Spartacists looked like they might win, the government ran ads in newspapers calling for soldiers to join the Free Corps and "prevent Germany from becoming the laughingstock of the world."

Thousands of men responded. We—yes, I quickly and proudly thought of myself as part of that "we"—all hated the government that had accepted the shameful Treaty of Versailles, but we hated the reds more. True, both the reds and we hated the rich and talked about fighting for the rights of the workingman. But our grandiose goals were different: revolution versus nation. We believed in the ordinary German who, given the chance to regain his dignity and earn a decent wage, would help rebuild German pride. The reds derided anything to do with the nation, pontificating about the need for the working class to destroy the state and join in an international movement.

"Never forget that only we can save our country," Hermann would lecture me. "Only we can stop those who want to destroy it. That's why we can't show any mercy." He paused. "Did you hear about the Red Cross nurses in the Ruhr? One of our groups caught a group of nurses there carrying guns, even though everybody had been warned that they'd shoot anyone carrying weapons. The nurses claimed it was for self-defense, but that's what all the reds say. They shot them all."

I was shocked and impressed.

Late one afternoon as we were returning to our improvised barracks, we found ourselves pinned down by fire coming from a factory build-ing across the street. Hermann and two of his buddies spotted where the shots were coming from and told me to stay put while they circled around the back of the building to surprise the gunmen.

"Let me go, too."

"No, we need you here," Hermann insisted. "You cover us in case anyone comes from the other side."

I was convinced that he was merely protecting me. But after they had been gone for several minutes, I began to feel lonely and nervous. I crouched behind an empty vegetable stall, gripping my gun tightly. I heard shots from inside the factory building, then nothing. Suddenly, some instinct made me look behind me. A man wearing a brown cap and carrying a rifle was moving in my direction. I fired wildly. He stood up straight and took aim. At that moment, his forehead disintegrated, and he dropped like a stone.

"Next time, you'd better steady yourself before you shoot," Hermann said, trotting up and slapping me on the back. "I might not be around to help you out."

"I'm s-sorry."

"You'll learn." He paused and sucked in his lower lip. "Men have to learn fast around here, or else they're not around for long."

He had called me a man.

I didn't have to wait long for the next chance to prove him right. A few days later we gave chase to four Spartacists, cornering them in a large warehouse. I was behind Hermann, walking down a dimly lit passageway, when he stumbled over some loose boards and fell. I saw the outline of someone rushing at us. I fired, and the figure collapsed, his hand releasing a large knife that went skittering across the floor.

Hermann picked himself up. "You're learning fast," he said. "Good for you." Then Hermann turned over the body, a boy probably no older than I was. The front of his shirt was soaked with blood, but he was still breathing slightly. His eyes were cloudy. A soft moan emanated from somewhere deep within him, an eerie, almost inhuman sound. Hermann looked at him, raised his gun in one swift motion and delivered a final shot to the side of his head. I looked away, tried to gulp back the vile fluid that pushed its way up into my mouth. I leaned over and puked.

"No time for that, kid," Hermann said. "There may be more of them to take care of."

There weren't. Our comrades had finished off the other three Spartacists. As we emerged from the warehouse, my forehead was wet from sweat, and I couldn't rid myself of the horrible taste in my mouth. But I felt calmer, my breath coming more evenly, my body temperature cooling.

"First blood." Hermann chuckled. "You know what they say about dogs: Once they taste the blood of any kind of bird or animal, they'll always hunt that species. I won't have to worry about you any longer—you can take care of yourself."

Those words marked Hermann's changed attitude toward me, a change that dispelled whatever lingering doubts I might have had about the violence I was coming to take for granted. I realized he wasn't treating me as just an inexperienced boy anymore, and taking their cue from him, the other men no longer thought of me as a mascot. I belonged.

Late one night in the barracks, Hermann brought me an article in a Free Corps pamphlet written by someone called Ernst Jünger. I remember his words made me feel proud: "This is the New Man, the storm trooper, the elite of Central Europe. A completely new race, cunning, strong, and purposeful."

Hermann's confidence that he had molded me into a New Man prompted him to introduce me to others, including Otto Strasser, who would eventually become my mentor. Strasser was a decorated veteran of the First Regiment of Bavarian Artillery in the Great War, a Socialist Party activist, a stocky, intense leftist student who had earlier organized workers' brigades to combat groups like ours in Berlin. But he was now connected to a movement forming in Bavaria, which was attracting Free Corps men from all over the country. He was searching for recruits willing to consider deploying to Munich.

It was Strasser who would first hook me up with and then set me on my collision course with a man in Munich called Adolf Hitler.

Chapter Two

Along with the rest of the small contingent of Free Corps men recruited by Otto Strasser in Berlin, I stepped off the train in Munich on a brisk November morning in 1920 and immediately felt that I was in a different Germany. A Germany that was, well, more German than Berlin. *Gemütlich,* in the best sense of the word—a cozy, snug world brimming with wonderful baroque architecture. Cleaner in every way, smaller yet more stately, less chaotic. Later I would discover that there were a lot of foreigners—Russians, Poles and others—in Schwabing, the city's famous artists' district. But there wasn't anything like the hordes of foreigners who were so evident everywhere in Berlin, babbling away in languages that generated a perpetual fog of irritating, incomprehensible sounds. There were Jews, too, but again far fewer than in the capital.

Maybe my initial impressions were shaped in part by what Otto had told me about Hitler's reaction after moving from Vienna to Munich in 1913. The city had immediately felt warm and inviting to him, "as familiar as if I had lived for years within its walls." But most important, as he told Otto and so many others, it felt like "a *German* city." For Hitler, the contrast was with Vienna, which he complained contained "not a drop of German blood" and was the center of "the Babylonian empire" of the Hapsburgs, an unruly hodgepodge of nationalities, cultures and languages. Later he'd also talk about how much better Munich was than Berlin, a city he never liked.

I hadn't disliked Berlin, but it was still a place where I was afraid of running into people who remembered me from the days before I became a Free Corps fighter. I guess I was afraid they would see through this identity—or worse, expose me in some excruciatingly embarrassing way in front of my comrades. In those days, I also longed for a clean start, for myself and for Germany. Munich seemed like the answer to my prayers.

Initially, I had shared the suspicious attitudes of my mates in the Free Corps when Otto came to talk about Hitler and his new party. But he returned several times, usually meeting with us as a group and always lingering afterward to strike up conversations with anyone who would listen. I was one who always stuck around.

It helped that Otto came with Rex, his young, frisky Irish setter who demanded nonstop attention. He'd nuzzle me and put his paw on my leg if I dared stopped petting him for a moment. I'd never had a dog, and I'd been jealous of my friends who did. Some of the other men laughed behind Otto's back about his preoccupation with Rex, wondering aloud why he had picked that breed instead of something fiercer and smarter. "Aren't setters a bit, well, you know . . ." Joachim asked him early on, not quite plucking up the courage to finish his thought.

Otto laughed. "A bit dopey?"

"That's what people say."

"Dogs are like people," Otto explained. "If you train them well, if they grow up with discipline, they're well behaved. An Irish setter can be just as smart as any other breed. Never blame a dog for bad behavior, blame his master."

"He's not much of a watchdog, though," Joachim added.

"No," Otto freely conceded. "People should watch out for themselves. He's a companion, the friendliest kind you can have."

I liked Otto's straightforward approach, and his self-confidence. He was equally relaxed in talking about his politics, acknowledging that he had been naive to believe in those who called themselves progressives. He was bitterly disappointed with the lame performance of the Weimar government, which was filled with Social Democrats. His faith in the German socialists was shaken when they held a meeting in Halle, where the Russian revolutionary Zinoviev had held forth for hours in his heavily accented German. Zinoviev—who was also president of the Third International, which wanted to enroll the German leftists—had come straight from Moscow to deliver an unambiguous message. "It sounded like a new messiah doctrine," Otto declared, his face flushing slightly. It was, he continued, a vision of a world socialist movement completely subservient to the rulers in the Kremlin. In other words, German socialists would be expected to allow Russia to dominate their country.

That hardly fit Otto's own sense of mission. As a result, he was in the process of abandoning his former allegiances and forging different ones. He was only a few years older than I was, but he had obviously given a lot more thought to political ideas. He wasn't thinking only about how to fight but why and for what. You'd think all of us would have been thinking along similar lines, but I can't say that I had at that point. And I'm not sure my comrades had, either. There was something impressive about someone who had really done some thinking. And about someone who seemed to have met everyone important and could tell a good story about them.

Otto, of course, benefited from special proximity to Gregor, his older brother who had returned to his pharmacy in Landshut in Lower Bavaria a true hero of the war. Gregor's fame as a commander had spread well beyond Bavaria; he had always led his men boldly into battle, and he was never tainted by the suspicion that he would demand anything of his men that he wouldn't do himself.

Gregor was putting together his own Free Corps brigade, consisting of infantry, artillery and machine-gun units. "He's convinced that all our units need a common goal and a common rallying point," Otto explained. "A common cause." This was exactly what Otto was looking for, a doctrine and movement that would not fail him the way the socialists had.

He hadn't known where to look, he told us. But Gregor claimed that he had already found the answer. He invited Otto to visit him in Landshut on a day when he was expecting two special guests for lunch: General Erich Ludendorff and Adolf Hitler.

No one calling himself a German in those days would have passed up the chance to meet Ludendorff, the commander who had nearly succeeded in leading our troops to victory in the Great War. Otto didn't know much about Hitler at that point, except that he was an agitator in Munich, an army corporal who had become famous for his speeches, which, even in those days of superheated political warfare, were considered unusually incendiary. Otto was as curious about the newcomer as he was awed by the prospect of meeting Ludendorff. As I listened, spellbound, he described the encounter.

The lunch was nothing like the way Otto had envisaged it. When he arrived at his brother's pharmacy, where the shutters were already closed, he saw a strikingly elegant black car parked outside. "Not exactly socialist transport," he said, chuckling. Otto had thought he'd arrive early and get a chance to talk to Gregor about what to expect, but now he had to walk into a meeting already in progress.

Ludendorff was as imposing as his reputation. Otto's first impression was of solid mass: a hefty individual in all parts of his body, topped by a face marked by extraordinarily bushy eyebrows and a defiant double chin. Otto was no scrapper himself, but he felt the near intimidating power of the general's handshake. This was a man to be reckoned with.

Hitler was a pale presence in a blue suit who projected both obsequiousness and resentment while remaining mostly silent. In fact, the first discussion about Hitler that day was one in which he never actively took part. Gregor had invited the three guests into the dining room where Else, his young wife, was waiting. Ludendorff proposed a toast to all those who had served in the Great War. Hitler raised his glass of water.

"Herr Hitler, I should explain, doesn't drink alcohol," Gregor pointed out. Just then the maid brought in a large roast. Gregor smiled weakly at his wife. "He's also a vegetarian."

As Otto tells it, Else smiled back, but her eyes flashed an unmistakable challenge at both her husband and the guest. "Like any true gentleman, Herr Hitler wouldn't refuse to eat the food that I have so carefully prepared," she said with mock charm. "I'm sure he'll find it delicious."

Hitler said nothing but did not object to being served the meat and dutifully ate it. Which may have explained his silence for most of the meal; he only occasionally spoke up to agree with Ludendorff.

When the men moved into the living room, Hitler acted jumpy, as if his previous silence had caused him to suppress too many feelings that were now bubbling to the surface. Ludendorff ensconced himself in a deep leather armchair and lit up a cigar, and the Strasser brothers sat opposite him, hanging on his every word. Hitler was pacing back and forth, his head down, until he abruptly broke into their discussion about the recent turmoil in Berlin with a furious harangue about Jews as the source of all the world's evils.

"Filth!" he shouted. "Jewish communists and Jewish capitalists— what difference does it make? They're all filthy Jews who are destroying our country. They're swarming all over this pathetic Versailles government, and they'll be Germany's ruin unless we act quickly and decisively."

"Aren't you overdoing it a bit, Herr Hitler?" Otto asked. "Sure, Jews latch on to any movement that they think will be profitable for them—whether it's socialism or capitalism. They'd even grab any opportunity to milk you and your followers. They're crafty, no doubt, cynical profiteers. But they haven't produced anything themselves, and they certainly don't control anything."

Hitler's face contorted in angry contempt. "You don't know anything about the Jew, what he's capable of," he sneered. Then, in a leap that was hard to fathom, he began talking about the need to whip the Germans into shape to crush France.

"Why France?" Otto asked. "If there's to be war again, it'll be with the Bolsheviks. And then we'll need the help of France to make sure we can get the job done."

Ludendorff intervened, saying that our task was to build a national socialist state. "We have to be strong enough to make any enemy think twice about trying to attack or humiliate us."

Hitler looked eager to respond but thought better of it. Before he and Ludendorff left, he patted Otto on the shoulder and attempted to make light of their disagreement. "I'd rather be hanged by a Bolshevik than dragged to the guillotine by a Frenchman any day," he said. It struck Otto as a strained attempt at humor by a humorless man.

When the two guests had gone, Gregor asked Otto about his impressions. The younger brother expressed his admiration for Ludendorff but left no doubt that he had hardly been awed by Hitler. "Why are you allying yourself with him?" he asked.

Gregor hesitated, frowning, then offered a complicated explanation. With the authority of Ludendorff, what he called Hitler's "magnetic quality" and his own organizational ability, he felt that they could create a powerful force in German politics—national socialism. Yes, he acknowledged, Hitler seemed more interested in the nationalism, but he would keep the socialist element in there as well. He knew Otto was sick of the socialists but not of socialism, and Gregor shared his commitment to helping German workers improve their lot. Besides, he argued, Ludendorff and he would control Hitler. "We need all sorts of leaders to make this work," Gregor insisted. "And you haven't seen Hitler in action in front of a crowd. He really knows how to excite them, how to make them rally to our side."

Otto was skeptical, but he respected his brother's courage as a soldier and his political judgment. He was also eager to make a leap of faith. But instead of making a full leap, he agreed to send some men from Berlin to help the Free Corps build up its strength in Bavaria. He'd see what use they would be put to in Munich, he said, and watch the direction this national socialist movement would really take before enlisting himself.

"A deal?" Otto asked.

"Sure," Gregor responded. "You won't regret it, and we'll get you on board soon enough."

So I went to Munich. Admittedly, I was more the exception than the rule, since very few fighters from Berlin were willing to follow Otto's advice and move south, even on a trial basis. I shared many of their doubts about all this talk of a new movement in Bavaria that could unite nationalists and socialists. "Come on, why should they man the same side of the barricades there when, everywhere else, they're at each other's throats?" asked Hermann, my friend and protector. "At least we know what we're fighting for here in Berlin, but what would we be fighting for there?"

I guess what swayed me about Otto was that he was honest enough to admit he shared our doubts. He didn't try to convert us, since he wasn't fully converted himself. But the heroic aura of Ludendorff was a powerful lure: If he was involved with this crowd, I thought, they had to be serious. And I had heard enough about Gregor—not just from Otto but from others —to be as impressed by him. He was a big, broad-shouldered bull of a man with a disarmingly low-key but decisive manner. With his natural sense of authority, he seemed born to command troops into battle. I believed Germany needed more such men in positions of power instead of the current appalling ranks of weaklings. Besides, the battles in Berlin weren't getting us anywhere. After the adrenaline rush they induced, we often felt depressed and frustrated. Nothing was really changing.

Now that I look back at it, however, there was a more important factor: the way Otto treated me. He singled me out as someone with promise who could help this movement. "I want you to be not only a good soldier down there but my eyes and ears," he said. "I want to know more about this Hitler and his party before I throw in my lot with them, even if Gregor says it's the right thing to do." I felt proud to be chosen and emboldened enough to strike out on my own without Hermann's protective presence.

Our small contingent from Berlin was put up in a dingy dormitory on the outskirts of town where the local Free Corps was already thoroughly domesticated. We were told that we'd sleep in a long, dark corridor where extra bunks had been deployed, since there was no space left in the rooms. Our new comrades hardly went out of their way to welcome us. They continued playing cards and smoking in their slightly less crowded accommodations, looking very much like the hardened veterans who weren't about to acknowledge our existence, much less greet us.

As I was putting away my small bag under my bunk, I felt a sudden shove that sent me sprawling, hitting my forehead on the floor. I slowly pulled myself out from under the bunk and saw a beefy man with stringy brown hair and a flattened nose standing over me.

"Watch where you're sticking your ass out next time," he said. A couple of his companions laughed.

"You watch where you're going," I shot back, my anger overriding any sense of calculation.

"What did you say, asshole?"

"You heard me."

"Teach the runt a lesson, Uwe," one of the other men demanded. "These Berliners think their shit don't smell."

Uwe calmly picked me up by the lapels on my jacket and spat in my face. Then, dropping me like a sack on my bunk, he ostentatiously brushed off his hands and turned to leave. I went flying at him, catching him full in the back and propelling him against the wall, his face making loud contact first.

He roared and turned around, his flattened nose streaming blood. His fist caught me in the solar plexus, taking my breath away. I thought I was finished, but suddenly Erich, Stefan and several other Berliners were all over him—and then the Bavarians were all over them. I found myself entangled in a mass of flailing bodies, absorbing random punches and throwing a few myself.

"Enough, enough," I heard someone shouting. "*Achtung!*"

Miraculously, the fighting stopped, and we all drew ourselves up into two scraggly lines facing each other, the Berliners on one side and the Bavarians on the other, as a short officer with huge arms tapped a riding crop in his hand.

"Who started this?" he asked.

Uwe looked at me defiantly. I kept quiet, and so did everyone else.

"You'll get enough action tomorrow night," the officer continued. "So I don't want to see any more here. This time, I'll let it pass." Looking up and down both rows, he added: "Don't let it happen again. I warn you."

He turned sharply on his heels and marched out.

Uwe stepped forward, and I tensed. "Not bad for a Berliner," he said, holding out his hand. I took it and he laughed loudly. "Welcome to Munich. My name is Uwe Passau. You know, Lieutenant Schmidt is right: You and your buddies will get plenty of chances to use your skills here at Hitler's rallies. That was just a warm-up."

Still laughing, he and the other Bavarians tumbled out the door.

That afternoon I set out with Erich and Stefan to celebrate the fact that we had survived our initiation in the barracks. We also wanted to take a better look at our surroundings. We hiked into town, arriving at the northern end of the famous English Gardens. And then we kept walking. I couldn't believe how large the gardens were, how well groomed, how elegant even the trees looked. Berlin has its Grunewald, but that's more a bit of forest with paths, unkempt and wild by comparison.

When we crossed Prinzregentenstrasse and entered the city center, the contrast was even greater. We walked through the inner city's huge gates and gaped at the stately palaces, theaters and, of course, the wonders of Marienplatz. I stared at the gold gilded statue of the Virgin and craned my neck to watch the mechanical figures that magically appeared on the clock tower of the imposing New Town Hall when the chimes signaled five o'clock. It seemed like a fairy-tale place, not the gritty Berlin that I had grown up in.

I wanted to keep walking and looking, but my friends had other plans. "I'm thirsty," Stefan said.

"Not yet," I pleaded. "Let's see a bit more."

We decided to split up. I'd do some more walking, then catch up with them at a beer hall that they pointed to down one of the streets leading off Marienplatz.

Heading south on Sendlinger Strasse, I did something I hadn't done in years. I stepped into a small church. Mine was never a religious family, and religion was not a subject I gave any thought to once my father went off to war. Before that, he had taken me a few times to a Protestant church in Berlin, which I remember as barren and cold. Something about the ornate exterior of the small church drew me in that day in Munich, and I was startled by what I saw. The inside was crammed with figurines, gold ornaments and twisting patterns and paintings all the way up to the ceiling. The people who came in to genuflect and make the sign of the cross seemed less awed than comforted by all this commotion. I sat there not knowing what I really felt, thinking that if I had grown up Catholic in a church like this, I would have either loved or hated it, I wouldn't have been indifferent, as I was to my own church.

As I walked back in the direction of the beer hall, I was struck by something else: The girls seemed prettier, their clothes lighter and brighter, outlining their curves better, and their faces seemed more animated. Maybe because I felt less inhibited than in Berlin, I found myself smiling at some of them, and—to my surprise—they often smiled back. There were fewer of the hard expressions that many Berliners, including the good-looking women, so often wore on their faces.

At the beer hall, I pushed my way past rows of long wooden tables crowded with drinkers and dodged the waitresses wielding liter mugs of beer until I found Erich and Stefan planted in a far corner. They were working on their mugs and wearing foam mustaches; a couple of empty mugs on the table made it clear that they were on round two.

"Hey, what a great place," I said.

"You can say that again," Stefan replied, wiping his upper lip with his sleeve. "But you'd better order quick. You've got some catching up to do."

We drank, and I felt happy to be in this world, happy that I had taken the leap and left Berlin, happy that I was with new friends and sure that I wouldn't encounter the past that I wanted to leave behind.

But I should have known not to be too happy. I should have known that Munich was far from a fairy-tale city, that its baroque and rococo facades contained an equally twisted past and present. Within its beauty lurked a history of madness. Only later did I hear the stories about mad King Ludwig who, a half century before, had conversed with imaginary guests in his palace and demanded that his valet wear a bag over his head in the king's presence. And the madness of the period after the Great War had swept Munich at least as forcefully as Berlin. It, too, had gone through its coups, assassinations and counter-coups. It, too, was seething with an anger that could suddenly transform friendly beer halls into combat zones, with the heavy glass mugs turned into dangerous flying objects.

We drilled every day, marching until we were in perfect step. Then our instructors made us sprint up and down the field next to our barracks until we were all gasping for breath. We had to drop to the ground for push-ups and sit-ups. We learned new ways to use every weapon in our arsenal—fists, truncheons, guns. At night we washed our uniforms and shined our boots until they gleamed.

We had recently been named the *Sturmabteilung,* the SA for short. We wore distinctive armbands with the party symbol, a black swastika enclosed in a white circle. It felt like a promotion from the Free Corps. "Storm Troopers," our officers would intone, "must be ready to attack at a moment's notice, without hesitation. When you hear the order, the Storm Troopers must move as one." Hitler would provide the political rhetoric, we'd provide the muscle.

It didn't occur to me to question why the muscle was needed. Berlin had already conditioned me to accept that it wasn't enough to proclaim a political message. You needed to fight to survive and to be heard. But I hadn't realized to what extent the Nazis, as Hitler's movement was quickly dubbed, were intent on not only being heard but silencing even those who had come looking for debate, not physical combat. It was a distinction I didn't get clear in my own mind until much later. For now I was in my instinctive combat mode and determined to prove to the Bavarians that I was every bit as good a fighter as they were.

"Private Naumann!"

I stepped forward out of the inspection line to face the short officer who had stopped the barracks brawl.

"This is your chance to show that you know how to fight your enemies, not your friends," he barked. "Join the others on tonight's detail."

I was pleased and nervous. Everyone in the barracks had known that a small detachment would be sent to Munich's famous beer hall, the Hofbräuhaus, where Hitler was to speak that night, but they had also heard the rumors that the reds and others were preparing to bust up the meeting. That made the evening's assignment a scary honor.

We numbered forty-five as we entered the Hofbräuhaus, and we found the *Festsaal,* the large meeting hall, already packed with people, many of them looking none too friendly. The police were in the process of closing off access, stranding many of Hitler's supporters outside. What exactly were we supposed to do if the crowd, which consisted of close to a thousand people, turned on us?

Our squad leader ordered us down into the vestibule. There was a commotion outside, and then the police opened the doors. Dressed in a brown leather coat and pistol belt and holding an imposing whip, Hitler strode into the room, quickly taking us in. He ordered the doors to the meeting hall closed and turned to us, lined up in front of him.

"Lads," he said, "these aren't easy odds, but this is the moment to prove your loyalty to the movement. No matter what happens, we stay in the hall. The only other way any of us will leave is as a corpse. I'm staying and you're staying. I'm sure you'll be with me, but if anyone runs, I'll be sure to tear off his armband personally. And then you can forget about ever serving the movement again. Now, remember, the best defense is a good offense. If anyone in that crowd tries to break up the meeting, if anyone tries anything disruptive at all, you move and you move fast. Understood?"

"*Jawohl*," we responded.

Apparently satisfied, Hitler led us into the hall. We lined up along both sides, and I surveyed the crowd. What I saw confirmed my worst fears. Entire sections were jammed with mostly young men, factory workers by the look of them, who were pushing the crowd toward the front, where Hitler was preparing to speak. Some of the men were already gathering empty beer mugs. I had little doubt what they planned to do with them. Some looked less dangerous but no less hostile. As soon as Hitler started to speak, they began heckling him.

At first Hitler managed to ignore the interruptions. I was too intent on watching the people in front of me to listen carefully, but I caught disjointed phrases: "The Versailles government has to be abolished . . . the stab in the back by traitors and Jews . . . fighting for a new Germany . . ." I could see that his odd, jerky body movements and intensifying voice were beginning to work a strange magic on the crowd.

But his enemies must have become aware of the same thing, and they were becoming increasingly agitated. I saw a few hasty consultations. Then, at a moment when Hitler faltered uncharacteristically in his speech, groping for the right phrase, several voices began shouting.

A man jumped up on a table. "Freedom!" he shouted.

"Now!" commanded our squad leader.

The hall erupted. The mugs flew, and the menacing young men broke chairs apart and attacked the crowd with the jagged pieces. Everybody was screaming. Then many fell silent as they tumbled to the floor, squirming and spitting blood.

My guts tightened, and I had to suppress a strong urge to turn and run. You're not running anywhere, I told myself, with more determination than I felt. The signal came to strike, and I was relieved to be surging forward with my comrades around me, with no more time to think about fear. In groups of about six each, we charged at the troublemakers who had started the attack. We swung our truncheons, mowing them down in bursts. I felt warm blood on my face and hands but didn't know how much of it was from me and how much from the people I was clubbing. I saw a couple of my fellow SA men go down, but most remained on their feet no matter how many blows they absorbed.

I moved as if in a trance, as if I were watching myself from somewhere above the action, noting with satisfaction that I remained focused on my task and that anyone who dared to stay in my path quickly paid the price. We truly were an army, and my comrades weren't going to settle for anything short of victory.

Our opponents saw and felt our determination, and more and more of them fled out the back door. But one group remained in a corner, refusing to accept defeat. A couple of shots rang out, followed by some wild firing. Dragging their wounded, they, too, made for the exit.

As we began helping our most bloodied fighters and tending their wounds, the chairman of the meeting declared, "The meeting goes on. The speaker has the floor."

Hitler, jubilant, resumed his speech. The room wasn't anywhere near as full as it had been, and we had to dispatch seven of our men to the hospital for broken bones, but there was no doubt about the outcome. We had won.

And where were the police during all of this? As the chairman was announcing the official end of the meeting, a police lieutenant rushed into the hall, waving his arms. "This meeting is dismissed," he shouted.

Hitler gave him a contemptuous smile. "Good job, Lieutenant," he said.

Looking nervously around him, the policeman left as hastily and clumsily as he had arrived. So much for law and order in Munich, I thought. We'd obviously be responsible for ensuring *Ordnung* at our meetings. And we had proven that we were capable of doing just that.

I emerged relatively unscathed, with a black eye, a few bruises and a swollen left ankle that I only noticed later in the evening back in the barracks. I had been lucky. That night Uwe and his buddies came out into the hallway and handed around a bottle of schnapps. I nearly gagged on a long swallow—it must have been the cheapest crap available. But I felt proud of our victory, relieved to see another sign of our acceptance by the Bavarians and more convinced than ever that I had made the right decision by coming to Munich.

The next morning, though, I woke up sorer than I had expected. And when I swung my legs off my cot, I was startled by the pain that shot through my left foot. Overnight, my ankle had ballooned and stiffened. Gingerly, I tried to put a bit of weight on it but quickly abandoned that plan and sat back down on the cot.

One of the Bavarians came over. "That's a good one. Did you put it in cold water last night?"

I confessed I hadn't even thought of it.

"Well, now I can't tell how bad it is. You'd better get to a doctor to check it out. Wait, I'll be back in a minute."

He quickly reappeared, carrying a pair of crude, battered crutches. "You'll need these," he said, explaining where I should go.

Uwe volunteered to show me the way. We took the tram a couple of stops, and I hopped along on my crutches for another block until we found ourselves in front of a two-story building. Luckily, the doctor's office was on the ground floor.

We knocked and went into a plain room with sterile white walls and no pictures. An elderly couple sat on one side and a young mother with a small child on the other. The receptionist's desk was empty. I backed slowly into a free seat next to the child, and Uwe remained standing. "I'll make sure they'll take care of you here," he said.

A young woman in a nurse's uniform came from the doctor's office to the desk in the waiting room. Her dark blond hair, not quite shoulder length, was brushed back in a way that accented her high forehead, nose that turned up ever so slightly and blue-green eyes set deep in a face that was both girlish and mature. She was medium height, slender and very well shaped. My eyes briefly scanned her blouse, and just as quickly I made sure they darted away.

"I'll be with you in a moment," she said to me. "Frau Schmidt, please bring Claudia in here."

Uwe grinned as the nurse turned around and led the mother and child into the other room. "Not bad, huh? Bet you didn't have girls like that in Berlin."

Before I could think of what to say, the nurse was back. "Yes," she said, looking our way. "What can I do for you?"

Uwe was immediately at her desk. "You can do something for my friend," he said, jerking his thumb in my direction. "His ankle seems to be in pretty bad shape. As for me, I don't need anything special— except maybe to know when you get off work."

"I'll pretend I didn't hear that," she replied brusquely. "As for your friend, the doctor will take a look at him as soon as he has time to. He'll have to wait for these other patients to finish first."

Uwe shrugged. Turning to me, he said, "Guess you're on your own, Karl. You know how to get back."

I waited, embarrassed by Uwe's behavior and trying hard not to stare at the nurse as she walked in and out of the room.

Finally, she told me to come inside. "Do you need the crutches?" she asked.

"No, I'll make it," I insisted.

I hopped across to the desk and supported myself, then hopped into the doctor's office behind her. He was a short, compact man with a broad mustache that curled up at the edges.

"Looks like you didn't do too well last night," he said, glancing at my black eye and smiling slightly. "Who started it this time? I'm sure it was the other guys. Always is."

I began mumbling a reply, and he cut me off. "It doesn't matter. I think this whole town is going crazy with all these fights. Doesn't any-one just talk anymore?" He didn't pause for an answer. "So show me the foot."

He examined it, prodding gently but still making me squirm. "I'm sure it hurts," he said, "but it doesn't look like anything's broken. Only a bad sprain. I'll wrap it up, and you'll have to watch it. Be careful; especially when it begins to feel better, don't go too fast. You've badly sprained those tendons, and they'll take some time to heal. No more rowdy stuff, at least until this heals, you understand?"

"Yes," I said meekly.

"God, if it were that easy to make all of you behave. Maybe we'd then be able to get this country back on its feet again." He laughed bitterly as he finished wrapping my foot tightly with a long strip of white cloth. "All right, Sabine, make sure this young hero makes it to the door."

I hopped behind her, but as we made it to the waiting room, I stumbled. She turned and grabbed me under my arms. As she steadied me, we were face-to-face, her arms still under mine and holding my shoulders. She blushed first, but I'm sure I was even redder. She stepped back quickly.

"You really do have to be careful," she said, not looking in my eyes. She reached for my crutches and handed them to me.

"Thanks," I said, failing to think of something more to say.

As I shuffled to the outside door, she held it open. This time she looked straight at me. "If it hurts, come back in a few days. If it doesn't, well, you can come back anyway." She averted her gaze and added: "Four is a good time, because I finish work then."

She turned away and returned to the desk, busying herself with some papers. I think I said something like "I'd like that" before going out, but afterward I wasn't sure whether it was to her or just in my own mind.

Chapter Three

Hitler ordered a large escort of SA men to accompany him to Coburg, a town about two hundred kilometers due north of Munich that had recently been incorporated into Bavaria. The organization was truly splendid. For the first time, a special train was put at our disposal, and those of us who boarded it in Munich were soon augmented by additional companies of SA troops who were picked up at stops along the way. In each case, the troops marched to the train in their smart uniforms, proudly carrying the flags bearing the bold black swastika set against a red background. I felt our gathering strength, and I was convinced the local townspeople couldn't help but be impressed. By the time we reached Coburg, our ranks had swelled to fourteen companies, or eight hundred men.

The occasion was a "German Day" organized by the town. Hitler had received an invitation from some of the *völkisch* parties of the right, but the town was dominated by leftists—trade union leaders and communists, he told us. During our train ride, he explained that those groups had effectively terrorized the town for the last couple of years, not allowing other voices to be heard. "Our duty is to break the terror and to guarantee freedom of assembly," he said.

To illustrate his point, he told us the reds on the organizing committee had demanded that the SA, if it were to serve as his escort, be as unobtrusive as possible. "Can you imagine they ordered me—yes, ordered—to make all of you keep your flags furled and not to play any music. I laughed in their faces. And you know what we'll do as soon as we arrive? We'll march sharply into town, our flags waving and the music playing. Just let them try to stop us."

That's what we defiantly did, and I felt as proud and inspired as any of my fellow troopers. Hundreds, maybe thousands, of angry reds were out on the streets to jeer us. "Murderers!" "Criminals!" they called out.

We ignored them as we marched into town behind a nervous group of local policemen. We made it to the center without any major incident, but when we turned toward our accommodations, a shooting range on the outskirts of the town, the mob switched from hurling abuse to hurling stones. When the order came, we moved swiftly, lashing back at our attackers with such organized ferocity that they were dispersed within minutes.

Our triumph was short-lived, however. In the evening, I stayed in our temporary quarters playing cards, but some men decided to walk around town, thinking it was largely pacified. Several of them were caught by larger groups of reds who pummeled them mercilessly, and they came back badly battered. I was furious, determined to exact revenge if I was confronted the next day. It was a sentiment we all shared that night as we dropped off to sleep.

In the morning, Hitler came carrying the local newspaper and pamphlets. They denounced our "war of extermination against the peaceful workers of Coburg" and called for "a great demonstration of the people" to prove that the town would not be "terrorized." Hitler waved the papers. "You see the kind of Marxist-Jewish slander we are subjected to?" he shouted. Then, dropping his voice so we had to strain to hear him, he declared: "They won't get away with this. Your duty is to make them understand that, using whatever means necessary."

Our ranks had swelled to nearly fifteen hundred men, as more SA reinforcements had arrived during the night and early morning. When we marched to the main square where the reds were to stage their demonstration, we formed an imposing force. Our message was simple: strength, strength, strength. It had clearly registered. Instead of facing thousands of reds, as we had been led to expect, we saw only a few hundred opponents. We could see the fear in their eyes. A few, probably outside reinforcements who had missed the previous day's fighting, were bold enough to taunt us. But as soon as we swung into action, most took to their heels. I got in only one or two swipes. Compared to some of our earlier battles, the finale was almost nothing.

As we marched back toward the train station that evening, some of the locals cheered us for the first time. "You did well, men," Hitler told us on the train. "We liberated Coburg from the reds."

It was a victory that increased our fame. More recruits joined our ranks: from a small band, we were gradually growing into a true army. I felt that I was making up for the experiences I had missed out on during the war. And as one of the early recruits, I already felt a special pride in my ability to welcome the newcomers. No one questioned my credentials anymore.

My ankle had healed, and I decided to meet Sabine as she got off work. To tell the truth, I had decided that right away and planned the meeting in my head over and over. The problem was that I didn't know whether she had meant the invitation seriously and if she remembered it. And beyond meeting her, I wasn't sure what to do. Should I invite her to a café? Certainly not to the kind of beer halls where I normally went with my buddies. And what would it cost to treat her to anything?

With the price of a beer now counted in millions of increasingly worthless marks, I was hardly in the position to afford much of anything. We were paid a small wage in the SA, never enough to keep up with the raging pace of inflation. It was as if your marks shrank every moment they were in your pocket or under your mattress. Hitler was right: Our enemies were intent on not only proving that they had won the war but also on destroying and humiliating us. Here I was worrying whether I could invite a girl for a cup of coffee. The demands for reparations, particularly by France, kept growing more and more outrageous.

I was standing in front of Sabine's office at four o'clock in the afternoon. Actually, I had arrived almost a half hour earlier and then walked up and down the street, not daring to go too far for fear of missing her. I wanted to seem like I was there by chance, especially if she looked surprised—or annoyed—when she saw me. In that case, I'd nod hello and keep going. No humiliation, purely an accidental meeting, was the way I'd play it. But if she seemed the least bit pleased, I'd invite her to a café, no matter what it cost.

The problem was that no Sabine emerged from the two-story house. I thought she may have been sick, and I came back the next day for another hour or so of nervous pacing. Again she never showed. The same thing happened on the third and fourth days. I suppose I could have gone to the doctor's office to ask about her, but I didn't have the nerve. The thought occurred to me that I could go in and ask the doctor to check my ankle again, but I quickly rejected it as too transparent a ploy. Maybe she had deliberately lied about her schedule. She probably had.

Angry and full of self-pity, I walked in circles near her office. I hadn't imagined it, I told myself. She clearly had said to stop by around four. Was this some kind of joke or a brush-off?

I looked at my watch for the umpteenth time. It was five-ten. All right, I told myself, I'll make the loop around her office this final time. After that, I'll never set foot on this street again.

The door to the doctor's office opened, but it was only a man with a bandaged head. I squeezed my right fist and, angry with myself and her, punched it into my left hand before I turned around to retrace my steps to the barracks. I put my head down and began walking at a brisk pace, seeing nothing of my surroundings.

"Good evening, Herr Patient, I see you're not limping anymore."

Startled, I looked up at the woman I had almost passed. Dressed in a plain brown coat, Sabine looked even prettier than I remembered her.

I guess I didn't say anything at first, because she laughed. Then she looked at me more closely and turned serious. "Why the glum look? Is something the matter?"

I didn't know what to say.

"Are you angry with me?"

"I've been walking around your office like an idiot for a week," I blurted out. "I mean, I stopped by a few times and never saw you."

She smiled. "You did? I thought you had forgotten about me."

"No, no. But why weren't you ever there at four o'clock?"

"The doctor changed my hours. I come in later and don't get out till five now. I thought of letting you know . . ." Her voice trailed off.

"And?"

She colored. "How was I supposed to do that? I didn't even know whether you wanted to come see me. Besides, you live in some barracks, with all those men like the one who brought you to the office that day. He's not exactly my type, you know."

"You mean you didn't tell me the wrong time on purpose?"

She laughed, pretending to feel my temperature by placing her hand lightly on my forehead for a moment. "Are you still sick? Besides, why didn't you just come in and ask for me?"

I shrugged, trying to mask the excitement that her brief touch had sent through me.

"Well, what now?" she added.

"Would you like to go to a café?"

"Would I?" She crumpled her mouth into an intense frown, as if carefully weighing her answer, but her eyes were still laughing. "Of course I would."

I hadn't known what to think about Hitler at first. There was something strange, even unsettling, about a man who was so mercurial— perfectly calm one moment and ready to explode from the emotions churning within him the next. But when he talked about all the guilty parties—the reds, the Jews, the cowards—who had betrayed Germany and allowed its enemies to defeat it, I couldn't help but feel moved. Here was the explanation for all the troubles so manifestly around us; here was the reason why the deaths of my father and brother had contributed not to a glorious victory but to Germany's humiliation.

It wasn't just Hitler's message that was convincing; above all, it was the way he delivered it. He increased his number of political meetings, and more often than not, our presence began to guarantee order without force, which meant I could watch him more. Initially, I found his behavior downright bizarre and the dyspeptic rhythm of his speeches unnerving. Looking back at those days, I now think I should have trusted my early discomfort, not allowing myself to gradually fall under his spell, at least when he was rallying his supporters.

But I was mesmerized, simply astounded by the physical effort that went into his speeches. He would sound calm at first, speaking so softly but intensely that his audience would lean forward in hushed attention. His voice would begin to rise, the accusations would grow angrier and angrier, and he would reach a crescendo by invoking his vision of a powerful, proud Germany for the Germans, which would no longer accept the humiliating conditions of a defeat engineered by treacherous politicians. By then the applause would be enormous, the hall electrified. I watched older women become enraptured to the point where they were aroused in a way they probably hadn't been for years, carried away by his words to near ecstasy. None of us who watched him elicit those responses again and again could remain unmoved.

In the course of his speeches, Hitler would down bottle after bottle of mineral water. They were small bottles, but I was taken aback by how many he could consume. Most people didn't notice, since they were focused on his speech. As someone who was there so often, I began to pay attention to such details. Usually, he drank at least a dozen, and once I counted twenty empty bottles after he spoke. In the summer, he'd sometimes keep a piece of ice on the rostrum to cool his hands. In any weather, his shirt was soaked through with sweat by the middle of his performance; by the end, it was dripping. Afterward he would rush off to bathe and change before rejoining the meeting. This was a man who gave his all, without fail, on every occasion, before every audience. I admit that I found that impressive.

So did many who came out of curiosity and left converts. He knew how to draw them in. I may not have understood his methods, but I could feel their impact. And now, after I've had the time to read in prison, I've developed a bit of understanding as well.

Take the question of timing. I finally read *Mein Kampf,* which he wrote during his own days in prison. He explained why he held almost all his meetings in the evening rather than during the day. He pointed out something I never thought about: how a play or a movie always seems better when you see it at night. People find it easier to absorb something new, and to submerge themselves in another world, in the evening. "In the morning and even during the day people's will power seems to struggle with the greatest energy against an attempt to force upon them a strange will and a strange opinion. At night, however, they succumb more easily to the dominating force of a stronger will."

From a tiny fringe party, the Nazis were growing into a movement in Bavaria. The leftist press angrily denounced Hitler, claiming he was a threat to everyone and everything, and printed scurrilous rumors. This made people curious about him, bringing more potential recruits to his meetings. Even the titles of his speeches—"The Future or Doom" was one frequent billing—aroused controversy, and he knew how to turn every bit of attention to his advantage.

One day I was ordered to deliver a letter from my SA commander to Hitler. I had to look up the address I was given, Thierschstrasse 41, on the city map. After making my way down past the English Gardens, I reached Maximilianstrasse, one of the most affluent streets in the city, and turned left to Maximilianplatz. At the proud statue of Maximilian II, I turned right on Thierschstrasse, a less imposing street with a tramline running down the middle. Just past a pharmacy whose window offered a huge array of brown bottles, I found number 41. The ocher-colored building featured windows with elegantly carved decorative peaks. Between two windows on the first floor, where Hitler lived, a statue of the Virgin was mounted in a recess. With her hands crossed, Mary gazed upward in prayer.

I was nervous pushing open the building's main door. I had seen

Hitler often enough, but until then only as part of a larger force. He had never had reason to single me out, and I assumed he wouldn't recognize me. Besides, I was entering his private world. I had heard he spent much of his free time in the mountains, in Obersalzberg, but this was his home when he was in Munich.

In the downstairs hallway, I noticed the usual wooden mailboxes on the wall and several bicycles parked along the walls. To the left was a long wooden stairway with a wooden banister held up by wrought-iron bars. The stairs creaked as I marched up to the door on the first landing. To its right was another bas-relief, featuring some saint I couldn't recognize blessing a woman. After a moment's hesitation, I knocked.

A middle-aged woman opened the door, the landlady, as I later learned. "Herr Hitler, he's over there," she said, pointing to the second door on the left. A slightly disheveled Hitler was already opening it. His hair was poking out at odd angles, and he wore only a loose shirt hanging out over his pants. I saluted. "A letter from Captain Wulff," I reported.

"Come in, Private. What's your name?"

"Naumann, sir, Karl Naumann."

"Well, Naumann, you've been doing a good job. I've seen you in action, defending me and my right to speak at our meetings."

I flushed.

"Just a moment," he continued, quickly reading the note. "I'll give you a reply right away for your captain."

Hitler sat down at his small desk, and I remained standing near the door. As he wrote, his head drooping over the paper in an almost bird-like position, I took in the surroundings. The room was small and narrow, no more than three yards wide, with a window overlooking the street and the tops of the trams as they rumbled by. There was nothing here to suggest wealth or power. A simple linoleum covered the floor. A bed. A desk and chair. A couple of bookshelves, with only a few books I recognized: Clausewitz's *On War,* Treitschke's *German History,* Spamer's *Illustrated World History.*

Hitler pushed back his chair and handed me an envelope. "Keep up the good work, Private."

As I leaned forward to take it, I was hit by a pungent, sour smell. It startled me, but my main thought was to salute and turn as smartly on my heels as I could before walking out the door.

Sabine and I rarely talked about politics. During our first few meetings, she expressed some interest, but more in the nature of the people I had become involved with than in their program.

"Your friend Uwe scares me," she told me. "I wouldn't want to be caught with him alone somewhere."

"He looks meaner than he is. Really. Of course, you have to be tough to be in the SA, but it's for a good cause."

Sabine arched her eyebrows and spooned more sugar into her coffee. She loved anything sweet, the sweeter the better. "You mean Hitler's cause? Whatever that is. All that ranting about Germany's enemies and German pride? What does it all add up to except the fantasies of a strange-looking man who wants to be kaiser?"

"What are you talking about?" I replied huffily. "I've watched Hitler. I've been to his apartment. It's one simple room. This isn't a man who is after personal glorification and wealth. He wants Germany to get back on its feet. To be proud again."

She laughed, and any offense I had taken melted away. "You're still so naive," she said, reaching over and rumpling my hair. "Only a couple of years between us, and I sometimes think I should be your mother."

"Some mother."

"Some child," she retorted, and we both laughed.

We met several times a week, whenever I could get away from my duties. Sometimes in cafés, where, to my relief, she immediately offered to pay her share of the bill. "I'm a working woman," she pointed out when I reached for the bill the first time. She made more money than I did, but, unlike me, she had to provide for her own living expenses. We went to the movies a few times. But mostly we just walked in the English Gardens or in the city center. Neither of us could afford much more.

If we had little in common in terms of politics, we quickly discovered a different bond. She was an only child, and her father had died, as mine had, in the war. Her mother had suffered from tuberculosis and died a couple of years later.

"You mean your mother is living and you don't keep in touch with her?" she asked accusingly. It was the one time in those early meetings when she looked genuinely angry with me.

"So what? You don't know what it was like in my house. She never stood up for me when my father hit me. What do I owe her?"

"Everything," she shot back without hesitation. "Absolutely everything. You have to promise me that you'll get back in touch with her."

I didn't reply.

"Promise."

"All right, maybe. Maybe next time I go to Berlin. At some point I will, you know."

Sabine took this vague statement as concession enough, and she didn't push me further. We saw more and more of each other. We designated a willow tree in the English Gardens as our meeting spot and began our walks from there. I learned that her surviving family member was a sick grandmother who shared her small attic apartment in a drab three-story building across the river from the English Gardens. Aside from feeding herself, Sabine had to feed and care for her. I felt worse about not being able to pay for even the small things, like a cup of coffee.

When it was time for me to report back to my barracks, I would walk her home. The second or third time, I worked up the nerve to kiss her on the cheek. "You can kiss both cheeks," she said with a soft laugh. And that became our regular good-bye.

Until a cold winter afternoon when she said she had to go home earlier than usual to check on the coal in the stove. At the door to the building, I leaned over to kiss her on the cheek and banged my mouth against hers instead, teeth against teeth. I drew back.

Sabine's eyes met mine. "I wanted a different kind of kiss."

"Oh, you mean . . ."

"Don't worry, I don't bite—yet."

She reached up and drew my face to hers, putting her lips firmly on mine.

"I know," I responded, and pulled her to me, kissing her again.

She looked up, her hands holding me lightly by the waist. "Look, it's cold. You should warm up upstairs."

I hesitated. "What about your grandmother?"

"She'll be asleep. Don't worry."

She took me by the hand and led me up the darkened staircase to the top floor. She unlocked the small door, and we went in. It was nearly dusk outside, and everything inside was already in semidarkness.

The apartment was no more than a room divided by a curtain. A slightly irritating odor filled my nostrils, a mix of coal dust and something else that I gradually identified as coming from the cot where the head of a small white-haired woman barely emerged from the covers. Sabine added a few coals to the oven, and we went to her side of the curtain, which also contained a cot, a small table and a washbasin. There wasn't room for anything else.

"I know it isn't much," she said, looking around nervously. "If you're hungry, I can offer you a bit of bread and cheese."

She turned toward me, and this time I drew her close. Our mouths met, and I felt the softness of her body pressing against mine, welcoming the reaction I couldn't hide. Then she sat down on the cot and reached both hands to me, pulling me down beside her.

"Sabine, I . . ."

"Shhh," she said, putting her forefinger on my lips. She took my right hand and placed it on her breast. "Grandma won't hear anything. She's asleep and almost deaf."

I reached into her blouse, and she pulled it off, loosening my shirt at the same time. "Wait," she said, sliding under the covers of the narrow bed. A moment later she pulled out her skirt and tossed it on the floor. "I'll turn around. You can throw your pants on that chair."

Awkwardly I took off my shoes and my trousers. I slid under the covers with my underwear still on.

Sabine pulled them down as she covered my mouth with hers, her tongue working itself around my lips and then meeting mine. Within a moment I felt a familiar panic, then the surge that left both of us sticky wet.

"I'm sorry," I said, desperately trying to pull away. "I'm really sorry. I wanted to tell you."

Sabine held me tighter than ever, pulling my head against her chest. "It's all right, it's fine. I'm glad you're here. Relax, just relax. Has any girl ever told you how handsome you are?"

I shook my head. In school, the girls were always more interested in the tough boys I had tried woefully to emulate.

"Well, they should have," she said, running her fingers down my face from top to bottom. "Let me be the first, then."

I suddenly remembered the "pretty boy" remark of the prostitute in Berlin. That only deepened my gloom.

We lay pressed against each other in the dark, but I couldn't shake my sense of shame. Again, I thought. How could this happen? Was I a normal man? Was I born with something wrong, something that could never be made right?

I must have fallen asleep, a remarkably deep sleep even if it turned out to be short. Still half asleep, I felt Sabine's gentle stroking and myself growing hard. She rolled me over, and as I came wide awake, she was astride me, her hands grasping my chest. This time I felt the surge within me rising gradually and then erupting, deep inside her. She leaned forward, her breasts brushing my body as she kissed me again.

"Feel better?"

I thought I would explode again with joy.

Back in the barracks, I wanted to say something to show that I was now one of the men in a way I hadn't been before. I told myself that I wasn't going to boast about what I did with Sabine the way some of the men talked about going out on the town. I won't tell, I can't tell. But it turned out I didn't need to say anything directly. I guess my self-confidence was evident, decipherable, to my companions.

"Hey, guys, I think Karl is getting laid," Uwe announced one afternoon.

I turned red, trying to decide whether I should take a swing at him or simply admit that he was right.

"Sure is," Stefan chimed in. "About time."

I couldn't help but grin. If I thought I had full membership in the club before, I knew that I was definitely in now.

For all the banter, the barracks still had their share of tensions. Our public shows of discipline at party meetings didn't always carry over; fights kept breaking out, and three troopers were stripped of their armbands and banished for knifings. One of their victims died in the hospital, and our superiors had to work hard to ensure that word didn't leak out to our enemies. Luckily, the authorities seemed inclined to look the other way whenever we were involved in violent incidents; they were used to covering up for us. There was little doubt that we had secret sympathizers in higher Munich and Bavarian circles who hated the reds more than they distrusted us.

Hitler understood those sentiments and was determined to use them to his advantage. Our meetings were fine as far as they went, keeping his supporters enthusiastic and attracting recruits to the movement. But he remained eager to prove that he could defeat the reds and drive them off the local political stage.

The opportunity, it seemed, would be on May 1, 1923, the traditional day for the left to mount a show of strength. The Bavarian government had given the communists and socialists permission to hold their May Day demonstrations, but Hitler announced that this would be an insult to the patriotic Germans who saw the red flags as "the painful symbol of the collapsing fatherland."

Early in the morning, all the SA troops in Munich assembled at Oberwiesenfeld north of the city. Several armed units from other regions joined us, bringing our number to over thirteen hundred men. Among them was Gregor Strasser, looking fit and very much in command of his troops from Landshut. We were well armed with rifles and machine guns, and we had a couple of horse-drawn cannons that I had never seen before. We shot out our right arms and shouted in unison, "*Heil* Hitler!" This was our new salute.

But any sense of security those numbers might have provided us gave way to nervousness as we realized that regular Bavarian troops had effectively surrounded us. Hitler looked more agitated than usual, pacing back and forth in a steel helmet. When he would take it off, we saw that sweat was streaming down his face. He looked uncharacteristically undecided. When he cast his glance in the direction of Munich to the south, he seemed to have no idea how to get us there.

At around eleven A.M., Reichswehr troops marched onto the field. In their midst, I recognized the face of Captain Ernst Röhm. At the time, I knew only that Röhm had served in the Army District Command in Munich, and he had joined the National Socialists even before Hitler. Later he had backed Hitler's efforts to take over the small party from the inside, and he encouraged Free Corps men to join and become part of SA units like ours.

But Röhm was now representing the Bavarian authorities, and Hitler was startled to see him. "Whose side are you on? Are you a traitor?" Hitler asked. "Why are you trying to stop us from dealing with the reds?"

Röhm looked him calmly in the eyes. "This isn't the right moment for what you have in mind. The government and the Reichswehr have decided that the May Day demonstrations can take place. No one is to interfere with them—no one."

Hitler fumed and resumed his pacing. I saw Gregor Strasser approach and argue vehemently with him. Later I learned that Strasser had urged him to open fire on the government troops and to proceed with his plan to attack the reds. Hitler did nothing. Finally he agreed to the government troop's order that we hand in our weapons to them.

Stunned, we obeyed. As we surrendered our weapons, Hitler tried to reassure us. "We've already shown the reds what we are capable of," he declared. "There's no need to shed blood now. Our day will come soon." Then we marched off the field.

On our way back through Schwabing, we spotted a couple of reds carrying a May Day flag. "Let's get them," Uwe shouted, and I joined in the brief melee that followed. The two reds never had a chance. By the time I reached them, Uwe was kicking one of them, already flat on the ground. The other terrified man was trying to retreat, his face bloodied. I punched him in the face and the gut, and he went down. I felt my blood pumping as I kicked him in his ribs, just as Uwe had done to his companion. "Here's the traitors' flag," I yelled, holding up their red banner. Someone struck a match and set it alight. Shouting, we tossed the burning banner on the ground next to the writhing bodies. But even as we celebrated our paltry victory, we couldn't hide our frustration. We had been humiliated that day. Publicly.

Chapter Four

Sabine and I began going back to her apartment almost every afternoon or evening that I could get away. Her grandmother seemed to do nothing but sleep. We would walk in as quietly as we could and jump in under the covers. The first time that Sabine moaned loudly, I froze momentarily.

"No, no, don't stop," she pleaded.

I put my mouth to her ear. "What about her?"

She giggled and tightened her arms around my back. "I told you, she's almost deaf."

I finally met her grandmother one evening after we had made love and Sabine was brewing tea. "I'd like some, too," the old woman said, her voice carrying from behind the curtain.

"Oh, Grandma, you're up," Sabine said, pulling back the curtain. "I want you to meet Karl."

A shriveled, tiny woman was sitting up on the bed, her face a mass of lines and furrows, her short, thin white hair pointing in myriad directions. But her eyes were a bright blue. They must have looked like Sabine's when she was young: lively, with a glint of amusement as she looked me over. I found myself blushing.

"Well, young man, I'm very pleased to meet you. Sabine has told me so much about you—and, if I'm not betraying any secrets here, I think she likes you. A lot, I'd say."

Sabine laughed. "Grandma, how do you figure such things out?"

"Just the wisdom of age, you know. Now, help me get up and over to that chair."

We sat down at the apartment's rickety table, and I was relieved that the two of them kept talking. Sabine must have sensed that I didn't know what to say. But her grandmother wasn't about to let me sit there.

"So what is it that you plan to do with your life?" she asked.

"For now I'm a soldier."

"What did you say?"

Sabine signaled for me to speak louder.

"I'm a soldier," I almost yelled.

The old woman broke into a broad grin, showing her gums and very few teeth. "I'm hard of hearing, not deaf."

"Sorry."

"That's all right," she said. "But I already know you're involved with a bunch of rowdies. That's what boys who think they are men do."

"Grandma," Sabine interjected. "Please."

But Grandma wasn't about to be stopped. "You know it, too, Sabine. Now let me finish. I was just asking what you really intend to do with your life once this business is over."

"I haven't thought about it much," I responded. "I guess my feeling is that it'll take quite a while before we straighten this country out. But then maybe I'd like to learn a trade. I'd like to fix automobiles or something."

"And you and your friends are going to fix this country first?"

"Grandma, not again."

I realized they must have quarreled about me before.

"I'm not starting anything," the old woman insisted. "And Lord knows this country could use some fixing. But even if I don't have much of an idea what's happening outside anymore, I know enough not to trust a bunch of boys running around playing soldiers."

She began to cough, a deep hacking that made her face flush red, then purple. Sabine rushed over and put a handkerchief up to her mouth; as the cough subsided, she gently wiped the spittle from her chin and cheeks.

"I'd better rest a bit more now," Grandma said hoarsely. "My apologies. And Karl, don't you mind anything I said. You look like a very nice boy, and I'm so happy for Sabine."

I stood up. "Thank you, Frau Koch."

Sabine led her grandmother back to bed, tucked her in and drew the curtain. "I'll be back soon," she said. "Get some rest."

We walked silently down the stairs. As we stepped outside, Sabine put her arm in mine. "She means well, she really does."

"I know," I said, although my pride had been wounded. "She can't understand what we're doing."

We walked to the corner where we normally parted before Sabine replied: "I'm not sure I understand sometimes, either." Then she quickly kissed me on the cheek. "But I love you, you know I do."

"Yes, I know. Someday you'll also understand why we have to do things we do—why Germany needs the help we're giving it."

When I recall those words now, I wonder what kind of a person I was not to hear how they sounded. And how Sabine put up with me at those times. But then I took my words seriously, very seriously. I was under Hitler's spell.

From the beginning of 1923, Germany had been in a constant state of crisis. Our enemies kept demanding more and more reparations, even though we had nothing available for payment. The French used this as an excuse to send in their troops to occupy the Ruhr, our industrial heartland. Hitler denounced the occupation at every rally, and even the normally spineless Weimar government called for a campaign of passive resistance. I don't think there was a single true German, no matter how meek, who wasn't incensed by this attempt to humiliate us further.

As of July 1, the exchange rate for one American dollar was 160,000 marks. A month later, it was a million marks. After that I lost track: The numbers were in the billions. People panicked. As soon as they came into any money, they rushed to buy something before their marks became even more worthless. There was rioting in Berlin over the price of bread; all normal commerce was breaking down. Many people raided potato fields. Others frantically sold whatever family treasures they had for suitcases full of money, only to discover that they couldn't get rid of it fast enough for it to be of much use beyond feeding themselves for a few more days.

One afternoon when I went to meet Sabine, I was startled to see her crying. This was something I had never seen before.

"What's the matter?" I asked.

"Oh, Karl, you have no idea what's happening in this city. I never thought I'd see anything like it. I was walking down Sendlinger Strasse and saw a totally hysterical woman picking up marks from the gutter. I tried to talk to her, but she was beyond that.

"I asked a shopkeeper who was standing in front of his door what had happened. He said that the woman had dragged a big basket of money and stopped in front of his store. She had seemed nervous but normal. Then she put her basket down, stepped into the almost empty store, glanced around quickly and came back out. But in that brief interval, someone had dumped the mounds of paper money into the gutter and stolen her basket." Sabine wiped away her tears. "What's happened to everyone?"

"I know—it's everywhere." Then I added: "That's why we have to fight to set this country right."

I was far from alone in thinking that way. Hitler kept signing up members to the Nazi Party, thirty-five thousand between January and October alone. The SA also kept attracting recruits, fifteen thousand in the same period. There were so many newcomers in our ranks that I already felt like a veteran. And then there were the women, not young ones but "the varicose vein squad," as we called them: the old ladies who hung on Hitler's every word at our meetings and, rumor had it, provided a lot of the party financing. Despite the economic hard times, we still paid for the meeting halls, the uniforms, the flags and the party publications that spread our message. Hitler was a master at loosening the purse strings of the rich, especially women. Some of them even auctioned their expensive jewelry for the cause. The movement was growing stronger and stronger as the nation got weaker and weaker.

I could tell that Hitler was energized by the crisis. He was increasingly impatient to strike, not just against some local group of reds but against the rulers who were responsible for what was happening. I remember his words from a rally in Nuremberg: "I can only take action where my fanatical belief for the entire German people leads me." Everyone took such declarations as a promise, a promise that we would help him keep.

Before dropping off to sleep at night, I often imagined what it would be like to march north and claim the capital for our movement, *Auf nach Berlin!*— On to Berlin! I'd be returning to my home city as part of a conquering, or liberating, army. I could see my old school friends—Jürgen, Peter and the others—lined up on Pariser Platz as I marched through the Brandenburg Gate. They'd be awed by the rows and rows of brownshirted troops. And wouldn't they be amazed to see me in the front ranks? And jealous. I wouldn't lord it over them, just give them a short, dignified wave. And I'd even visit my mother to make sure she was all right. To show her that I had made something of my life, that all her worrying was for nothing. And, of course, I could tell Sabine that I had kept my promise.

In the barracks, we played guessing games about whether the Bavarian leaders would join us or not. Their support could transform our fantasy into reality, and for a while, it looked like the Bavarian leaders might be among those succumbing to Hitler's powers of persuasion. Bavaria was the only state in Germany that hadn't banned the Nazi Party at the time, and the authorities often winked at our behavior. They were diligent about arresting leftists who attacked or assassinated their opponents. You had a much better chance of getting away with such behavior if you were with us. "They know we're all on the same side," Uwe had explained to me early on. "You don't have to worry much about the police here."

For those of us who wanted to believe that the Bavarian authorities were on our side, the signs of tensions between Berlin and Munich were good news. The Weimar government demanded that Bavaria ban our newspaper, the *Völkischer Beobachter,* and arrest several officers who sympathized with our cause. But Commissioner von Kahr, the man who had recently been granted broad powers by the Bavarian government to keep control over the situation, was a German nationalist. He wasn't about to accept orders from a government he hated as much as we did. Nor was General von Lossow, the commander of the army in Bavaria. Both refused to carry out the orders from Berlin. This was what fueled the talk that we might soon be marching north together.

Uwe didn't believe it, though. "We're going to have to conquer Munich before we can seriously think about taking Berlin," he warned.

Stefan, who was as eager to get back to Berlin as I was, tried to argue, but Uwe wouldn't budge. "Remember, it was von Kahr who banned some of our meetings."

"Yes, but only for a while," Stefan pointed out. "It wasn't as if he was serious about closing us down."

"I don't trust them or anybody here," Uwe insisted. "Not von Kahr, not von Lossow, not that von Seisser," he added, referring to the police chief who was another key figure in Bavaria. He was equally dismissive of the *Kampfbund,* the right-wing parties who should have been our allies. "Some of them just want to make Bavaria an independent state. Instead of making us the rulers of a strong and proud Germany, they'd break the country apart."

At the rallies that I helped guard, Hitler sounded increasingly angry with the Bavarian leaders, especially after they sent emissaries to Berlin and seemed to be losing their enthusiasm for challenging the government. He confirmed Uwe's skepticism. "The halfhearted and the lukewarm have remained the curse of Germany," Hitler shouted. His attacks were directed at the Weimar government—or the Versailles government, as he always called it—but we realized they were aimed at Munich as well.

We sensed we were on the brink of some momentous action or huge letdown. Hitler, I believed, wouldn't permit the latter. We had come too far and fought too hard to let everything unravel now. Something had to happen, I was convinced. Something very big.

I didn't see Sabine as often as before. As the tensions in the city and the country mounted, we were frequently kept on alert several days at a time, without permission to leave the barracks except for official duties. Falling asleep in my bunk at night, I missed her. I wanted to reach out and draw her to me, to feel her body against mine. Occasionally when I was half asleep, her image would blur and then change altogether. I found myself envisaging someone I had seen on the street or in a shop, a girl I didn't know at all. Or one of the women who would show up at the beer halls and drink with the likes of Uwe or Stefan and then disappear with them for an hour or so. They'd boast about those escapades in the barracks later, the way Jürgen did about Ulrike back in Berlin. I'd laugh with the others, but it was a forced laugh. I still couldn't imagine going with such women: They scared me. But they were also tempting, and I couldn't block them out of my mind, either.

All of which left me feeling sheepish the next time I saw Sabine. She embraced me so trustingly, holding nothing back. And there I was fresh from some sordid fantasy, even if I hadn't acted upon it. When we were together, those thoughts evaporated quickly; she was too real a presence to allow for fantasy substitutes, at least in those days.

On a Tuesday morning in early October, I was given permission to leave the barracks until the evening. I had stood guard at a big meeting the night before, and I had no particular duties that day. So I decided to surprise Sabine at work, then walk around the city until she got off and we could head back to her apartment. It had been about a week since I saw her last, which seemed like forever. Just the thought of her rushing into my arms made me slightly giddy.

The weather had turned cool, and the path I used to cut across the English Gardens was already strewn with yellow leaves. As I left the park, I nearly tripped over a small furry object that came rolling out of a pile of leaves. An older man sitting on a tattered blanket quickly snatched it back, and it was then I saw that he was keeping tabs on a whole litter of puppies, all of them a mangy brown. He still had the puppy I had narrowly avoided, grasping him casually in a large, gnarled hand from which a cigarette protruded from the other side.

"Hey, want one?" he asked, holding the squirming puppy up higher. "A fine specimen—almost a purebred. And you can get him cheap."

I laughed. "A purebred what?"

"Well, since you're obviously royalty, the likes of him is too lowly for you." The man turned his back on me and began to gather up the puppies in the blanket.

"Listen," I said, "sorry. I'm broke. And I don't have anywhere to keep one."

The man didn't seem to hear. I watched him walk down a street that led away from the park to a corner where he put down his blanket again and let the puppies play so passersby would see them.

I didn't stick around to see if he had any luck. I headed quickly toward the doctor's office. I paused before I composed myself and knocked. When the door opened, I wanted to grab Sabine and kiss her right there, even if she had always warned me against any such displays near her patients or her boss. This had been one of our longest separations, and I figured she'd forgive me. Just this once, anyway.

But when the door opened, I found myself facing a heavyset nurse with a broad, flat face fixed in what looked like a permanent angry scowl.

"What do you want?"

I found it hard to get an answer out.

"Well?" she demanded.

"Is Sabine here?" I asked, trying to clear the frog in my throat.

"No, she isn't. Who's asking?"

"I'm Karl Naumann."

Her face softened ever so slightly. "Oh, yes, Karl. She said if you dropped by to tell you what happened. You see, her grandmother died.

And the funeral is today, or was today. It's probably over by now. She won't be back at work until tomorrow."

"I see," I said, turning away. "Thanks."

I walked off, heading in the direction of Sabine's apartment. How would she feel, I wondered, all alone in that place. Sure, it had been hard to care for her, but her grandmother had been the only family she had left. I had known enough to realize they had been very close.

After a few steps, I stopped. I turned around and headed back toward the English Gardens. At the corner where I had last seen him, the old man with the puppies was still there. A little girl with frizzy blond hair was playing with one. She pleaded for her mother to buy him, but the woman yanked her away. "Would you want me to starve your little brother so that you can have a pet?" she scolded. The girl's eyes filled with tears as she looked back at the puppy before they disappeared down the street.

"Would you sell me one of them?" I asked, stepping up to the man.

He looked at me with guarded eyes. "For what? You said you had no money."

I emptied my pockets of a few million marks and held them out. "That's all I've got."

"That might be enough to buy me a roll," he said contemptuously.

"I'm sorry, but I really don't have anymore. And I need a puppy badly—for my girlfriend. I just found out her grandmother died, and she has no one else."

The man turned away, looking up and down the street. A few people were walking by, but no one was paying any attention to his puppies.

"All right," he said. "At least it's one roll. And I'll probably have to drown them anyway. Certainly can't feed them."

I was delighted. "Thanks, you've really helped me out." I handed him the money and scooped up the closest puppy. "Boy or girl?"

"A boy," he replied. "Can't you see?"

"Oh, yeah." I laughed. "By the way, what kind of dogs are these?"

The old man shrugged. "Hell if I know. I found them yesterday abandoned at a garbage dump."

The puppy snuggled up on my chest as I walked quickly back in the direction of Sabine's apartment. It was a long walk, and he squirmed only occasionally. But just before I reached Sabine's building, I felt a trickle of moisture on my shirt. I pulled the puppy away and looked down at the wet spot. "Now look what you've done," I admonished him. He looked back with his innocent brown eyes, and I felt my face break into a broad grin.

Sabine wasn't home yet, so I sat on the top stair and let the dog explore the small landing. I put my head down and must have dozed off. The next thing I remember is Sabine shaking my shoulder gently. "Karl, Karl, what's this?" she asked. She was holding the puppy and looking at him with puffy red eyes that were filling up with tears.

"I thought you'd like some company. I mean, your grandmother, I'm sorry, I really am. I bought him on my way here."

"Come," she said, pulling me up with one hand and still holding the puppy with the other. As we stepped into her apartment, she threw her free arm around my neck and was both laughing and crying. "You're crazy. How am I supposed to care for a dog?" she said. "I love him already. God, I'll miss her."

"I know," I said, holding her tightly. "I know."

We talked for hours that afternoon; rather, Sabine did most of the talking while I listened and stroked her face and arms or played with the puppy. She talked about her parents, her grandmother, even told stories she had heard about her grandfather, who died before she was born. I've never been good about listening to family stories, but I let them wash over me, hearing enough to realize how much warmer a family this must have been than mine ever was. But it wasn't until she was back on the subject of her grandmother that I abruptly started to focus.

"You know, she heard us all those times," Sabine was saying.

"What, you mean when—"

"Yes, dummy. She pretended not to, but she did."

"You told me she was nearly deaf."

"Her hearing wasn't good, but it was good enough. A curtain across the room hardly qualifies as a major sound barrier."

I was angry. "Why didn't you tell me?"

"And if I had, what would we have done? She didn't admit she heard everything exactly, but she dropped enough hints. You know what she said? 'Bravo child, life is short. I don't want to prevent you from enjoying as much of it as you can.' Then she told me how she and Grandfather used to do it in the apartment they shared with her mother because they didn't have a place of their own for a long time after they were married. 'Some things never change,' she said. 'It's life.' "

I thought about those blue eyes that had sparkled in the old woman's tired face, and I no longer felt any resentment. "She was a good woman, a very good woman."

I picked up the puppy and let him dangle over my head as I lay back on the bed. Sabine was sitting on its edge, her hands cupping her face.

"But I still feel like an idiot," I said.

Sabine turned around and grinned. "So do I. Remember the time that you put . . ."

"Stop, I don't want to hear about it," I said beating my chest with my free hand in mock agony. "Don't do this to me."

I put the puppy back down on the floor, reached for her shoulders and pulled her back until she was lying beside me again. At first she was very still. Then she kissed me, long and insistently. I forgot all about the dog.

I saw Sabine only once more that October, late in the month. We were almost always on alert, and the barracks were buzzing more than ever with rumors that Hitler was planning a major operation soon. When I explained to Sabine that I might not be able to see her for quite a while, that we were likely to be involved in a showdown of some sort, she pleaded with me to quit the SA and find a normal job.

"Quit now, when they need us most?" I retorted. "No way."

Sabine didn't say anything more, but I knew she was trying hard not to show how worried she was. For the first time, I detected a bit of anger or disappointment, although that, too, was suppressed.

Back in the barracks, I quickly convinced myself that I had exaggerated whatever Sabine was feeling. Besides, there was too much else to think about. If we had been expecting something for a long time, by early November there was little doubt. Our officers kept drilling us, and we remained on full alert without any passes. We were supposed to be ready to move out at any time.

On November 8 the order came. We donned our uniforms, checked to make sure our pistols were loaded and lined up in front of our barracks. Winter had arrived early. Snow was already falling in the hills just outside Munich. The city air was cold and damp; I shuddered as I stood at attention. Our orders were to accompany Hitler to the Bürgerbräukeller, the beer hall where the triumvirate of von Kahr, von Lossow and von Seisser were addressing their supporters that evening. We had heard that Hitler was trying to convince them to join him in a rebellion against the national government, but so far he hadn't succeeded. This, we realized, could be the decisive confrontation.

We were loaded on trucks for the short drive away from the center of town across the Isar River to the huge beer hall. Hitler had already arrived in his red Mercedes, along with several members of his entourage. We followed shortly afterward, arriving at the hall but remaining in the trucks. At the signal from our officers, we jumped out and surrounded the building. I looked at the fear in the eyes of the regular police who were supposed to be maintaining order, and I immediately felt sure they'd do nothing. They meekly let us through, and we marched into the building.

We pushed our way into a huge, noisy hall; a couple thousand people must have been there. Von Kahr was speaking from the platform at the front of the cavernous room. I could hear him droning on but couldn't make out his words. People were drinking beer, laughing and largely ignoring the proceedings. "One billion marks," I heard one of them complaining. "Could you have ever imagined that we'd be paying one billion marks for a mug of beer?"

Hitler was suddenly standing in front of us. I had become used to his unusual appearance, but that evening I was startled. It wasn't just his black morning coat with long tails that made him look more like a waiter than a revolutionary, despite the Iron Cross he had pinned to its breast. It was the unnerving movement of his eyes as they darted about the hall. He saw us, but I felt he was looking through us or not focusing at all. But he must have been emboldened by our presence, because he abruptly waded into the crowd as we formed a phalanx behind him.

We didn't get very far. The crowd pressed together, blocking our progress, and the room became even noisier as people began to notice us. Hitler jumped onto a chair and waved his pistol in the air. "Quiet!" he shouted. To no avail. Then he fired a shot at the ceiling. "The national revolution has begun!" he declared in a quivering voice.

The room fell silent, with the beer drinkers looking on in bewilderment. I tried to project a look of confidence, but I felt as shaky as Hitler seemed. The sweat pouring down his face didn't help steady my nerves. But I stood as rigidly as I could.

Hitler ordered the triumvirate on the platform to follow him into a side room. At first they didn't move. Hitler assured them and the crowd that they were in no danger and could work everything out in ten minutes of discussion. Still they sat there. Hitler began pushing his way toward the leaders, with our phalanx right behind him. Von Kahr was the first to get up, and the others slowly followed. Hitler turned to us. "The first six men, come with me," he ordered. I was the sixth man.

We entered a side room where Hitler invited the leaders to sit down at a large table. The six of us stood at attention along the wall.

Hitler began on a conciliatory note, asking forgiveness for breaking his word that he would not try to stage a putsch on his own. The crisis in Germany was too severe to be ignored. The time for action had come, he told them. Once he had taken power, they would all hold top positions: Von Kahr would become regent of Bavaria; von Lossow would become minister of the army; and von Seisser would be head of the national police.

Seeing that the three men remained unmoved, Hitler pulled out his pistol again. This time he pressed it against his head. "Nobody is leaving," he announced. "If I fail today, I have exactly the number of bullets I need—four. Three for you and one for me."

I was amazed to see von Kahr shrug. "What difference would our deaths make?" he asked.

The three men looked uncertain what to do next, as did Hitler. "Good, so it's decided: We'll go back into the hall," he said after an awkward pause.

What was decided, I wondered. But I didn't have time to figure it out. Instead, the six of us led Hitler and the Bavarians into the hall as he had ordered.

The room was once again noisily chaotic. The drinkers obviously had had enough time to regain their courage, and many of them hissed and jeered when they saw us. Looking more confident, Hitler ignored them and announced from the platform that he expected total silence. "Otherwise I'll order a machine gun placed in the gallery," he declared.

Then he began working his magic. He announced the roles he had assigned to the Bavarian leaders, who stood behind him without objecting. The crowd now assumed they were all in on the plan together. For good measure, Hitler announced that General Ludendorff—who had just arrived—would command the army. And, he promised, once he had assembled his national government, they would march on Berlin. "We will save the German people!" he shouted. "We will save the German nation!"

The crowd was already with him. Knowing he had won them over, he harked back to how he had been blinded in a gas attack at the end of the war: "I am going to fulfill the vow I made five years ago when I was a blind cripple in the military hospital: to know neither rest nor peace until the November criminals have been overthrown, until on the wretched Germany of today there arises once more a Germany of power and greatness, of freedom and splendor."

The crowd was applauding wildly. I stood even straighter, convinced that I'd be marching through the Brandenburg Gate in a matter of days.

Things quickly began to go wrong. I had heard Hitler and the others talking about SA troops entering the city, but there was total confusion about where they were supposed to go. Shortly after his speech, Hitler rushed out to deal with some kind of dispute that had arisen when one of the storm-trooper units had tried to occupy a barracks that housed engineers. He left Ludendorff in charge at the beer hall, and the audience began streaming out. When Hitler returned half an hour later, he was shocked to discover that von Kahr, von Lossow and von Seisser had been allowed to slip away as well.

"How could you let them leave?" he snapped at Ludendorff.

The proud general drew himself up and shot Hitler a disdainful look. "They gave us their word that they are with us. There's no danger."

More of our troops arrived. I saw one SA unit shoving a group of frightened Jews into the beer hall's cellar. They had been caught putting up posters for the Social Democrats, and a couple of them were also carrying prayer books from a local synagogue—proof enough of Hitler's charge that the Jews were behind the government we hated.

Most of them went quietly, but one young man protested, screaming at his captors to let him and the others go. A huge sergeant kicked him hard in the shins, then—as the man bent over to grab his leg—brought a fist up squarely into his descending face. The man tottered backward into the arms of a private, who roughly dragged him down into the cellar along with the others.

I looked away. I felt squeamish, but I didn't want to show it. Seeing Ludendorff and Hitler across the room, I got closer. The general was ordering one of his men to telephone von Lossow or von Seisser, but they were nowhere to be found. Hitler left, saying he needed to check on what was happening elsewhere.

It was after midnight, and officers from other units came in seeking orders, but no one knew what to tell them. They brought disturbing reports of telegrams from the triumvirate denouncing the putsch, explaining that they had been forced into the apparent approval at gunpoint and that they were ordering government troops into the city to stop us. I felt uneasy. It was one thing to talk about a triumphant march to Berlin with the backing of all the patriotic forces; it was quite another to contemplate an actual battle with the local troops and police.

I dozed fitfully as we sat in the beer hall awaiting orders. Early in the morning, we drank lukewarm coffee and munched on some bread and cheese. Then it was out into the cold again, another gray uninviting day. "Shit, I don't like this," Uwe complained, rubbing the stubble on his chin. "It doesn't feel right." I tried to laugh it off. "You're always the pessimist," I replied. But I was trying to convince myself as much as him.

We clambered aboard our truck and drove a short distance, only to stop on a largely deserted street and wait for further orders. The wait stretched into several chilly hours. I rubbed my hands and jiggled my legs but couldn't generate any warmth. At one point a breathless messenger shouted that we were supposed to help free Captain Röhm's unit, which had taken over the local military headquarters only to be surrounded by government troops. But then another messenger delivered an order to wait.

Finally, our drivers turned on their engines and deposited us back at the beer hall. By then the area was swarming with storm troopers, and I could see Ludendorff and Hitler talking and gesturing. We were once again ordered to be ready to march right behind Hitler. As I came closer to the two leaders, I heard Ludendorff explaining that the army would never turn against him.

"Time to march," Hitler ordered.

We quickly formed up, parade-style. Hitler and Max Erwin von Scheubner-Richter, his closest aide, and Ludendorff made up the front row, along with Hitler's bodyguard Ulrich Graf and the air force captain Hermann Göring in a long leather coat. As the most experienced SA unit, we marched behind them. Other units followed, but they were a less than impressive sight. Everyone had swastika armbands, but many of them wore only bits and pieces of old war uniforms.

We numbered a couple thousand in all. As we set out across the Ludwig Bridge, where a police unit quickly backed down, clusters of onlookers waved swastika flags and cheered us on.

About fifteen minutes later, we reached the Marienplatz, where a bigger crowd awaited us and our Nazi flag was flying from the city hall. There was even a bit of singing, and the mood felt better than at any time since the night before. But when I looked at Hitler in his trench coat, I saw that none of the tension had drained from his face. He was pale, and his eyes once again seemed to be looking through rather than at the people around him. He seemed uncertain of what to do next.

But Ludendorff never hesitated. He turned right, marching away from the Marienplatz in the direction of the Odeonplatz. Beyond that was the military headquarters where Captain Röhm's troops were surrounded. As we squeezed together up the narrow Residenzstrasse, I caught a glimpse of police with their guns at the ready. The familiar knot formed in my gut.

Hitler was walking arm in arm with Scheubner-Richter. A police captain gave the order to his men to move forward. I heard a single shot, I wasn't sure from where, and then several volleys. Everyone was pushing to get out of the claustrophobic street, and I found myself sprawled on the pavement. "Come on, let's get out of here," Uwe shouted, and he yanked me back up before turning and running.

As I steadied myself, I looked to where Hitler had been standing. Scheubner-Richter was lying on the street dead, along with several other people. Ludendorff was still marching straight into the police cordon, where he was immediately arrested. As for Hitler, I caught sight of him holding his arm as if injured, then scrambling away with Graf and one of our medical officers.

I took off after them, figuring I should help if I could. But when they reached Max Joseph Platz, Hitler's car was waiting, and he jumped in, followed by Graf; the medical officer rode on the sideboard, his pistol at the ready. As they roared off, I stood there, still shaken. It wasn't just the gunfire, the confusion and the dead bodies. It was as much the sight of our leader fleeing as soon as those first shots were fired. Instead of leading a successful putsch, he had led us into a disaster and then run at the first opportunity.

I heard another burst of gunfire from the vicinity of Marienplatz. I turned and ran in the opposite direction.

Chapter Five

What if the shot that felled Scheubner-Richter had hit Hitler instead?
What if Hitler had been blinded permanently in the poison-gas attack
during the war? The what ifs have driven me nearly crazy as I've served
my seven years here. Not so much what any of them would have meant for
the party, but for Geli. And, of course, for me, for my life. I know it
doesn't make sense to think in those terms. Once my mind gets going about
this, it's off and running on its own, and I can't do anything to stop it.
I'm tormented by those thoughts as I follow my mindless prison routine
and, even at night , I wake up with the same thoughts. What if, what if,
what if. . .

My return to Berlin was not at all as I had envisaged it. Instead of a triumphant entry as part of a victorious army, I arrived alone, frightened, more uncertain of my future than ever.

In Munich after the debacle of the putsch, I had hidden in Sabine's apartment for several days, not knowing how extensive the manhunt was for anyone associated with it. Sabine brought me the news that Hitler had been caught and arrested two days later in Uffing, about fifty kilometers south of Munich. He hadn't been wounded in the brief exchange of shots that had killed fourteen Nazis and four policemen, but he had dislocated his left shoulder, probably when his bodyguard yanked him to the ground. There were stories, too, of my panicked SA comrades burying or even destroying their weapons—in one case, smashing their rifles against trees. I found all this hard to believe, harder still to imagine how we could recover from such a defeat.

When I took the train to Berlin, nervously eyeing anybody in uniform, the socialist papers were proclaiming the end of the Nazi movement. One, which I picked up off the seat, quoted *The New York Times:* "The Munich putsch definitely eliminates Hitler and his National Socialist followers." That meant me, I thought gloomily, and everything that I had been fighting for during the last three years. What was I going to do now?

Sabine didn't come right out and say it, but I knew she was secretly relieved by our defeat, hoping it meant I would put away my uniform and my fantasy about marching to Berlin and overthrowing the government. When Otto Strasser sent a message asking me to come to Berlin both for my own safety and to consult with him, she wholeheartedly supported the idea. She was worried that I was still in danger in Munich, and she knew from what I had told her earlier that Otto was no fanatical supporter of Hitler. He had expressed misgivings from the beginning, and in his occasional letters, he had sounded skeptical about my glowing accounts. At heart, Otto remained a socialist. And while he was impressed by Hitler's ability to appeal to the workers and the unemployed, he was troubled by the highly visible flirtation with the rich and powerful—the big industrialists and others who provided financial support.

I wrote a cryptic reply to Otto saying only that I'd see him soon. So when my train pulled into the Anhalter Station in Berlin on a cold November morning, I wasn't sure yet where I wanted to go. Straight to Otto for what would undoubtedly be an accounting of what happened in Munich? I wanted to see him, hoping to find some guidance there, but I also didn't feel quite ready to rehash our defeat. Or should I follow Sabine's advice and head for my mother's apartment, finally putting her fears to rest that I had disappeared altogether? But what would I say to her—how would I explain my long disappearance? It would have been one thing to do so as part of a victorious army, but now what did I have to offer as justification? Here I was back in the city of the Versailles government, as Hitler always called it, and I felt only anger at myself and my powerlessness.

I took to the streets, staying away from Neukölln, where I had grown up and where I feared I might encounter the same former class-mates I had earlier envisaged applauding my glorious return. I headed instead for the downtown areas, what I remembered as the exotic world of fancy shops, theaters and restaurants. But the reality was harsh. I stepped around war veterans missing arms or legs, either beg-ging or selling matches. Sabine had given me some money for the trip, and I handed a few thousand marks to a couple of them, but I soon re-alized that I had to spend it on my own needs—and fast. It was dwin-dling in value every hour that it was in my small bag. In Berlin, I quickly learned, prices were increasingly expressed in anything other than money. Passing a theater, I was startled to see a sign announcing: ORCHESTRA STALLS: THE SAME PRICE AS HALF A POUND OF BUTTER. REAR STALLS: TWO EGGS.

I would see my mother later, I told myself, even if it meant finding some other place to stay. I decided on an initial investment: I paid an old woman who owned a grimy pension—a three-room apartment in Wedding where she packed in whatever visitors she could—for a cou-ple of nights and meals in advance. As soon as I handed her the pay-ment, she plopped down my dinner, a bowl of cabbage soup, and rushed out to buy more cabbage and potatoes before the cash became worthless.

My room was no more than a closet, and its small window looked out at the gray wall of the building next door. Although it was early afternoon as I settled in, it was almost dark inside. I lay back on the cot, shivering, and pulled a filthy blanket over me. This wasn't much better than when I had lived on the streets and slept in stairways be-fore joining the SA and becoming part of a group that cared for its own.

I must have drifted off to sleep for some time, because when I awoke the room was completely dark. I threw off the blanket and went out. It was early evening, and I headed back toward the city center where I could at least watch the wealthier Berliners on their way to the shops, restaurants and cafés. I had a strong urge to get as far away from my lodgings as I could.

I didn't want to pay for the tram, so I walked all the way to the Kurfürstendamm, where I knew the rich would still be at play. There were even more women and young girls out on the sidewalk than before, hoping to attract the attention of the well-dressed men leaving the restaurants or cafés. A couple of them gave me a perfunctory look but recognized another hard-luck case and didn't waste time propositioning me.

About halfway up the Kurfürstendamm, I hesitated in front of a bar. The clientele didn't look wealthy, but I knew I couldn't afford to squander whatever cash I had left on a beer. Still, I was tempted and stood there for several minutes. Finally, I turned away just as a redheaded woman stepped outside.

"Karl?" she asked. "Karl, my God, is that you? I haven't seen you in years."

I turned back. It took me a moment to identify the thickly powdered face, still young but sallow and defiant in a way I didn't remember, the dark brown eyes much wearier. "Ulrike, I'm sorry—I didn't recognize you," I stammered. "I mean, you look great, all grown up."

Ulrike pulled out a cigarette and offered me one. I shook my head but lit hers with one of the matches I had bought from a disabled veteran that afternoon. She exhaled slowly, locking her eyes on mine until I looked away. "You don't have to tell me stories, Karl. I know what I look like."

I shivered in the cold.

"Hey," she said, "you must have been standing here for a while. Come on, let's go inside."

I hesitated.

Her face stiffened and her eyes narrowed. "Embarrassed to be seen with me?"

"No, no," I protested.

"Can't afford a drink?"

When I didn't reply, her face relaxed. "I'm buying—for old time's sake. It's not often I see anyone I knew in those days. Besides, I always liked you."

"You did?"

She laughed and put her hand lightly on my shoulder as she guided me through the door to a corner table in the back of the bar.

We sat there for I don't know how long. I certainly wasn't in any hurry, and to my surprise, Ulrike wasn't, either. "A night off," she said. "I deserve it. Besides, these days there's only a fifty-fifty chance of making anything on the street." She looked at me across the table, under which our knees touched. "Do I shock you?"

I shook my head.

"Don't lie. Look, this is the way it is now. Foreigners come here and buy up whole blocks of buildings because our money is worthless. People sell their apartments and then commit suicide if the buyer is a week late with the payment, because by then the money they get isn't worth anything. The rest of us just survive any way we can. That's the way it is. You think my mother would be alive today if it wasn't for me? She's sick and couldn't find work even if she were well."

"You don't have to explain," I said. "Really. I know what's happening here. It's all the same—in Berlin, in Munich and I guess everywhere else."

We drank some more, and Ulrike ordered me a thick sausage. As I looked at her, I couldn't help thinking about Jürgen and his talk of "the Ulrike treatment."

Ulrike met my gaze. "What?"

"Nothing, nothing at all."

"That's what I liked about you: You were always a bad liar." She wiped the beer foam from her lips with the tip of her fingers. I noticed her bitten-down fingernails. "Time to go," she added. She stood up and paid the bill.

I followed her out the door. "Thanks," I said. "That was great."

Ulrike smiled, but she looked less certain than she had all evening. "Take me home," she said softly. My eyes betrayed my confusion. "I know, you've got a girl. But just this once. I haven't wanted to be with someone—I mean for me, not for work—in so long."

So I found myself on the familiar tram to Neukölln, after all, not to my mother's place but to Ulrike's tiny room. I don't want to talk about any Ulrike treatment, but she did things Sabine had never done and I had never dreamed of. I guess she had learned her trade well, but that night I tried to blot out those thoughts. It was only I, she told me, who made her so excited. And for those few hours, I believed her as much as I had ever believed anything. As much as I believed my own inner voice saying that this would be just this once, that Sabine didn't ever have to know, that it wouldn't hurt her. I'll make it up to you, I silently promised her, by never being unfaithful again. It's just this once. God, she was good.

I made my way back to my grimy room in Wedding around four in the morning, but when I woke up at ten I felt determined, energetic and no longer afraid of my old haunts. If I ran into anyone else I knew, so be it. It wasn't as if many of them, or any of them, could boast that they had made much more of their lives. At least I had traveled, lived in another city, fought for a cause—even though that cause was lost. And I was no longer an inexperienced boy but a man, a man who knew something about women, different kinds of women. But when I thought briefly about fulfilling my promise to Sabine by visiting my mother, I felt a flicker of the old doubt. I'll do that later, I decided. First I needed to focus on the reason for my coming, Otto's summons.

Otto had kept his political activities discreet enough not to jeopardize his day job at the Reich Food Ministry. Since it was Saturday, I didn't need to wait until evening to find him at home. When I knocked, I heard a shuffling of papers and a chair scraping the floor, and then he was there in the open doorway, his arms stretched out and grasping my shoulders in greeting. "You've grown up," he said, sizing me up with bemusement. "Looks like Munich hasn't treated you all that badly."

Rex jumped up in greeting, and I dropped down on one knee to pet him. He gleefully offered me his stomach. "Hey, I've got a dog, too, now. Or at least my girlfriend does. I gave it to her."

Otto grinned. "Yes, Munich is treating you well."

Looking up, I saw a small table overflowing with a typewriter, papers, books and pamphlets. Some I recognized as Nazi publications from Munich, but many of the others didn't look familiar. *The Capitalist Menace,* one proclaimed. Another read: *The Case for Nationalization.*

Otto motioned me to sit and followed my gaze. "Yes, I'm still working on the socialist part of the agenda. I hope you didn't forget that down in Munich, with all the talk about just the nationalism part."

I shrugged, still playing with Rex, who had followed me to my chair. "Well, I'm not sure either part matters much anymore. It's pretty much over, I guess."

"Look who's the pessimist now," Otto said. "In your letters, you were always saying Hitler was really on to something, that his movement could succeed, and I was the skeptic. You're almost as bad as Hitler himself."

"What do you mean?"

"You haven't heard about your führer's second great moment after fleeing Munich?"

I shook my head, and Otto told me the version of events that he had somehow already learned from his other sources in Munich, clearly ones a lot higher up than I was.

Hitler, it seemed, had taken refuge in Uffing, in the Hanfstaengls' house. I had heard stories about Ernst "Putzi" Hanfstaengl, or "the American," as we called him. He was a member of a wealthy Munich family of art publishers, and he had introduced Hitler to many of his rich friends. His wife, Helene, a tall elegant woman, was the one with the real American family background, but Ernst had studied at Harvard and entertained Hitler by playing university sports songs on the piano. Anyway, Otto explained that Ernst and several other Hitler advisers had already fled across the border to Austria when they got word of the shoot-out. So it was Helene who was at home when Hitler arrived, still in pain from his dislocated shoulder and deeply despondent.

"You know, I think Hitler may be a bit in love with Helene," Otto said, chuckling. "He's always been in awe of some women, and she seems to be one of them. In any case, word was out that the police were already approaching the house when Helene found him standing in his bathrobe and holding his pistol. I don't know whether he actually pointed it at his head, but she was convinced he had decided to kill himself. She lit into him: She told him he didn't have the right to abandon his followers that way, that he'd better not take the easy way out. And she actually took the pistol from his hand. After that he accepted his arrest peacefully when the police came. He just threw his trench coat on over his bathrobe and made sure he had his Iron Cross pinned on it. The police treated him with a lot of respect, as if they were escorting a patriot instead of a criminal.

"So what do you think of that?"

I shook my head. "Not exactly encouraging. If Hitler was thinking about shooting himself, what are the rest of us supposed to feel?"

"You've missed the point," he lectured me. "Sure, there have been plenty of arrests. My brother, Gregor, marched his men back to Landshut and faced down a Reichswehr detachment that wanted to stop them. 'Make way or I fire,' he told them—and they backed down. But he, too, was arrested at his own home the next day. Although, as in Hitler's case, the arresting officer was almost apologetic about having to carry out such an order. The point is that a lot of people consider von Kahr and the others the real traitors here. They were going to back our revolution, and then they turned on it. We may have lost this round, but I'll wager we've gained a lot of sympathy."

I still wasn't convinced, but I was impressed by Otto's passion, his strong belief that the Nazis had a chance to stage a comeback.

"What's crucial here is how everyone behaves at the trial," Otto continued. "We can use it as a platform. We can put the government on trial instead of it putting us on trial. But that depends on how smart Hitler is, whether he'll know what to do."

No matter what happened, Otto insisted that he'd keep producing propaganda for the movement—or simply against the government. In fact, he told me, he was thinking of quitting his bureaucratic job and devoting himself full-time to writing. So much needed to be done, he explained, and the written word was so important.

"What can I do? Can I stay here and help you out? There's nothing left in Munich."

"Not yet," Otto said. "The time may come soon when you can work for me here, but I need to get my operation going first. And for now you can be my eyes and ears in Munich, much more so now. With Hitler and the others arrested and about to face trial, we'll need to send messages back and forth and watch every step of these proceedings. And see how Hitler really performs. He may not have been much of a leader when the shooting started, but the real battle is just beginning. And words are going to be just as important in this battle as bullets. You can travel back and forth, but I want you most of the time in Munich."

We talked about the kinds of information Otto would be looking for, and as I was leaving, he solemnly shook my hand. "Look, I'm not saying everything is going to work out. But maybe because I'm far enough from what happened in Munich, I can see the possibilities. Don't give up. And yes, don't give up on Hitler. You and Gregor were right: He does know how to reach people. Now he's got to show that he can do that even from a courtroom or prison."

I didn't lie to Sabine about Ulrike when I returned to Munich; I just didn't say anything. I felt almost virtuous in my conviction that what had happened was and would be the only exception. The first night after I returned was almost like our very first nights together, both of us finding that we couldn't get enough of each other, our brief separation pulling us even closer together. But when we had exhausted ourselves and I was already half asleep with my arms tightly around her, Sabine asked: "So how is your mother? What did she say when she saw you?"

"She's fine," I said sleepily. "I'll tell you about it tomorrow."

Sabine pushed back to look at my face. "You saw her, right?"

"Yes, of course."

"Good, I was worried there for a moment."

One lie of omission and one direct lie, I thought. But no need to hurt or disappoint her, no need to be stupidly honest. What happened didn't really matter, I told myself. It was just a delayed initiation into manhood that I almost had earlier, before I ever met Sabine, except for the fact that I wasn't ready for it then. As for my mother, I'd see her the next time.

In the morning I was saved by the fact that we woke up late and both of us needed to rush off. Sabine was going to work, and much to her disappointment, I had my first assignment—to make contact with members of the now underground Nazi movement in Munich and to plan coordination with Landsberg, the town west of Munich where Hitler and the others had been imprisoned. Otto had been precise: I was to report on the prisoners, how they were treated and what they were doing. If he was going to commit himself to the party—he hadn't formally joined yet—he wanted to know how they dealt with the setbacks as well as the victories.

One thing became clear quite early: The authorities weren't going to mistreat Hitler and the other Nazi prisoners. Word came that Hitler's cell number seven was comfortable, bigger than his small room on Thierschstrasse. Its window had the requisite double bars but offered a pleasant view of trees and bushes. His colleagues were allowed to visit him and to talk as long as they wished.

The real worry, however, was not the conditions but his state of mind. Alfred Rosenberg, whom Hitler had designated as the Munich leader of the party during his absence, was distressed by news that the prisoner wasn't eating. A German who had grown up in the Baltic city of Reval, Rosenberg was an intellectual, one of the smartest men we had. But he also knew he could hardly fill Hitler's shoes. That's probably why Hitler had chosen him. He wouldn't be a threat.

He was loyal and genuinely concerned. "They say he's pale and listless and that he hasn't eaten in almost two weeks," he told me. "He just stares out the window. The doctor is warning the others that they'd better get him to eat or he'll die. I want you to go there and try to talk to them. And, if you can, to him. I'll give you a letter for him. You have nothing to worry about: They have no specific charges against you and probably won't have any idea who you are."

I set off for Landsberg the next morning, hitching a ride with a driver who dropped me off near the small town wedged between steep, wooded hills. I crossed an old wooden bridge over the Lech, more like a small stream than a river at that point, and headed for the prison complex. It sat atop a hill and was surrounded by imposing stone walls.

As I approached the gate, I tried to remain calm, but I felt warm and sweaty under my worn jacket despite the early December chill. It was one thing to say that I wasn't in any danger and quite another to test that theory. Was it true that the authorities had no interest in arresting any more of us?

"Your business?" the guard asked, his florid face impassive behind elaborate waxed whiskers.

"I'm here to deliver a letter to Adolf Hitler."

His expression didn't change. "All right, hand it over."

I took a breath. "I'd like to give it to him personally."

The guard gave me a contemptuous look. "Hand it over."

I reached into my pocket and pulled out the letter from Rosenberg.

The guard tore it open and read slowly. His face softened for the first time. "Why didn't you tell me you were one of his people? How was I supposed to know that? We've got to guard the prisoners and to make sure nobody gets to them who shouldn't." He paused. "I'll take you to Drexler—he'll tell you whether you can see Hitler. Follow me."

We walked down a long corridor until we reached a locked door. The guard drew out a large key and opened it. "This is where we keep the politicals," he said. He laughed. "Sure beats the other side, where the criminals are."

I didn't get to see Hitler that day. Anton Drexler, the original founder of the party that Hitler took over, drew me aside. "He's resting now," he said. With evident satisfaction, he added: "He ate today for the first time."

Drexler explained that he had spent hours in the cell convincing Hitler not to give up. He wanted me to know that his persuasive powers had done the job, with the result that Hitler finally gobbled down some rice. Later, I heard another version of events. Helene Hanfstaengl had intervened again, according to this account, by letter. She told Hitler she hadn't stopped him from taking his life at her house only for him to do so behind bars. She warned him not to disappoint his supporters, not to take the easy way out. And to ignore all the gleeful press accounts of his political demise. Prove them wrong, she insisted.

Whoever deserved the credit, Hitler's recovery was remarkable. He not only began eating again and regained his physical strength quickly, his outlook changed radically. By the time his stepsister Angela came to visit from Vienna later in the month, she found him brimming with optimism. His left arm was almost completely healed, and he showed her gifts he had received from well-wishers, including Winifred Wagner, the daughter-in-law of the composer and a great admirer. There were flowers, his favorite cakes, books, all delivered without any interference from the prison authorities. "Victory is only a matter of time," he assured Angela. Those words spread quickly throughout our camp and outside it. While the socialist press continued to ridicule Hitler and his coconspirators, I realized we were far from isolated.

As Christmas neared, I asked Sabine to come with me to a café in Schwabing, Munich's favorite district for artists. I wouldn't normally have thought to enter one of those more fashionable cafés, but Rosenberg suggested it, saying that the owners had invited members of our movement for something special.

I wasn't sure what to expect, and I didn't explain the party connection to Sabine. But she was happy for a rare night out. When we entered, the café was arranged with a darkened stage near the window at the front; the audience was invited to sit in the back. I recognized a few faces from party meetings, but the crowd seemed to be mostly artistic types.

"What's this all about?" Sabine asked as we sat down.

"I'm not sure," I whispered, "but I think it has something to do with Hitler."

Sabine rolled her eyes.

"Just wait, let's see," I pleaded.

A low light was turned on the improvised stage as male voices sang "Silent Night" from somewhere on the side. We couldn't see the singers. A man was sitting at a table in front of the window, his face buried in his hands. I couldn't make out who he was, but then I noticed the fake bars in the window as a light snow fell outside. The man slowly turned, and in the dim light, his familiar features, slicked-down black hair and narrow but thick mustache stopped me short. By the time he had turned fully, I knew it wasn't Hitler, but I still felt slightly in shock. As did much of the audience. I saw several people, both men and women, with wet eyes. Even Sabine seemed oddly moved. "It's too bad he has to spend Christmas in prison," she said. "I wouldn't wish that on anyone."

At the end of 1923, none of us could quite figure out what the government was doing, but somehow it managed to halt the crazy inflation and stabilize the mark again. Rosenberg and others warned us not to believe the economic situation had really improved. I took those warnings to heart, I guess, because it was easy to be cynical about anything going right for a change. Nonetheless, I had to admit that life began to feel a bit more normal again. And it was nice to know that when I had a few marks in my pocket—most often from Sabine—they would be worth just as much tomorrow as they were today. But plenty of people who had seen their life savings evaporate weren't going to forgive the government, no matter what it had finally managed to achieve. There was no doubt that the rage fueling our movement was still there.

Which was what Hitler was counting on when he and the others were put on trial in Munich in early 1924. The charge against him was high treason, but his plan was to turn the tables on his accusers. That much of his strategy I had heard beforehand from Rosenberg and others.

The trial, held in Munich in the old infantry school building on Blutenburgstrasse, opened on February 26. I was able to get into several sessions with the help of a press card that Rosenberg had secured for me from one of the right-wing newspapers. I had protested that I'd never get away with pretending to be a journalist, but he claimed all I had to do was take notes along with the others and no one would examine my credentials too closely.

"They'd recognize one of us, but you're a young unknown face," he assured me. He gave me an appraising look. "It's not a typical face, I'd say, not like most of the muscle around here."

"What do you mean by that?"

"Take it as a compliment. You're handsome, young, clean-cut. You don't look like someone who grew up fighting in beer halls. Besides, many of the people in there are on our side and wouldn't give you away even if they knew."

And that proved to be Hitler's secret weapon during the twenty-four-day trial. The Bavarian authorities had insisted on the trial taking place in Munich to cover up their involvement in the plotting that had preceded the putsch attempt. Hitler wasn't about to let them get away with that, especially in front of a sympathetic audience. The judge was a nationalist who let Hitler go on as long as he wanted, and even the prosecutor seemed wary about pushing his case very aggressively.

Hitler quickly put to rest any remaining doubts about his eagerness to fight. At first I was stunned when he admitted to leading the putsch. "I alone bear the responsibility," he declared. But he hammered home the point that he was fighting for a noble cause. "I am not a criminal because of that," he said. "If today I stand here as a revolutionary, it is as a revolutionary against the revolution. There is no such thing as high treason against the traitors of 1918."

About his accusers, the Bavarian triumvirate, he declared what all of us knew—that they had turned against us only in the end. "If our enterprise was actually high treason, then during this whole period, von Lossow, von Kahr and von Seisser must have been committing high treason along with us, for during all these weeks we talked of nothing but the aims of which we now stand accused." All around me, I saw nods of agreement.

I felt my faith in him restored, almost forgetting the chaos of the putsch and how he had fled as soon as the shooting began. In his rendition of events, I saw a pattern that had eluded me then, and I felt a growing pride that I had been one of the participants. I put all this down late at night in letters to Otto. "Hitler is proving that he is a real leader after all, just as you predicted," I wrote.

The press was carrying long accounts of the trial, providing Hitler with an audience far beyond the courtroom. You could tell from his words that he was aiming to convince more than the court of the justice of his cause. "Gentlemen, it is not you who pronounce judgment upon us, it is the eternal court of history which will make its pronouncements upon the charge that is brought against us."

On the day of the verdict, I arrived early. A crowd had already formed outside, and I saw several women with flowers, begging the guards to give them to Hitler. I laughed when I heard one of them ask whether she could take a bath in Hitler's tub, but I also felt happy to be on the side of a leader who could inspire such adoration.

Everyone began shoving when the defendants showed up. They paused in front of the courthouse for a photograph. Hitler, I realized, had gained so much weight in prison that he looked almost chubby. This is going to turn out just fine, I thought. He's got everyone on his side.

Inside the courtroom, only Ludendorff was acquitted. Hitler was sentenced to five years, minus the time he had already spent in pretrial detention. I felt dejected, wondering whether the movement could survive his absence for so long. But then I listened to the other parts of the ruling. The court announced that, although Hitler was an Austrian and should be eligible for deportation, they wouldn't send him away. Citing his bravery during the war when he fought for the German army, it declared that "a man who thinks and feels as German as Hitler" should not be expelled. And the presiding judge specifically mentioned the possibility that Hitler might be released on probation before the end of his sentence, which was the minimum he could have received if found guilty. Most of the other defendants were found guilty of lesser charges and emerged with light sentences. It could have been worse, I thought, much worse.

Or much better, depending on your point of view. Once again the socialist press was quoting foreign newspaper accounts to buttress its angry condemnations of everything about the trial—how it had been turned into "a propaganda circus" for Hitler, how it had been a mockery of justice. One of the papers I looked at quoted the London *Times:* "The trial has at any rate proved that a plot against the Constitution of the Reich is not considered a serious crime in Bavaria."

I no longer felt endangered because of my small role in the putsch. "It looks like I can do anything I want," I told Sabine cheerfully. "I'm in the clear."

"Does that mean you'll look for a normal job and forget about politics?" she asked.

"How can I do that? I'm not sitting in jail, so I have to do what I can to keep things going until Hitler and the others get out."

"And then?"

"And then I'll see."

Chapter Six

In leather shorts and a Tyrolean jacket, he was standing in the middle of cell number seven, drenched with sunlight on this late April morning.

"*Heil* Hitler!" I saluted from the open door. "Happy birthday."

He cast me an amused glance. "I'd invite you in, but as you can see, there's not much room."

The cell was overflowing with flowers, gifts and letters, and more were stacked in neighboring cells. The festive air made it easy to forget we were in a prison. Every few minutes someone would call out "Happy thirty-fifth!" and deposit another bunch of flowers or boxes. There must have been enough poppy-seed strudel in cell number seven to feed Hitler his favorite dish three times a day for the next four years that he was supposed to serve. There were packages of ham, bacon and sausages from admirers who didn't know he was a vegetarian. Hitler had them distributed among the common criminals downstairs, where the rules and conditions were much harsher. Hitler and his fellow Nazi prisoners seemed like boarders whom the management was intent on pleasing.

Hitler stepped around some of the parcels. "Any messages?"

"Other than everyone's greetings, they wanted you to know that the preparations for the national elections are going well," I reported. "The National Socialist Freedom Movement will field thirty-four candidates in the May elections."

His face seemed to darken. "Good, that's very good. Who's on the list?"

"Strasser, Röhm, Feder, Frick, Ludendorff. I can bring you the complete list next time."

"Yes, Strasser." He paused. "Gregor is the organizer here, I take it." It wasn't a question.

Anton Drexler was at my elbow, nudging me away. "Come join us for the noon meal," he said. "Herr Hitler will come along shortly."

Hitler looked at me as if I had just arrived. "Yes, go to the table," he said brusquely, then turned away.

I followed Drexler to the common room, where the other prisoners were gathering. They stood behind their chairs, chatting. Drexler pointed to a chair, and I took up the same position, finding myself between Drexler and Rudolf Hess, who had given himself up after the trial—although he could have stayed in Austria, where he had fled. People said that he desperately wanted to be at Hitler's side.

I introduced myself, but Hess hardly appeared to notice. His square face and close-set eyes were fixed on the door. Abruptly, the talking stopped, and all eyes turned in the same direction.

No one moved. Hitler walked in, and someone shouted, "Attention!" He stepped to the head of the table.

Hess was the first to rush up. "My most heartfelt wishes for your health and happiness," he declared, bowing slightly. "May you live a long life and, for the sake of Germany, achieve all your goals."

Hitler nodded, and Hess hastily stepped back behind his chair. One by one, the others came up with greetings for Hitler.

"Do I go, too?" I whispered to Drexler as quietly as I could.

"Everyone does," he shot back. "Not just on his birthday but every day."

After all of the regular diners had paid their respects, I followed. "Birthday greetings from everyone in Munich," I said stiffly, feeling foolish about repeating myself. "Especially from my comrades in the SA who look forward to serving you again soon."

"They will have their chance soon enough," Hitler responded as he pulled back his chair and sat down.

Much to my surprise, that was it as far as any reference to politics or the party's prospects was concerned. As we ate our meal, Hitler visibly relaxed, steered the conversation to the subject of cars, music, plays. I knew nothing about those subjects, so I ate mostly in silence.

Hess finally acknowledged my presence. "Are you surprised by anything here?" he asked.

"By the pleasant atmosphere. It's almost as if this weren't a prison at all."

"It is and it isn't," Hess sternly replied. "Prisons are meant to intimidate and humiliate, but no prison could intimidate or humiliate Hitler. He doesn't allow it to feel like a prison."

"Is anything not permitted here?"

Drexler jumped in. "We can't leave, but short of that, we're able to do just about everything we want. Not officially, mind you, but it isn't hard to get around the rules. After we eat, I'll show you the newspaper we put out."

"And there's no limit on visitors?"

"Visiting hours are six hours a week. Don't tell Hitler that, though. He must have visitors six hours a day."

Hitler pushed back his chair and stood up. We all rose, and he looked in my direction. "Wait for Emil—he'll provide you with my messages for Munich."

He turned and left. Emil Maurice, his driver, grinned and scrambled after him. The others began to disperse.

"He likes to do his writing now," Drexler said. "So you should get your messages in a little while."

We sat back down. "What's the rest of the day like?"

Drexler shrugged. "Nothing special. Free time until coffee and tea at four. Afterward, another walk around the garden or sports. Dinner at six in our cells, but we can buy beer or wine if we want. Then it's more exercise, a final gathering in the common room and lights out at ten. With the exception of Hitler. He often reads till midnight."

"What kind of sports?"

"Wrestling, boxing, workouts on the parallel bars or the vaulting horse."

"And Hitler—" I ventured.

"No, no," Drexler cut me short. "He'll referee occasionally, but he never takes part. You know what he once told me: 'A leader can't participate in sports because he can't be seen to lose.' Makes perfect sense, don't you think?"

I nodded eagerly to acknowledge this bit of wisdom.

Emil Maurice arrived, carrying a small bundle of letters. Unlike the other party prisoners, he looked almost foppish with his thick hair rising in waves above his forehead. He flashed the amused grin that I had noticed earlier.

He stuck out his hand and grinned again, as if we were sharing a joke. "We were never introduced. I'm Emil, the driver, the fixer, the guy who delivers clean shirts for the boss. A lot of shirts, I assure you. Anything you need to communicate or get done, any special requests, I'm at your service." He bowed slightly.

I smiled back. "Yes, sir, I'll remember that."

"It's not 'sir' but Emil."

"Fine, I'm Karl," I added, delighted that someone was willing to treat me as an equal on a first-name basis.

I took the letters and stuffed them in the inside pocket of my jacket. Then I checked out with the guards, who waved me through without asking what I was carrying, and headed back to Munich.

My life with Sabine had taken on a domestic routine. I no longer made any pretense of looking for a place to live; it was too comfortable treating her place as ours. Besides, Sabine was happy with the arrangement, dismissing my halfhearted talk of finding somewhere else to live. "Why bother? You'll pay for some place where you'll never sleep anyway." She would laugh and blush slightly. More often than not, those conversations took place in bed or ended up in bed. She didn't have to do much convincing, but I liked to bring up the subject just to hear her objections. It became a game we both played.

We had another playmate during those games. Leo, the mutt I had bought for her, was more than six months old, a scruffy, medium-size dog who didn't want to be left out, whatever we were doing. Whenever I reached for Sabine and began kissing her, he'd be up and barking furiously. His jealousy made us laugh, and we teased him mercilessly, making our kisses noisy and long. At night, though, after he'd settle down at the foot of our bed and go to sleep, we'd try to make love under the covers so that he wouldn't interfere. But no matter how quiet we tried to be, he'd be up as soon as he heard or felt the bed moving. Before I could do anything to stop him, he'd plant his front paws on the bed and push his head under the covers, his cold nose pressing against our legs or reaching for the center of the action. "Down," I'd shout, pushing him away. Sabine's face would be contorted with laughter whether Leo had staged his attack in the worst or best moment.

During the day, when Sabine was at the doctor's office, I had time on my hands. I began visiting the beer halls, sometimes meeting Uwe, who was usually between part-time jobs as a housepainter. My work for the party wasn't regular enough to keep me all that busy, although I didn't like to admit this to Sabine.

"You know, you could look for a job," she told me one morning as she ate her roll before going off to work.

"I've got a job. Besides, have you seen the lines at the unemployment office? I go by every day, and they're always huge."

"I know, but somehow many of the husbands and boyfriends of my friends manage to find something."

"You're ashamed that you have a boyfriend who doesn't sit in an office somewhere or shovel coal?"

"That's not what I meant."

"So what did you mean?"

"Forget it. Do what you want. I have to go to work."

We made up that evening and pretended that nothing had happened. Leo went after us again, and we both ended up laughing so hard that I finished with more of a whimper than a bang. We held each other tightly afterward, falling asleep intertwined and happy.

A couple weeks later, Sabine came home from work and announced that we were going out the next evening. "Petra, Karin and I decided we should organize a party. We haven't done anything like this for so long."

"Go ahead. I'm not stopping you."

"But this isn't just a girl party. You and the other guys are coming, too. It's about time we all met."

I had met Petra, a nurse in Sabine's office who struck me as rather officious, and I had heard about Karin, who had been a classmate of Sabine's. But I had never spent any time with them, and I had no particular interest in doing so now.

"We can't afford a party," I objected. "And you can't be thinking of having it here."

Sabine wasn't about to be deterred. "I'm not stupid, you know. We've got it all worked out. Karin's parents have a nice apartment, and they're away in Garmisch for a few days. She says to bring just a little bit of food and beer."

I couldn't think of any excuse.

"Come on, Karl," Sabine pleaded, "this once. We never go out anywhere anymore."

It was true. Since I'd moved in, we hadn't been to a movie or even a café. My explanation was always that we couldn't afford it, but what spending money I had tended to disappear in the afternoons in the beer halls. Sabine took care of most of the household expenses.

"Sure, I'll go if you want to."

Sabine began gathering up some sausages, tomatoes and beer that she had brought home. "You'll see, it'll be fun. I know you weren't impressed with Petra, but she's warmer than she looks. And Karin is great. She's the only girl from my class I've stayed friends with."

Karin's parents lived near the university, where her father was a professor of German literature. We went by tram, and Sabine—who normally had a terrible sense of direction—led me easily through a maze of streets to their building. "I visited here often when we were in school," she explained. "Now I usually meet Karin somewhere closer to work. Her parents were always so nice to me: They insisted that I eat

with them whenever I came over, even in the hardest times. They knew I was much worse off than they were."

The building looked normal enough from the outside, except for a fresh coat of gray paint and sparkling white-framed arched window that made its neighbors look drab. As we walked up to the third floor we passed elegant, massive wooden doors with shiny brass handles and locks that suggested wealthy owners. The staircase was impeccab clean and well lit, with nothing like a laundry basket or a bicycle the landing, as was usually the case in the buildings I knew.

I looked at the names on the apartments we passed: Finkelste Rosenblatt, Mandelbaum.

"Is Karin Jewish?" I asked.

Sabine, who was ahead of me on the stairs, turned her head half but kept climbing. "I don't think so, but I've never thought about don't remember her ever talking about religion."

"Sure looks like a Jewish building to me."

Sabine stopped and turned around completely. "Look, Karl, difference does it make? I don't know what Hitler and your Nazis put into your head, but whatever she is, Karin is my friend."

"Right."

"Karl . . ."

"Look, I can leave. You're the one who dragged me here in th place."

Sabine reached out with both hands and took hold of my face ing it forward and gently kissing me. "I don't want to fight. I w to come, you know that. Let's forget politics. Please?"

Still sulking, I nodded. "Your friends, not mine," I could adding.

"Oh, Karl, just stop it."

We had reached Karin's apartment. Sabine knocked, and was flung open. I caught a whiff of enticing perfume and a glin tall, slender woman, dark hair swept up in a bun, as she Sabine. She pulled back, allowing me to see her broad smile a

dark eyes. "So this is the mysterious Karl," she said, extending her hand. "I'm so glad you could come."

Petra offered a short greeting as she paced around the huge living room, admiring everything in it. "These chairs with the wicker backs and wonderful curved forms, what are they?"

"Thonets. My mother ordered them from Vienna."

"And that painting of the beer garden? The one with those smudged colors."

"That's by Max Liebermann."

Sabine laughed. "I've been coming here since I was a kid, and I never realized those chairs had a special name. I certainly had no idea who painted the beer garden. I knew that everything in Karin's place was fancy, but that's all. Leave it to Petra to come here for the first time and identify everything."

"I'm a nurse, after all," Petra reminded her. "I work with things that are clearly labeled."

"So am I, but you're the one who's always organized."

I had sunk deep into a couch, cradling a beer. Karin had laid out a spread of food on the coffee table—our sausages along with several others, herrings, pickles and salads. "Help yourselves," she urged us. "We'll have something warm later."

"This was supposed to be simple," Sabine protested. "An evening where we all pitched in."

Karin smiled and brought out another dish, some kind of vegetable mix that I didn't recognize. "But you did pitch in. I just added a few things."

"Right. Just a few."

Most of the others were drinking white wine. I had declined, not quite knowing how I was supposed to hold the ornate glasses. Beer seemed safer, since it was served in glass mugs—fancier than I had ever seen, but at least a familiar shape.

I was sitting between Andreas, Karin's boyfriend, and Petra's friend Klaus. They were both finishing their medical studies and working as interns.

"I agree with Schumacher: He's a dangerous influence on parents," Andreas was saying to Klaus.

"Who are you talking about?" Karin asked.

"Daniel Schreber from Leipzig."

"Oh, him. Herr Discipline. He had crazy ideas."

"Yes, him," Andreas continued. "But his crazy ideas, as you call them, are what most German parents believe in: Don't coddle children, never hug them or stroke them. Just discipline them so you command complete obedience. Do you know that Schreber fired a nanny who offered a slice of a pear she was eating to one of his children? Children aren't supposed to ask for a piece of food when adults are eating, no matter how hungry they are."

"It's just like you train a dog not to beg at the table," Klaus added.

"Not exactly," I ventured. "You discipline dogs, but you pet and reward them for good behavior."

Sabine looked pleased, and Andreas nodded. "You're right. Schreber forgot that part when talking about children, which is why German children grow up to be so aggressive. They never get any rewards, just punishment. That's what Schumacher says, anyway."

Karin turned toward me. "Schumacher is the doctor Andreas works for—he's always complaining about him."

"He isn't bad, really, even if he's chasing his nurses while I do the work," Andreas said. "But it'd be nice to both do the work and make the money."

Karin popped a herring into her mouth. "And you're not chasing the nurses?"

"Not yet, anyway."

"Better watch it," Petra warned. "We nurses have a pretty good reporting system. That's why Klaus is always on his best behavior. Right, Klaus?"

Klaus spread his arms in a gesture of innocence. "It never occurred to me to chase more than the one nurse I've got."

Petra playfully swatted him on the head. "Sure, I believe you."

Everyone laughed.

Andreas looked at me and then Sabine. "How about you, Karl? You seem to have done a pretty good job chasing a nurse yourself. And you're not even in medical school."

I sat there uncomfortably, and Karin jumped in. "It works both ways. I don't have anything to do with medicine, either, and somehow you landed up with me."

But Andreas wasn't about to be deterred. "Karl, tell us what you do. I mean, when you're not chasing nurses."

"When I'm not chasing nurses, I'm chasing nursery school teachers."

It was Karin's turn to blush. "See, Andreas, you'd better watch out. You, too, Sabine."

Sabine smiled, but she cast a questioning glance my way.

It took a moment for me to figure things out. "Hey, I didn't know that's what you do, Karin. Honest."

"Tell that to Andreas," she said, laughing again. "Let's go to the table and get something more substantial."

Andreas didn't look amused, and I was relieved to see that the move to the table seemed to make him forget his question.

Dinner was a delicious *Tafelspitz,* a boiled beef dish that tasted better than anything I remembered eating. Having watched the others drink, I also screwed up the courage to switch to the wine and was amazed how smoothly it went down. I had hardly ever drunk wine before; all my friends drank beer, which was cheaper. Andreas kept making the rounds with the bottle, and my glass was never empty for more than a minute.

The talk had switched to the economic problems. "It's a bit better now," Karin said. "But my mother says she prays every Sunday for all those people she sees in the unemployment lines."

"Better now for whom?" I asked.

"For a lot of people," Karin replied.

"You don't see people carting around wheelbarrows of money anymore," Andreas added. "I assume you see that as progress."

My head felt fuzzy, and I suddenly had a longing to lie down far away from everyone. "I guess so," I mumbled. "At least the Jewish bankers are happy."

There was an awkward silence, and then Karin slowly stood up. "I'll get the cake. By the way, Karl, I guess you could call me half Jewish."

"But you said your mother prays on Sundays."

"She does. My father doesn't, though. He doesn't pray any other day of the week, either, since he's not a practicing Jew. But he grew up in a Jewish family."

I rubbed my neck and saw Sabine looking away. "I didn't mean anything personal, Karin. But there are real problems in this country."

"And the Jews are to blame? Maybe they're just maggots, vermin, lice, as that lovely man Hitler says," Andreas interjected, his voice rising.

"You don't understand."

Andreas wasn't about to be stopped. "I don't, do I? Who are you, anyway? A brownshirt?"

I felt their eyes on me when I didn't reply.

Karin sat back down. "Oh my God."

Andreas looked triumphant. "Somehow I just knew it."

Sabine was on her feet. "We're going, Karl."

Karin rose, too, and started walking us to the door.

"Good old Heine, he was right—how did he put it?" Andreas smirked, pausing as he took aim. "Ah, yes, I remember: 'When I consider Germany at night, then sleep for me takes flight.'"

Karin shot him an icy look, but I wasn't sure it was directed only at him.

I was already in the outside hallway when I heard part of Sabine's soft parting words with Karin. " . . . sorry, really sorry . . ." And something of Karin's long reply: " . . . he's confused, I understand . . . yes, we're friends, don't be silly . . . always will be . . . give him time . . ."

Sabine and I walked back to the tram stop and rode home in silence.

The first time I heard of the book, *his* book, was from Emil Maurice on my next visit to prison. The driver complained that his boss was forcing him to take dictation of his autobiography and manifesto, which he would call *Mein Kampf*. "Once he gets going, there's no stopping. You can't imagine the number of times my hand cramps up. Thank God for Hess, though. He's so eager to be the chosen one that he'll take dictation until he drops, which means I have to do this only some of the time." Emil winked. "The rest of the time when the boss is in his cell, we're all free to do whatever we want. He gives a lot fewer speeches now that he's working on the book. And he can't be bothered with the politics outside. Can't think of a better occupation for him."

Emil was right. Hitler seemed less and less interested in hearing about how the party was doing, even when it got around the government ban by joining with other right-wing parties and winning several Reichstag seats in the May elections. Among the winners was Gregor Strasser, who was playing an increasingly important leadership role while Hitler remained in prison. When I delivered a letter from Gregor, Hitler didn't bother sending a reply.

"I'm not sure why Hitler behaves this way," I wrote Otto.

Otto's reply was terse: "Hitler doesn't like anything he doesn't control completely. But he'll have to learn to live with the fact that Gregor and the others are leaders, too."

As Emil had pointed out, the other prisoners looked relieved to be on their own, more relaxed than on my early visits. They still met Hitler for meals, but his appearances were briefer.

One evening before I was about to leave, Emil and I looked on in astonishment as a group of prisoners, their faces smeared with black dust of some sort and their bodies wrapped in bedsheets, rushed by. Several of them waved brooms in the air and loudly hooted and yelped.

Emil gave me a puzzled look—and then broke into a broad grin. "I think I know what's going on. Follow me."

We ran after the group, which was heading directly for cell seven. Bursting in without knocking, they left the door open behind them. I caught a glimpse of a startled Hitler, who was standing in front of the small table where Hess was writing.

"Hear ye, hear ye," one of the invaders proclaimed, pointing a poker at Hitler. "Now you will stand trial for all your foul deeds. Get ready to hear the charges of the court."

The writing of *Mein Kampf* would have to wait, but Hitler didn't seem to mind. His initial scowl gave way to a look of amusement. "May the court be merciful with its humble subject," he pleaded mockingly.

"'Mercy' is not in our vocabulary," one of the men solemnly intoned. "We mean to judge, and to judge severely."

"What is the charge against the accused?" asked another.

"Treason, treason most foul."

"Treason against what?"

"Against the glorious Versailles government, whose accomplishments are beyond dispute: humiliation of the German people, ruination of its economy, the elevation of Jews and foreigners as its masters."

"Horror, horror," the first judge replied. "How could the accused dare to raise a hand against so noble a government? How does the accused plead?"

Hitler hung his head. "Guilty, most guilty, your honor."

"And what is the verdict of the court?"

"Guilty, most guilty," all the men draped in sheets chanted in unison.

"Then it is up to me, the chief judge, to hand down the verdict." The man paused ostentatiously. "After careful deliberation, I sentence you, Adolf Hitler: Your punishment for your heinous crime shall be to travel all around this country, Germany, by automobile. You must not—and cannot—cross any borders. Instead you have to wallow in this country's wretchedness that you dared to oppose. So rules this high court."

"I humbly accept the verdict, although it is harsh beyond measure."

"Harsh it is, but harsh it must be."

Then, with more whoops and yells, the men in blackface ran out of the room, leaving Hitler smiling and shaking his head as he signaled Hess that it was time to get back to work.

Emil tapped me on the shoulder, and we stepped away from the door before Hess closed it.

"The men must be getting a bit bored with all this time on their hands," Emil said as we walked toward the gate.

"Looks like it," I said listlessly. I was thinking about the prospect of another awkward evening with Sabine.

Emil stopped and looked at me directly. "What's wrong?"

"No, nothing. It was funny, really."

"Got a girl?" he asked.

"Yes, sort of."

"What do you mean 'sort of'?"

"It hasn't been going too well," I admitted. "She's not very happy with the way I've behaved recently. Actually, she's really angry."

Emil grinned and told me to wait. He was back in a couple of minutes with a huge bouquet of roses, which he held out to me. "Here. It works every time, believe me. I've perfected this method. Every girl I've been with has had plenty of reasons to be angry with me."

I hesitated. "You sure? I mean, where did you get them?" As the words came out, I knew the answer.

"Where do you think? The boss gets so many deliveries we don't know what to do with them." He thrust them into my hands. "Take them. It's for a good cause."

"Thanks, Emil. Maybe this will help."

He punched me lightly on the shoulder. "It's guaranteed."

As I turned to leave, he said, "Oh, I'll need you back here on Tuesday morning. I've got—or the boss has—a little assignment for you."

"What kind?"

"You'll see." He smiled. "It won't be difficult—or painful."

Chapter Seven

It was shortly after I arrived here that I ran into that Jew Bruno. He was in on lesser charges than mine. I don't remember the details, but I think he was involved in some kind of swindle, cheating his customers. Not surprising for a Jew, not surprising at all. What did surprise and anger me was the nerve he had. He congratulated me. "You did a wonderful thing for my people," he told me, holding out his hand. Of course I didn't shake it. I felt like hitting him, and he must have read my expression, because he immediately backed off. Can you imagine him saying that? Can you imagine believing that the reason I did what I did was to help the Jews? Bruno was clearly unbalanced, and I'm not referring to the way he limped. I'm glad he steered clear of me after that, at least for a long while.

After Sabine's grandmother died and Sabine took down the curtain that had divided the apartment, it felt larger, almost spacious, even if it was still a dingy small room. But when we began quarreling, the space once again felt claustrophobically tight, with nowhere for us to retreat from each other. In between the tears and the recriminations, I tried to explain a few of my beliefs. It wasn't easy.

I suppose it didn't help that I was constantly resentful. I resented the condescension of someone like Andreas, who was so smug in his ways just because he was in medical school and, I bet, came from a rich family. And who had so little respect for his country that he dug out that shameful line of Heine. I had found Karin attractive and less stuck up than I expected, until she had reacted so personally to what I said about Jewish bankers. All of them had taken on such superior airs, as if I'd done something truly shocking. You'd have thought I had suddenly pulled my trousers down, turned my back to them and bent over. When all I did was mention something that everyone knew to be true.

I didn't want to dwell on the subject with Sabine because she didn't understand politics. She saw everything in personal terms, and since Karin was half Jewish, she was ready to take offense at any discussion of Jews. I told her that I'd never said all Jews were guilty. And I reminded her that I had told Karin I had nothing against her personally. I had no reason to blame Karin for anything.

But that didn't mean other Jews weren't guilty. I knew enough about those other Jews. Yes, the bankers. And the landlords, the politicians and the liars who wrote for the socialist press. Let's face it: Why shouldn't they have been held to account for what they were doing to Germany? Who wrote the Weimar constitution? Someone called Hugo Preuss, a law professor from the University of Berlin. A Jew. You didn't have to dig very hard to see what was happening. It was all spelled out in our newspapers and pamphlets.

One moment Sabine would say she couldn't stand me for saying these things, and in another she'd admit she was confused, uncertain what to think. She certainly didn't understand my political convictions and didn't want to. She knew only that she hated the way they drove wedges between people. She hated hate, she said.

"Why should I have to make a choice between you and Karin?" she asked.

"Do you love Karin better than me?"

"You're missing my point entirely."

I came back from Landsberg with the huge bouquet of roses. Emil was right: It was better than any medicine. She was amazed at first; I had never done this before. Then she was suspicious. I had told her after earlier visits about the flood of gifts Hitler received, including flowers.

"You didn't bring these from the prison?" she asked warily.

"No, of course not."

"I don't want Hitler's flowers, if that's what they are."

I couldn't retreat to the truth now; I couldn't disappoint her. After all, I told myself, it's the intention that counts.

"I'm telling you, they aren't his."

"You swear?"

"I swear."

She kissed me, long and hard. "I don't know what to make of you at times. But I do know I love you."

"I love you, too."

Her eyes filled with tears again.

I put my finger on the tip of her nose. "Why are you crying now?"

"You never told me that before. First you bring me flowers and then you tell me you love me. What next?"

I stroked her hair and pulled her toward me, pretending not to understand the question.

The sky was gray when I headed back to Landsberg on Tuesday to find out what assignment Emil had in mind for me. The chill in the morning air was a reminder that summer was just about over. I buttoned up my light jacket as I rode in the back of a cart. The farmer had allowed me to hop in for the last part of the journey, almost up to the prison gates.

I rushed in a little later than I had hoped and found Emil engrossed in conversation with several other prisoners in the commons room, gesturing with some papers he held in his hands. He gave me a distracted wave when I poked my head in, which I took as a signal that he was busy. I stepped back into the hallway to wait.

It was about twenty minutes before the other prisoners left and Emil called me in. "Interesting news today," he said with no preliminaries. "Look at this."

He had laid out several sheets of paper on the table. I peered down. "What is it?"

"A copy of Leybold's report about the boss."

It took me a moment to place the name. "How did you manage to get the report of the prison's governor?" I asked in astonishment.

"You have no idea how many sympathizers Hitler has won for the cause here." Then he laughed. "A few more months in this place and he might become the governor himself."

I picked up a page and read:

. . . is contented, modest and accommodating. He makes no demands, is quiet and reasonable, serious and without any abusiveness, scrupulously concerned to obey the confinements of the sentence. He is a man without personal vanity, is content with the catering of the institution, does not smoke or drink and, though comradely, knows how to command a certain authority with his fellow inmates . . .

"Not bad, huh? That's our leader. Couldn't have written it better myself."

I nodded.

"Here's the part I like," Emil added, winking and offering me a conspiratorial smile. " 'He is not drawn to the female sex. He meets women with whom he comes into contact on visits here with great politeness, without becoming engaged with them in serious political discussions.' "

"Is that true—I mean, the part about him not being drawn to the female sex?"

"Nothing's that simple with the boss," Emil replied. I sensed he was going to say more but then thought better of it.

"Here's the really important part," he said, pointing to the last section of Leybold's report:

He will not return to liberty with threats and thoughts of revenge against those in public office who oppose him and frustrated his plans in November 1923. He will be no agitator against the government, no enemy of other parties with a nationalist leaning. He emphasizes how convinced he is that a state cannot exist without firm internal order and firm government.

"Does this mean they'll release Hitler early?"

"It doesn't depend on Leybold alone," Emil said. "The court has to rule if he can be granted parole. And there are plenty of people who think Leybold is crazy to believe this. The prosecutor is already fighting to prevent any early release. One of the police reports we've seen claims that if Hitler is released, he'll represent 'a constant danger for internal and external security of the state.' "

"You've seen those reports, too?"

"It's incredible what you can get your hands on when people wish you well."

"So what are his chances?"

Emil shrugged. "I don't know how much longer it'll take. But there's no chance he'll have to serve out his full term. It won't even be close. And I wouldn't bet on him being in prison next September."

"A year from now? Based on Leybold's report, I would have thought he'd get out much sooner."

"Remember, he still has enemies. You know what the prosecutor is saying? He's accusing us of smuggling letters out of prison."

"He is?"

Emil playfully covered his mouth with his hand. "I'm shocked, truly shocked, aren't you?"

"Seriously, Emil, have I done something to get him in trouble?"

"They'll use whatever they can against him, but all the guards here know what's going on. And you're not the only one who smuggles letters, if you can call this smuggling at all. Don't worry about it. It's only a pretext."

I wanted to believe him. After all, I had shown that first letter to the guard, as instructed, and afterward casually walked in and out without anyone ever checking. I had almost forgotten that what I did on each visit was technically illegal.

"But none of this was the reason I asked you to come back so soon," Emil said.

"I didn't think so."

I had become used to Emil's almost automatic amused looks, but this time he was clearly enjoying himself. "You know about Hitler's half sister, Angela Raubal?"

"Yes, the one who came here earlier."

Emil nodded. Angela was due to visit the prison today, and he wanted my help. She'd be coming with her daughter, who would briefly see her uncle and then would need care, since Angela would be staying for a longer visit.

"So I'm supposed to be a baby-sitter?"

"Not exactly." Emil laughed. "She's sixteen."

"Great, so what do I do with her?"

"There are a couple of bicycles out front, which the guards will let you use. It's all arranged. Take her for a nice ride somewhere. Hitler needs some time with Angela. Go to town, go for a ride or walk in the woods, whatever you want." He paused, looking at me more seriously than ever before. "Not whatever you want. Don't ever forget she's Hitler's niece. And that she's just a kid."

"Of course not."

"I know you're not much more than a kid yourself, so watch it."

"I'm twenty-one," I replied indignantly.

"I know. Precisely my point. It's not that big a gap."

I caught sight of Hitler's visitors before they went in. His sister couldn't have been that old, but she looked tired and dowdy, a small, worn-out woman, her eyes downcast as Emil led them to cell number seven. Her daughter, who was taller, was chatting with Emil, which meant she was turned away from me as she passed. I caught only a glimpse of her short light brown hair before they disappeared down the corridor.

The wait was longer than expected, and I must have nodded off briefly. Suddenly, Emil and the girl were standing in front of me, and I bolted from my chair. "So here's your energetic escort," Emil said, relishing that he'd caught me drowsing.

"I hope my company won't tire him out too much," the girl said, releasing a loud giggle. She held out her hand, and Emil made the introduction: "Angela, meet Karl. Karl, meet Angela."

"Oh, Emil, no one calls me Angela. That's my mother's name."

"It's yours, too," he said teasingly.

She turned back to me, still holding my hand. "I'm Geli."

She wore a plain pleated skirt and a carefully ironed white blouse with a fraying collar. She wasn't as tall as I had thought before, but she stood very straight, which probably contributed to my first impression. Her short, curly hair descended in a wave over her forehead, giving her almost a boyish look; there was nothing remarkable about her round face, which still contained a childish puffiness. Except for the big dark eyes. When she smiled, her face was transformed into something mischievous, those eyes radiating impish energy and warmth.

"Do you have a jacket or a sweater?" I asked. "You may need it."

She shook her head. "I have a sweater, but I left it with my mother. It's warmed up out there."

Emil took us as far as the guard gate. "See you later in the afternoon, then." Turning to me, he added: "Get her back safely."

"Jawohl," I responded.

Geli waved as we made our way out the gate. "I'll try to make sure he doesn't fall asleep on his bike," she called back over her shoulder. "Tell Uncle Alf not to worry."

We picked up the bicycles on the other side.

"Are you all right on one of these?" I asked. "We've got to go down a rather steep hill from here."

"Maybe," she said, mounting the rickety bike and pushing off. "How about you?"

She was already accelerating down the hill when I jumped on my bike to catch up. "Hey, wait for me."

I began pedaling furiously and then became alarmed at my downhill speed. I'd never owned a bike in my life, and had ridden one only a few times. The distance between us was widening instead of narrowing. The hill really wasn't that big, but it looked huge to me. I felt as if I were flying and close to out of control. I saw Geli reach the bottom at full speed, her bike wobbling once over a bump before she slowed down. I came roaring after her, hit the same bump and went sprawling.

I looked up from the dusty road to find her standing over me. "Karl," she managed to say, then bent over laughing. She tried to look serious. "Are you all right?"

I picked myself up slowly, examining nothing worse than a bruised forearm and a scuffed-up sleeve. "Very funny." I straightened my jacket, still embarrassed and angry. But when I saw her stuffing her fist into her mouth trying to stop from laughing more, I began laughing, too. "All right, can you take pity on me and ride a little slower?"

She grinned. "Yes, sir."

I got back on my bicycle and pushed off, carefully watching the ground to make sure I wouldn't hit anything that would trip me up a second time, although I tried to look and sound relaxed. I blurted out the first question that came into my mind. "Why do you call him 'Uncle Alf'?"

"What's wrong with that?"

"I don't know. It's just that . . ."

"He's too important here?"

"I never imagined him as somebody's uncle."

Geli rode slowly. "When I called him that in prison today, he seemed to like it. He certainly is treated with respect in that prison. It's fun having a famous uncle."

I almost always avoided talking about my family, but she didn't seem ashamed of hers. They lived in a tiny apartment in a dump of a building in Vienna, sleeping on straw mattresses. Her father had died when she was two, leaving Angela to provide for three children—Geli; her older brother, Leo; and her younger sister, Elfriede. Angela worked as a cook in a dormitory for Jewish students, where she had to prepare kosher meals.

I asked if her mother resented cooking for Jews.

Geli looked surprised. "Why should she? It's a job, isn't it?"

We bought some bread and cheese from a farmer and sat down by a stream to eat. Earlier, the sky had almost cleared, but now a thick cloud cover had moved in again. Geli talked about high school, how she wanted to study music afterward. "But you know what I really want?" she said, shooting me a coquettish grin. "I want to marry someone rich and famous. I want to go to the theater as often as I please and eat in fancy restaurants. I want the maître d' to take my coat and the waiter to pull out my chair for me."

"Have anyone in mind?"

"Not yet, but I'll find him." She paused. "So what about you?"

"What about me?"

"Got a girlfriend?"

The first raindrops splashed down before I could answer, and then the skies opened up, letting loose a downpour.

"Let's run," Geli said, pointing toward a cluster of trees perhaps a couple hundred meters away. We were drenched halfway there, and the field was turning to mud. Geli stumbled, and I grabbed her hand at the last moment, preventing her from falling. "We're even," I shouted above the noisy downpour as we made it under the nearly protective covering of the thick trees.

"Not quite," she said, panting, her wet hair plastered flat on her head and her blouse clinging to her body. I noticed how full her breasts were. I averted my eyes but not fast enough.

"I caught you," Geli gleefully announced.

I felt myself coloring. "You're wicked," I said as sternly as I could.

"Thank you," she said, with a mock curtsy. "I'll take that as a compliment."

I couldn't help but smile; it was impossible to be angry with her. "What do you mean that we're not even yet?"

"You haven't told me: Do you have a girlfriend?"

"Sort of," I said, lamely parroting my earlier answer to Emil.

"That means yes?"

"Guess so."

She shivered in her wet blouse, and I pulled off my equally wet jacket and offered it to her.

Her lips curled into a sarcastic grin as she wrapped it around her shoulders. "What a gentleman—thank you. But if I were your girlfriend, I'd kill you for talking about me that way. You'd be proud of being my boyfriend, or I'd send you packing."

"Well, good thing you're not my girlfriend."

She shook her forefinger at me. "A very good thing indeed."

The downpour ended as quickly as it had begun, and we made our way back to the prison fortress. We dropped off the bicycles with the guards and headed through the gate. Before we rejoined the others, Geli thanked me in earnest. "I had a good time, Karl."

"So did I." I meant it.

Her eyes took on their mischievous look. "You know, I think I'd like to have an older brother like you. Leo's too busy with himself to ever listen to me. Too bad we live so far apart."

"Yes, too bad. But maybe we'll run into each other again, sister."

She laughed the throaty laugh I had heard several times now. "Maybe we will," she said, squeezing my hand before we stepped back into the closed part of the prison.

Emil didn't let me forget about our return for a long time. We had stomped in still wet and muddy, and Geli had been in visibly high spirits. So had I. We had both laughed our way through our answers to him about what we had been doing. Seemingly amused, Emil had listened and laughed, too, but he also shot several questioning looks in my direction.

"You sure nothing happened? You know . . ." he asked the next time we met.

He seemed to be joking, but I began to have my doubts when he kept talking about how giddy we had been. I finally told him to stop it.

"All right, fine, don't get testy. I believe you," he said. Then he winked. "At least I think I do. But you know, I'm one of those new doctors they call psychologists—you can't fool me about anything."

"Right," I replied. "And where did you earn this degree in—what is it?—psychology?"

"The best place there is: the nightclub where I worked as a bouncer before Hitler discovered my talents. You can't be a good bouncer unless you can size people up in an instant. And I sized you up real fast."

"So?"

"So I'm not fooled by your shy, polite handsome-young-man routine. You obviously can bash heads; otherwise, you'd never be a brownshirt. I'd also watch you real carefully if you came into my nightclub. You're the kind of guy who might drink quietly all night and then do something crazy."

"Thanks for the compliment."

"I'm just being realistic."

"Great."

But on my next visits to the prison, we talked less about Geli as Emil and the others became increasingly preoccupied with the battle to win Hitler's release. The weather grew colder, and the early-release rumors were accompanied by fears that the Bavarian authorities would try to deport Hitler to Austria. Since he didn't have German citizenship, this looked like a realistic possibility. The police were pushing for it, and in the summer, it had appeared that the Austrians might be willing to cooperate. But by the fall, Emil told me they had reliable information that the Austrian government had rebuffed the Bavarians, arguing that Hitler's service in the German army meant he had effectively forfeited his Austrian citizenship.

Hitler's routine changed little. He was still dictating his book to Hess, occasionally reading a chapter aloud to other inmates. He grew more emphatic in his refusal to take part in party politics outside the prison. In his absence, the party had no clear leadership—and those at liberty were at odds with one another, weakening their position. By December 7, when the second national elections of the year were held, the coalition known as the National Socialist Freedom Movement won only half of the votes it had in May. I felt discouraged by the paltry 2.9

percent showing, which meant the group's number of seats in parliament would drop from thirty-two to fourteen, only four of whom were Nazis. Once again the press proclaimed that we were sinking into oblivion, and I wondered if I would have to find a new job.

In Landsberg, Hitler looked unfazed. When I asked Emil for an explanation, he was enigmatic. "Be patient," he told me. "Everything is working out."

Another person in good spirits was Sabine. I had brought her flowers twice more. Once they were even flowers I had bought after receiving my small monthly pay. She protested that I shouldn't be spending my money on such luxuries, but I could see how delighted she was. Our nights together were better than they had been in some time, and Leo was barking so loudly that the old woman downstairs complained regularly.

I realized that Sabine was relieved to see our party losing ground. I couldn't blame her for feeling that way, but I wasn't about to give her the satisfaction of telling her my worries. I didn't want to admit defeat, and she didn't want to let on how fervently she hoped that I'd forget about politics altogether. So we avoided the subject.

I felt happier than I had for quite a while. As long as the party didn't collapse completely, I figured, I'd still have something to do, and it was a relief not to be quarreling with Sabine. If only nothing changes, I thought, I'll be all right.

It was then that everything began to change.

For several days, Sabine had been acting testy again. Not exactly angry but distracted and irritated by small things. When I forgot to put the cheese on the outside windowsill at night and it spoiled, she lectured me about how we couldn't afford to waste food. When she came home to find that I hadn't tidied up the bed after getting up late, she remarked, "You'd think you could do one small thing in this house." But when I asked her what was bothering her, she quickly apologized for her irritability and claimed it was nothing.

Until the evening, when she came home with a strange, almost frightened look in her eyes. She took off her wet coat and, uncharacteristically, flung it on the bed. "I need to talk to you, Karl."

"Sure, go ahead."

"There's something . . ."

I had picked up her coat with the intention of hanging it on the stand near the door. "Yes?"

"I'm pregnant."

She was biting her lower lip as I stood there, still holding her coat, not moving, certainly not knowing what to say.

"Karl, say something, please."

"Are you sure, absolutely sure?"

"Come on, I work in a doctor's office."

I hung up the coat. "Sabine, sit down. We need to think this through."

"You don't want it?"

"No—I mean yes. It's just . . ."

Her face flushed. "I don't know how I'll manage. I'm scared. But look, go if you want. You don't have to stay."

"Sabine, stop, please."

I coaxed her into her chair. And then, without thinking, or maybe thinking too much, I frantically argued my case—a case that I constructed as I talked. It wasn't a question of not wanting to have children with her, I explained. I wanted children, many children. "Hitler says Germany needs more children," I added.

"Keep your Hitler out of this," she snapped.

My point was, I insisted, that I wanted us to embark on this important part of our lives the right way. We should have more stability first. My future was tied to a party with an uncertain future. We'd know soon whether I'd continue with this work or have to find something else. Then we could marry, which was the right thing to do first. When I saw her hurt look, I went further. We could get married soon, very soon, I promised. And then we'd have those babies.

I found myself dramatically dropping to my knees. "Will you do me the honor of marrying me?"

She pushed my head into her lap and stroked it. I could feel her hands trembling. "Yes, but I want my baby."

"You'll have your baby. Just not now, not yet. Let's get married first."

She cried some more, and she pleaded. But when I stood my ground again and again, she finally agreed.

Hitler's behavior only grew stranger. Or so I thought. In the Reichstag, Gregor Strasser denounced his continued imprisonment, claiming that the country was run by "a gang of swine, a mean, disgusting gang of swine." Instead of expressing his gratitude, Hitler angrily let it be known that he didn't want his supporters using such heated rhetoric. He seemed to be turning peaceful, almost apologetic, suggesting that he was no longer interested in anything but employing legal methods to advance his political views. Not for him the politics of violence. Not anymore.

"What's happening?" I asked Emil. "Doesn't Hitler want to fight for his release?"

"Of course he does. That's what he's doing."

"How? By acting like a lamb instead of a lion?"

"You're finally beginning to figure it out."

It was then I began to see another possibility: that Hitler wanted his party to look weak to convince the authorities he no longer represented a danger. I dismissed this reasoning almost as soon as it occurred to me. It seemed a betrayal of everyone on the outside. Later, though, I came to believe this was exactly what he was doing.

Whatever the reason, the Bavarian supreme court ordered his release on parole less than two weeks after the elections in which our candidates had fared so poorly. Emil had sent me word in Munich as soon as Hitler was informed on December 19, and I rushed to Landsberg early the next morning. I arrived just before noon.

The guard on duty urged me to hurry. "Everyone is ready for the send-off," he said.

He was right. I knew how sympathetic most of the staff was to our cause, how persuasive Hitler had been with his jailers. Still, I hadn't expected the sight that greeted me that day. The guards and administrative staff, headed by Governor Leybold, were lined up in formation. Hitler stepped out of cell number seven for the last time, holding his cap in his hand and wearing a raincoat over his shorts. Leybold, his eyes filling with tears, wished Hitler well and shook his hand, and several guards shouted, "*Heil* Hitler!"

Hitler didn't linger. His photographer, Heinrich Hoffmann, and the printer Adolf Müller were waiting outside with a car. Hitler looked up at the dark gray sky, ordered Hoffmann to snap his picture before the prison gate and jumped in.

Hitler had spent a little over a year in prison. I heard later that someone in the state prosecutor's office had calculated how much time he still should have served: three years, 333 days, 21 hours and 50 minutes. Much later, sitting in my own prison cell, I had often thought about what would have happened if he had served that time, how differently everything might have turned out.

Chapter Eight

I was walking home one evening shortly after the New Year when I ran into Uwe. We hadn't seen each other for a couple of months, and I almost passed him by.

"What's the matter, Karl? No time for your friends anymore?"

I looked at him in disbelief. He was as big and brawny as ever, but instead of the usual scruffy coat and workman's pants that he wore for his housepainting jobs, he was outfitted in a plain but proper navy blue overcoat and gray slacks. His hair was combed neatly to one side, and his chin no longer had the permanent stubble that he had cultivated since our SA unit had fallen apart.

"Forgive me, Herr Passau," I said, bowing with mock formality, "for confusing you with our capitalist masters."

Uwe grinned. "Jealous? Come on, let's get a beer, and I'll fill you in on my secret."

He steered me toward a nearby pub that was both smaller and tidier than the sprawling beer hall where we usually drank. It was also more expensive. Uwe quickly read my thoughts and patted me on the shoulder. "Fret not: The beer is on me." When he opened his coat, I glimpsed a white shirt and tie. "Patience, my friend," he said.

We settled onto our stools on opposite sides of a small round table, and a waitress took our order, returning with the two frothy mugs.

"Cheers," Uwe said. One thing hadn't changed. He still wiped off the foam on his upper lip with the back of his large hand.

"All right. What's the big secret?"

Uwe leaned across the small table and motioned for me to do the same. He whispered, "Work."

"Work?"

"Yes, full-time work. Not this here-and-there stuff I was doing but a real job with real earnings. It's incredible how that can change your life."

"Just like that, you got a job where you make real money?"

"Maybe not just like that. I had a bit of luck, but the times are getting better, and there are opportunities out there if you look for them. Things have changed, Karl. Haven't you noticed?"

Uwe explained that renovation and construction companies were hiring again. Now that inflation was back under control and the pressure on reparations from the victors in the war against Germany had eased, more and more people had the money and the confidence to fix up their old apartments or to invest in new ones. His boss, who had started with a small crew of part-time workers like Uwe, now employed several crews. He had taken a liking to Uwe, saw that the other workers respected him and made him the office manager. Uwe's job was not only to organize the schedules of the crews but also to deal directly with customers. Hence the more respectable clothes, the haircut and the shave. And the income.

"Look, Karl, I might be able to find a job for you, too."

"Full-time?"

"Sure, we're a serious operation now."

Uwe looked at me quizzically when I didn't respond right away.

"You see, I still have other commitments," I said.

"To Hitler, to that crew?"

I nodded.

"You can't be serious. What have they done for you? Don't you get that it's over? We're long past the stage where playing soldier accomplishes much of anything. You saw the results of the last elections. All of those groups put together, including the Nazis, couldn't get three percent of the vote. No one takes Hitler seriously anymore. His party isn't even legal."

I tried to respond forcefully, but my reasons sounded less than convincing even to me as I trotted them out. Hitler was already looking for ways to rebuild the party, which had fallen into inevitable decline while he was imprisoned; he was talking to the Bavarian authorities about winning approval to relaunch the party legally, and he seemed to be making headway. Most important, he had learned his lesson in the putsch. From now on, he repeatedly promised, he'd stick to only legal methods. We weren't going to be bashing heads anymore, just working to build a political base.

"You miss the point," Uwe countered. "Even if Hitler can put some kind of party back together, it won't count for anything. I admit that Hitler knows how to talk. I was as much under his spell as you and the others were. He made sense in a lot of ways. But now that the times are getting better, I don't need him." He paused. "Nor do most Germans, which is why he'll be the leader of only a fringe protest movement at best. People just want to live normally for a change." He drained his mug. "Shouldn't you be thinking about living normally, too?"

"I don't know. I'm not sure what normal is anymore."

"You're missing an opportunity. I bet Sabine would be happy if you took it. You've got a terrific woman. Why not make her happy?"

"We're going to get married soon."

"Good God, man, why didn't you tell me earlier?" He turned to the waitress, who was wielding several more mugs on her way to a bigger table. "Give us two more—my friend is about to be married."

The walls were a dirty brown, and the ceiling was covered with large damp spots. The room's single window let in almost no light; it looked like it hadn't been washed in years. From somewhere nearby came the pungent smell of cabbage and pig's knuckles on the boil.

Sabine shivered. "Are you sure this is all right?"

I reassured her yet again that Dr. Stein came highly recommended. She had been too embarrassed to ask any of her fellow nurses or the doctors she knew for help. Maybe she had hoped this would prompt me to reconsider, to abandon the whole idea. But I had confided in

Emil, who seemed pleased to be consulted in such a matter. "No problem," he assured me. "I know the right man. He's reasonably priced and very discreet."

"And good? Safe, I mean?"

"Absolutely. You have no idea how many satisfied customers he's had." Emil smirked. "And satisfied men who needed to send the women his way. Yours truly prominently among them. I'm a regular."

I had wanted to believe him, but now, sitting in what passed for the waiting room, I couldn't help but share some of Sabine's doubts. I wasn't about to admit them, however. There have never been any complaints against him, I told her. There was no need to worry. And once we had this taken care of, we could get married.

Sabine sat rigid, glumly staring ahead of her but seeing nothing. When she spoke, it was in a dry, low whisper. "Maybe we should just walk out and have the baby. Would it really be so bad to get married when I'm pregnant?"

"We've talked about all this before. It's about having a child before we're ready. Let's do it right."

A small bald man, wearing thick glasses and a stained smock, stepped into the room. "Stein," he said brusquely. "Is the fräulein ready?"

Sabine looked at me with pleading eyes. "I don't really know. I . . ."

"If you're undecided, then why are you here? I don't have time to waste."

"No, no, we're decided," I assured him. "Right, Sabine?"

Her eyes met mine and then, not finding what she wanted there, once again went out of focus as she looked straight ahead. "If you say so," she whispered.

"Well, then," Stein said, "I'd like the money now, if you don't mind."

I paid without a word.

Stein quickly counted the bills and shoved them under his smock. "You won't be needed till later. Come back around five."

Sabine didn't look at me as she followed Stein through the door.

I spent the next few hours walking around the city. When I felt cold, I stopped off in a café, and once I returned to the apartment, thinking I'd do some reading. I couldn't concentrate.

I was cutting though the English Gardens when a ball rolled near my feet. I leaned over and picked it up. "Give me," a small boy said, his hand out. He was bundled in a worn coat with a scarf wrapped tightly around his neck, but the face that poked out from under his cap was a work of art: a precisely chiseled mouth, a snub nose and light blue eyes.

"Ask the man nicely, and I'm sure he'll give your ball back."

I tore my eyes away from the boy and saw the mother smiling uncertainly. "Of course," I said, handing the boy the ball. "Of course."

"Thank you," the woman said, taking her son by the hand.

"How old is he?"

"He'll be three next month."

"He's very . . ."

"Yes?"

"Nice, handsome."

"I know."

I stood there watching them walk away. As the boy lifted the ball and showed it proudly to his mother, I suddenly recognized what I had done—how much of a mistake it was, how horrible a mistake. I raced up the path, passing the mother and child without a word, tearing through the rest of the park, through the streets and squares that were nothing more than a blur to me, until I arrived, breathing hard, at Stein's door.

I knocked and, when no one responded, banged hard and kept banging. The door opened a crack, and I shoved it hard and stepped in.

"What do you think you're doing?" Stein demanded.

"Don't," I said.

"Don't what?"

"Don't do it—the abortion."

"It's a little late for second thoughts. I told you two earlier that you have to know what you want." He looked me up and down. "Are you trying to get your money back?"

"You mean it's done?"

"Yes, it's done, goddammit. No refunds."

I sat down, feeling sick. "I don't want a refund," I managed to say. "That's not the point."

Stein's face relaxed, but only slightly.

"How is she?" I asked.

"A little wobbly."

"Is everything all right?"

"Yes, fine. She's a bit weak. Some women take this harder than others." Leaving me in the dark room where Sabine and I had sat earlier, he ordered: "Wait here."

I waited and waited. Maybe it wasn't so long, but it felt endless, and all I could think of was why hadn't I come back earlier, why hadn't I realized that Sabine had been right all along.

I was almost ready to barge in when the inner door reopened and Stein led Sabine out. Her face was drained of all color, her eyes had shrunk into the far recesses of her face and she shuffled forward.

I reached out to steady her, allowing Stein to step back. "Sabine, I'm sorry," I pleaded, my eyes suddenly wet. "I'm so sorry. Maybe we should sit down here and rest some more before we go. You don't mind, Doctor?"

Stein stood there impatiently.

"For God's sake, you can see how weak she is," I said.

"Right, stay if you want to." He turned his back toward the inner door. "I've got work to do."

I began leading Sabine to a chair. "No. I want to leave now," she protested in a barely audible voice.

We negotiated the way out and started down the street. Leaning on my arm, Sabine tried to keep shuffling ahead. But before we had managed to turn the first corner, she collapsed onto the sidewalk like a puppet whose strings had been cut. Not knowing whether I should try to lift her alone, I put my coat under her head and shouted for help. A man ran over from the other side of the street. "Just keep her head up," I pleaded before darting back to the abortionist's office and banging on the door. Once again the door opened a crack, and once more I immediately shoved it wide open. "Not again," Stein seethed. "I've had enough of this."

"You'd better get help for her fast or you'll need the help yourself," I shouted. "I'll have every brownshirt in Munich here."

I must have looked like I meant it, because Stein didn't argue. He peered out and saw Sabine lying on the pavement. "Go to her," he commanded. "I'll get help."

A car pulled up on the quiet street a few minutes later. The driver, a young man with the square jaw and huge hands of a boxer, leaped out. "We'll get her to a hospital," he said, swiftly lifting Sabine in his arms. I tried to help, but he already had her maneuvered into the backseat. I jumped in and put her head on my lap. As the car lurched forward, I caught a last glimpse of Stein looking out his partly opened door then slamming it shut.

I held Sabine as steadily as I could, but it wasn't easy. My own body trembled as tears flowed down my cheeks onto her face.

Sabine's initial condition, a nurse told me, was critical; she had lost a lot of blood. "If you hadn't brought her here right away, she probably wouldn't have made it," the nurse said. It wasn't much of a consolation.

Feeling that I had no choice, I went to Sabine's office and told Petra what had happened. She stared at me in disgust and disbelief. "You mean she relied on you to find a doctor for this?"

"She was embarrassed to go to her friends."

"And you agreed to take care of it? You?"

"I was told he was a good doctor."

"Good God," she muttered.

From then on Petra was a regular visitor to the hospital, seeing to it that Sabine received the best care possible. After a few days she reported tersely: "She'll make it." Then, seeing my expression of relief, she added: "No thanks to you."

Unlike Petra, who could use her nurse's connections to visit as much as she wanted, I was consigned largely to waiting. The two or three times I was allowed in, the floor nurse ordered me out after a few minutes. "She needs her rest. Go on, now, you'll have plenty of time for talking later."

I have to admit I was secretly relieved; Sabine said so little and usually had the same faraway, unfocused look she'd had in Stein's waiting room, even when I apologized again and again. I didn't know what more to do or say. Something stopped me from telling her what had happened on the day of the abortion, how I had changed my mind.

Shaken, I went to see Emil. He protested that he'd never heard anything bad about Stein. "I'm sorry about what happened, but you know I wouldn't send a friend's girl there unless I thought he'd do a good job. What do you take me for? Besides, there's always a risk in these operations. But she'll be all right."

"I should have let her have the baby."

"You're just saying that because of what happened," Emil said, placing his hand on my shoulder. "Really, she'll be fine."

"You don't understand. I decided that I'd made a mistake when I still thought there was time to stop Stein."

Emil sighed. "I'm sorry if that's what you felt. But you sounded very decided when you asked me for a doctor. I was just trying to help."

I nodded. It was hard to be mad at Emil, since I knew he meant it, and he certainly hadn't intended any harm. Besides, he treated me better than anyone else in the party, except for Otto.

When he saw I wasn't blaming him, he changed the subject. He told me that Hitler was working hard to rebuild the party organization in Bavaria. Since he couldn't speak in public, he was holding private meetings everywhere he could.

"That reminds me: I've got another job for you to do."

I shrugged. "I'm not sure I care about politics anymore."

"All right, I can understand that you're upset now and can't think about it. But the job isn't political—it's the kind you like."

"What is it?"

"Geli will be in town in less than two weeks. She'll be on a school trip, and she's never visited Munich before. I have to drive the boss to a meeting that day, so she could use an escort to show her the city. He thinks the school won't do a good enough job, so he's arranging to get her released from the tour for part of the afternoon. It won't be a lot of time, just enough to give her a few of the highlights." He paused. "You did the job so well last time that I suspect she'd like you to handle these duties. Do you think you can manage it?"

"Sure, why not?"

Emil looked at me carefully. "Is that all you have to say? I thought you liked Geli—in fact, I thought . . ."

"God, you always jump to conclusions. Yes, I think she's a nice girl, but that's all. I've got other things on my mind at the moment."

"All right. But it'll do you good to think of something else."

"Fine, I said I'd do it."

"And, Karl," Emil added, his lips curling into a grin, "I don't want you bringing back Hitler's niece all muddy this time."

Sabine returned home a few days later. Late the first evening, when the awkward silences got longer and longer, I told her everything about the boy in the English Gardens and how I had tried to stop the abortion. "I was so stupid not to have understood earlier, not to think about the baby we could have had." I felt the tears welling up and looked away, but Sabine drew me to her, stroked my face and kissed me for the first time since her return. She wept, too.

"I'm sorry, I'm so sorry."

"Why didn't you tell me before?"

"I thought I'd only make everything worse, since I was too late anyway."

She hugged me tighter. "You were, but you changed. I needed to know that."

"I think I have. At least I'll try to show you that I have."

"Good," she murmured.

We sat silently holding each other, but there wasn't anything awkward in the long silence that followed.

Sabine finally lifted her head, drawing back just enough to look at me directly. "Does this mean you're changing in other ways, too?"

"If you mean taking a job with Uwe, I'll do it if you still want me to."

She smiled. "You know I do."

We had quarreled about Uwe before the abortion. I had told Sabine about his transformation, which had astonished and pleased her. She suddenly saw Uwe, whom she had dismissed as an incorrigible rowdy who could only be a bad influence on me, as an ally. She had argued that I should go to work if he could provide me a job, and she had been delighted with his new views about politics, that it was time to drop out. Although I was already uncertain about my future in the party, I had become indignant, arguing that I was still committed to the cause.

Now I was more willing to yield. "All right, I'll ask him. Maybe he'll have some part-time jobs."

"Why part-time?"

"Because I have, you know, other duties." As the words came out, I realized I was echoing what I had told Uwe, even less convincingly than before. When Sabine pushed me to explain, I avoided responding by agreeing to consider full-time work if Uwe could arrange it.

"I have to do one thing first," I insisted, finding that I didn't want to capitulate completely.

"What's that?" Sabine asked.

"I need to talk or at least write to Otto."

"Don't start again," she pleaded.

"I'm not saying I'm starting up anything again. But I owe it to Otto."

"You owe Otto? He led you to Hitler."

"I've told you: Otto is a very rational person. I respect his judgment. He's not blinded by Hitler—he's not even a member of the party. And now that all the other party leaders are lining up behind Hitler again, Gregor isn't saying anything yet."

Sabine was far from convinced, but she backed off slightly. She didn't like to fight and, while suspicious of Otto, wasn't sure where he stood.

"I don't know, Karl, it's your sense of judgment I sometimes worry about."

"I'll write him a letter. What's the harm in that?"

Her eyes, still sunken deeply into her face, clouded over slightly as they took me in. "All right, I want to believe you. Maybe this is something you should do—to help you get away from all of them."

I bit my lip and nodded. "I'll do my best to sort this out, really." I meant it.

As instructed, I waited in front of the pharmacy downstairs from Hitler's old room at Thierschstrasse 41, where he had returned after prison. Emil had told me Geli would visit her uncle first and then be free when he left for his meeting. About six trams rumbled by on the narrow street before Emil pulled up in Hitler's red Mercedes. "Been waiting long?" he asked.

"I was here exactly when you told me to be. I'm a brownshirt, remember? I follow orders."

Emil laughed. "Well, the young lady must be entertaining her uncle well, because I'm a couple of minutes late, and he's still not down here. Thank God for that. He doesn't like waiting, not even for a minute." He looked nervously at his watch. "And if we're late someplace, he doesn't like that, either. It's always my fault, no matter how long I had to wait for him."

Just then the front door to the building opened. Hitler stepped out, followed by Geli. "*Heil* Hitler!" I saluted briskly. Hitler nodded, and

Emil got out to open the back door. Geli, who was bundled in a faded brown coat, caught Hitler by the arm before he stepped in. "You promise, Uncle Alf?"

"Yes, I promise," he said, settling into his seat. "Now, be a good girl and do some sight-seeing with this young man. You'll want to tell your mother what you saw in Munich when you get back."

Emil closed the door and got back in, offering a quick wave as he drove off. Hitler was already immersed in some papers.

"What was that all about?" I asked Geli as we watched the car disappear around the corner.

"Uncle Alf promised to take me on a ride in his car next time I come," she responded happily. "I've never been in a car like that."

I looked at her and was startled by the fact that my memory must have played a trick on me. Although I remembered her from our previous encounter as alluringly attractive for a young girl, she was certainly no beauty. I could see that she was wearing the same pleated skirt as last time, since the brown coat failed to cover it completely. Her short, wavy hair still had a somewhat boyish look, and I even glimpsed something of her mother's dowdiness in her. But then her dark eyes playfully locked on mine, and I realized that in her case it didn't matter.

"So let's do something fun today," she said. "I don't care what I'll have to tell my mother. She's always too tired to listen to me anyway. But I want to tell my girlfriends I did something exciting."

"Like what?" I asked cautiously.

"I don't know. Up to you."

"Well, we could start out by visiting the German Museum. It's just opened, and people say it's very good: lots of displays of the first cars, steamships, that sort of thing."

"Boring," she shot back, with a smile that took the sting out of her remark. "I don't want to see old cars; I want to drive in new ones, like Uncle Alf's."

"Afraid I can't help you there, since my Mercedes is in the garage."

To my relief, she laughed loudly.

"Look, we can't just stand here. I'll take you someplace you might like. But we need to go quickly, since it's twenty to eleven."

"What's that got to do with anything?" she asked. "Do you have a date?"

"Yes, with you."

We set out in the direction of Marienplatz. Geli wanted to stop at some of the small clothing shops along the way, but I kept prodding her along, telling her she could look at shops later. "I'm not like you, you know," she complained about the pace. "I'm not one of my uncle's soldiers."

"I noticed."

We reached Marienplatz with a couple of minutes to spare. People were already stopping to look up at the clock tower of the New Town Hall. "Isn't that a marvelous building?" I asked.

Geli nodded, taking in not just the building but the impressive square with its elegant gilded statue of Mary. But then her eyes began darting around to what else the square had to offer. "Fine, so what next?" she asked.

At that moment, the clock chimed the hour, and the doors on the tower flipped open. The mechanical knights began jousting, and brightly colored dancers twirled about. Geli craned her neck to catch the performance. Since I had seen it several times before, I watched her watching, delighting in her little-girl look of joy.

"That was wonderful," she said when the figures had once again disappeared behind the closed doors. "And now what—shopping?"

I had been thinking ahead, knowing I wouldn't get much of a reprieve. "Not yet. Let's go right nearby. Besides, I don't think you have money for the kinds of shops we have here."

I led her a few blocks to the *Viktualienmarkt,* the biggest—and fanciest—open-air food market in the city. Women dressed in traditional Bavarian country costumes offered a profusion of fruit, vegetables and meats. Maybe there wasn't much difference from other markets, but

Geli pointed to a red hat with a feather. "I'd like to try that one on."

The saleswoman took it off the shelf and pointed to its price tag. "Are you sure?"

"Yes, absolutely," Geli said, already taking it from the woman and placing it at a jaunty angle on her head. She looked at herself in the mirror on the counter. "I don't know," she added. "This may not do. It's for a rather formal occasion, after all. Do you have anything of better quality?"

I turned away as if examining other hats, but I caught the look of surprise in the saleswoman's eyes when she began to recognize that she might have miscalculated. Suddenly she was eager to help, pulling down several more hats of different shapes and colors. Geli tried each one on and rejected them all. "What about the fur hats?" she asked.

"Yes, of course, we have lovely fur hats. Mink or sable?"

"I really prefer sable."

The saleswoman disappeared into the back room, and Geli gave me the mischievous look I remembered so well from our first outing.

When the woman came back reverently holding two sable hats, Geli looked at them scornfully. "They're so simple, you know," she sighed. "And the colors aren't as rich as the ones I saw earlier."

The saleswoman stood there, speechless.

"Karl, you have to drive me to my lunch. We mustn't keep the baroness waiting." She turned back toward the woman. "I'll come back when you get another shipment. When will that be?"

"We should have some new hats in next month, but—"

"Fine, till then," Geli gaily replied. And we were out the door.

She grabbed my hand and pulled me away from the store, snorting with laughter. "You see why I can't shop in Vienna? This is so much fun."

"Your car, Fräulein," I said, holding open an imaginary door.

"Yes, hurry," she replied, pretending to step in and sit down. "My servants are waiting to dress me for lunch with the baroness."

I checked the time. "We should get back, really. It's a bit of a walk across the English Gardens—and I don't want anyone reporting to your uncle that I didn't get you back to your group on schedule."

We walked toward the park just as we felt the first misty drops of a cold drizzle. Dark clouds moved in, bringing along a more insistent rain, and we stepped up our pace. With the pension already in sight, the rain started to come down very hard.

"Is this going to happen every time we meet?" Geli asked, not seeming to care.

We sought cover under a couple of big trees, but they didn't offer the kind of shelter the trees in the countryside had, only a bit of patchy protection. Geli unbuttoned her coat, slipped it off and held it over her head as a shield from the rain that was still getting through. I saw that she was wearing the same white blouse with the frayed collar.

She caught my glance again. "Don't you want to come under here?" she asked, motioning me under her coat.

I stepped toward her. "You must be cold. I know I am."

"This should warm you up," she said, taking my right hand in one quick motion and placing it on her left breast. She pushed it away just as quickly. "That's it, no more. Thanks for the tour. I knew you wanted to do that."

I stood frozen.

Her lips lightly brushed my cheek, and she ran off to the pension through the rain. "No need to take me the rest of the way," she called over her shoulder.

After she had disappeared with a final wave, I reluctantly turned around and headed back slowly through the park. The rain was coming down harder than ever, but I didn't mind.

Chapter Nine

The ceremony was simple. Of necessity. It wasn't just the fact that we had so little money. Sabine would have liked a church wedding, and she would have somehow scraped together enough to pay for it if that had been a possibility. But no priest would marry a Catholic and a Protestant. And she knew that there was no chance I'd convert to Catholicism. I've never had much use for any religion, and I wasn't about to pretend for the sake of a wedding. So we had a plain civil ceremony officiated by a squat, dour bureaucrat with thick glasses that kept fogging over. Although it was a cool autumn day and the room wasn't overheated, he kept wiping sweat from his narrow brow and flaccid cheeks as he took care of the formalities. He dabbed at the drops of sweat that plunked down on his papers with the same wet handkerchief, only smearing the ink further. I could see the disappointment on Sabine's face at first, but then our eyes met, and she put her hand up to her mouth to suppress an attack of the giggles.

The official stopped in midsentence. "If the fräulein cannot control herself, no wedding will take place," he intoned solemnly, leaving no doubt that Sabine had offended the dignity of his office.

I stared straight ahead, afraid to look in her direction. I could hear her trying to stifle more laughter and coughing to disguise it. "I'm sorry," she said. "I really am."

I heard Uwe behind me, coughing through his laughter as well.

"Maybe everyone here is too sick for these proceedings," the official added. "Perhaps all of you would be better off recuperating at home."

I bit my lower lip, and somehow Sabine pulled herself together. Uwe fell silent.

"Well, then, let's see if we can proceed."

We barely managed to get through the rest of the ceremony. When it came to the exchange of rings, I was so nervous that I extended my left hand to Sabine instead of my right. She tried to slip the ring on my finger, but it got stuck halfway; evidently the ring finger on my left hand was thicker than on my right, but I still had no idea why she couldn't get it on. I could see she was trying to suppress a new burst of giggles, and I desperately jammed the ring on myself. Later it would take a lot of painful pulling, with the help of soap, to get it off. By the time the ceremony was over and Uwe and Petra had signed as official witnesses, I was sweating as profusely as the bureaucrat. He brusquely took his documents and left.

"Haven't you forgotten something, Karl?" Uwe asked.

"What?" I asked, and then blushed. Sheepishly, I kissed Sabine.

Uwe shook his head. "I have to remind that boy of everything."

"You'd better keep reminding him," Petra added with a strained smile.

Sabine looked as close to radiant as I could remember. Certainly much happier than since she got out of the hospital. "Don't worry," she said playfully. "I'll remind him from now on."

Nonetheless, it was Uwe who not only reminded me what to do next but also thought of it in the first place and then made it possible. He had told me to arrange something special for Sabine after the wedding. If the ceremony was going to be simple, he explained, it was all the more important to have a memorable experience afterward.

I had looked at him blankly.

"Karl, ever hear of a honeymoon?"

"Sure, for rich people."

"I know, and I'm not proposing anything fancy. But Sabine once told me she'd love to visit Weimar. I'll fund a short trip: It'll be my wedding present."

"God, Uwe, that's incredibly generous of you. I've never taken her anywhere. But why Weimar, of all places?"

Uwe read my mind. "It's not just the place where they wrote a constitution you hate . . ."

"Yes, of course, I should have thought of it sooner. It's Goethe, isn't it? She's always reading his poems."

Uwe punched me lightly on the arm and rumpled my hair. "You're a real genius."

So it was thanks to Uwe that we rode the train north to Weimar, the town where Johann Wolfgang von Goethe spent fifty-seven of his eighty-three years, as Sabine informed me. Countess Anna Amalia brought him and then Friedrich von Schiller to her court, transforming the town along the Ilm River into Germany's literary capital. It was also a town where Bach played the organs for Saxon royalty, and Liszt served as music director. When Sabine saw how little those names meant to me, she embarked on a crusade to educate me, at least about Goethe, her idol. "They forced me to recite his poems in school," I protested. "I always wanted to get him off my back."

But I dutifully trooped to see his mahogany casket, which lay along with his friend Schiller's in the crypt of the cemetery chapel. Sabine placed a single red rose between the two caskets, which were simpler but more elegant than the elaborately carved caskets of the local princes and princesses in the same crypt. We walked by the majestic bronze statues of the two writers in front of the national theater, and we went up and down the stairs of Goethe's house. Sabine admired the classic busts and the views of the garden where the poet's wife had spent many of her days. The baroque mansion, now a museum, still contained many of his books and art. "It pays to be a poet," I noted, looking at the lavish surroundings.

"Oh, Karl, for such a great man, he lived modestly."

When we reached the room with the narrow bed where Goethe died, Sabine whispered: "His last words were 'Open the window and let in some light.'" She turned to me. "Do you think the light simply goes out when we die?"

"I don't know." I shrugged. "You're the believer."

But nothing could discourage Sabine from trying to share her sense of wonder about the man and the place. "Just think, he lived within these walls, walked the streets we've been walking, admired some of these same houses," she marveled.

And when I was less than awed, she began reading me his poems in bed at the small guesthouse that Uwe had arranged for us. She was sitting with her back propped up against the pillows, and my head was on her stomach. We had made love, gently, slowly, somehow more soothingly than we ever did at home.

"Listen to this:

> *"Why do you wander further and further?*
> *Look! All Good is here.*
> *Only learn to seize your joy,*
> *For joy is always near."*

She leaned over and ran her tongue around my lips. "Isn't that what we have now?"

"Yes, your Goethe isn't all bad."

"Or this," she went on.

> *"Hate, begone, and Envy, vanish!*
> *All that is not joy we banish."*

"Are you trying to tell me something?"

"What do you think?"

"What I'm doing is not about hate, you know. Just justice."

"I've told you I don't understand politics," she said. "But I think I do understand Goethe, and I love his approach to life. Maybe you'll like this more." And she began reading me "The Diary," which, she explained, wasn't included in the regular Goethe anthologies.

My eyes had begun to close, and I only half heard the beginning, something about the narrator having to spend the night in a hostelry rather than return home to his wife because of a broken wheel. But then a young girl serves him dinner, and Goethe finds her every movement irresistible.

> *"A heavenly promise blossoms from her eyes;*
> *I watch her rounded bosom's splendid swell*
> *As it is filled with little half-checked sighs;*
> *And to her ears and throat and neck as well*
> *I see the fleeting rosy love-flush rise."*

Sabine paused, her eyes laughing at me. "You like that, do you? Not exactly what you remember from your school days, is it?"

"No," I conceded. "Don't stop now."

Sabine read on. Goethe described how the lovely creature came to his bed at midnight, confessing her love—but explaining, too, that she was a virgin. She settled her "sweet body" into his arms, allowing him to do whatever he wanted. He was at first delighted, then tormented.

> *My master player, hitherto so hot,*
> *Shrinks, novice-like, its ardor quite forgot.*

The virgin falls peacefully asleep, satisfied only with kisses.

> *So the dear angel lies, and as if all*
> *The bed was hers, spreads each commodious limb,*
> *While he, still powerless, squashed against the wall,*
> *Must forfeit what she freely offered him.*

"You mean nothing happened?" I asked, now more awake than ever.

She read to the end of the poem, from the girl's scurrying away from the bed as soon as she awoke in the morning, to the departure of the poet who was "soon homeward and wifeward bound."

"Ah," I said. "Now I think I understand."

"Bravo," Sabine responded. "In case you didn't, here's the translation of the message in Latin at the beginning of the poem: 'I held another woman in my arms, but as I was about to take my pleasure, Venus reminded me of my lady and deserted me.'"

She pushed the pillow from behind her head and lay back. "Meet your lady," she said, opening her arms. I rushed into them with a new urgency, and she held me tightly as our bodies fused again, this time faster, more explosively, than before. With her arms still wrapped around me as I lay spent on top of her, she laughed gently. "And watch out for those young maidens."

"I will," I promised. "I will."

I wrote to Otto, explaining that I was no longer sure what to believe and was thinking about dropping out of the party altogether. In his reply, he asked me not to make any firm decisions until we had the chance to talk. He was planning a brief visit to his brother's house in Landshut and asked me to meet up with him there.

I agreed, although Sabine tried to talk me out of it. We didn't quarrel, but she didn't hide her disappointment when I insisted on going. "I've talked to Uwe about a job," I said. "He'll probably know something when I get back."

She didn't respond.

"I'll take Leo with me. He'll keep me company on the train."

"Keep an eye on him, Leo," she said, a trace of a smile creeping back across her face. "Make sure he behaves."

"I will," I said, leaning over to kiss her.

Gregor was out when I reached his house, but Otto was waiting for me. He greeted me with a bear hug and motioned me into his brother's study. He greeted Leo just as enthusiastically, mentioning that he had left his Irish setter in Berlin with a friend and missed him already, although he'd be away for only a few days.

As always, Otto exuded an edgy energy as he paced around the small room. "Look at these books," he said, proudly pointing to several well-worn volumes with indecipherable lettering. He picked one up. "Do you know what this is?"

I shook my head.

"Homer, in the original Greek. My brother may be the big warrior to a lot of people, but at home he likes to be the scholar." He tapped the book's cover. "This is where he gets his inspiration. No one should underestimate him."

We settled into two comfortable armchairs, but Otto was up in a moment to offer me tea and strudel. "Sorry not to have anything more elaborate, but Gregor had to go off on an urgent trip, and no one else is around at the moment. So tell me, what's the mood in Munich?"

I told him briefly what I knew, that Hitler was working to rebuild the party and had staged the first big rally since his release from prison, putting on a show of unity with most of the movement's major figures who were attending to lend their support. Otto listened with a distracted air; this obviously wasn't new information for him. When I asked him why his brother hadn't been at the rally in Munich, he brushed the question aside. "That doesn't matter now," he declared. "There's something more important to talk about. I've joined the party."

Otto grinned broadly, relishing my surprise.

"What made you finally do it? You no longer have doubts about Hitler?"

He shook his head. "It's not that. Gregor asked me to help him by signing up. You see, Hitler has asked him to organize and lead the party in the north. Since Hitler can't make public speeches, he needs someone like my brother to be the public figure, especially in areas where he's less known. You know how the workers love Gregor. They know he's on their side."

"And you're convinced Hitler is on their side, too?"

Otto patted Leo, who had planted himself at his feet. "Let's put it this way. The Strasser brothers, if I may say so immodestly, are now in a position to make sure we build a party that puts the workers' interests at its center. We want national socialism to live up to its name, to offer real socialism. Nationalism *and* socialism. I don't know if Hitler has that in mind, but we do. And now Hitler has to rely on Gregor, and maybe even on me, which means we have the leverage we want. You know what Hitler said to Gregor when he heard I'd joined the party?" Otto laughed softly. "He said: 'Whatever he does, he'll do well. Two men like you cannot fail.' We don't intend to."

"So the two of you are going to steer the party toward socialism?"

"Not just the two of us. We're recruiting people. Gregor just converted Goebbels—you've heard of him, the one with the clubfoot?"

I hadn't.

"He's a young Rhinelander, an excellent speaker, even if he's pretty unpleasant to look at. He was against us, working with our opponents in the movement before. But now he's on board. And there are others. We need you, too, you know."

I hesitated, then summoned my resolve. "Otto, I don't think so. I'm a married man now."

He was up in a flash, pumping my hand. "That's wonderful news. Congratulations." He looked me over again. "I thought I detected a new maturity. Yes, now I see—the married man. Excellent."

He seemed to forget about his political pitch, busying himself with inquiries about Sabine, our wedding and the honeymoon.

Only when it was turning dark and I indicated that I needed to take Leo for a walk did Otto return to his earlier topic. He pulled out copies of articles he'd published under the pseudonym of Ulrich von Hutten in the *Völkischer Beobachter,* the party paper, during the time Hitler was in prison. He also showed me more recent manuscripts. "Seen these?" he asked.

"Some of them, but I haven't read everything," I replied, admitting—not for the first time in my life—that I wasn't the most conscientious of readers.

He and Gregor were about to launch publications in the north, he explained, that would offer the opportunity to disseminate their ideas.

He slapped his knees and stood up. "Sorry, let's not keep Leo waiting. I'll gladly take a walk with you."

It was chilly and overcast when we stepped outside. The streets were almost deserted, with everyone probably at home getting ready for dinner. As Leo loped happily along, sniffing his new surroundings, Otto spelled out the ideas he and his brother were propagating. "Call them Strasserism," he said with a self-conscious smile. "It's a doctrine based on our opposition to both Marxism and capitalism."

Of all the historical models, he explained, feudalism was the closest to what he and Gregor had in mind—of course, feudalism adapted to a modern industrial economy. Big industries should be nationalized. The state would be the sole owner of land, which it would lease to private citizens. The big estates would be expropriated from their rich owners, leased to and utilized by small farmers. People could do whatever they wanted with their leased land except sell or sublet it. This would prevent exploitation and the emergence of another rich class.

Political power would be decentralized, and Prussia no longer allowed to dominate the other German states. Instead the country would be divided into self-governing cantons, following the Swiss model. There would be only a small professional army, not the Prussian military machine. Germany needed harmony at home and abroad, which meant a fair system that threatened no one, and an end to oppression. Economic oppression was the worst enemy, not any racial group. But, Otto continued, Jews and others who exploited ordinary Germans would be put on notice that their reign was at an end. The new state would care for the well-being of all Germans, with no favors for the rich.

"An idealistic vision?" Otto asked, not breaking his brisk stride. "Yes. A practical vision? Also yes."

"I haven't heard a lot of those ideas from Hitler," I ventured. "Not the way you put them."

"Not yet, for certain. But we can use Gregor's position to see that they gain acceptance. We have pretty much a free hand in the north, and we want our publications to circulate in the south as well. That's where you—"

It all happened very fast. A blurry black form bolted from the shadows, Leo emitted a piercing yelp and Otto—already a few steps ahead of me—shouted, "Get off him! Get off!" I rushed forward only to see Otto clutching his hand, which he had jerked away from the snarling black dog who had attacked Leo. The dog, a rottweiler, quickly turned his attention back to Leo, who had retreated to a hedge with blood trickling down his neck. I tried to reach for him, to pull him away. The rottweiler caught my thumb in his teeth, and I yanked my hand back as the pain surged through my body. As I did so, I realized Leo was next and that I wouldn't be able to save him.

Otto stepped in between the two dogs, faced the aggressor and swung his left fist directly at his jaw. The dog lunged, his teeth ripping through the skin on the back of Otto's hand. At the same moment, Otto brought his right hand down on the back of the dog's neck, his fingers plunging into the coarse fur. The dog went limp.

Otto looked up. I must have been a sorry sight: I was holding my torn left thumb with my right hand, which was pressed against my chest, but I couldn't apply enough pressure to stop the blood dripping down the front of my jacket. Then he glanced at Leo, who was whimpering near the hedge.

"What the hell do you think you're doing with my dog?"

I heard the voice before I saw its source, a tall, disheveled middle-aged man who appeared from the shadows.

I saw something in Otto's eyes I'd never seen before. Cold fury. He moved his right hand to the prone dog's chest, found whatever he was looking for and pushed. The rottweiler emitted a low gargling sound before lying completely still.

The tall man dropped to his knees and tried to lift the dog's head, but it was too late. "You son of a bitch, you've killed my dog."

"Get out, get out!" I found myself shouting. "Out of here quick, or I'll kill you."

The man looked at me contemptuously, seeing my bleeding hand. "Sure you will."

Still clutching my thumb with my right hand, I swung my joined fists at his face. But he was ready, deflecting them easily with his left forearm as he punched me squarely in the face with his right. I felt the warm flow of blood from my nose and stepped back dizzily. Otto rushed between us, doubling the man over with a series of punches to the midsection and kicking him hard as he went down. "I told you once, and you didn't believe me. Now your dog will never attack anyone again."

Otto turned to me. "Come on, I know a doctor down the street who will look at these injuries, both yours and Leo's."

"And yours," I managed to remind him.

"Mine, too."

Luckily, the injuries weren't as bad as they looked. My thumb required a few stitches, and the wounds on Otto's hands weren't very deep; painful, I'm sure, but not dangerous. The doctor also examined Leo's neck, disinfecting and bandaging it, and assured me that he'd recover quickly.

"Otto, how'd you do it?" I asked once we were back in his brother's house.

"Do what?"

"You know, kill the dog."

Otto looked away and shook his head. "I shouldn't have done it."

"Shouldn't have done it—are you kidding? You saved Leo, all of us."

"Maybe. But the dog is never at fault; it's his master who is to blame."

"But when the dog is out of control?"

Otto shrugged and said nothing.

"You haven't answered my question: How did you learn to do that?"

"I know dogs; you know I love dogs. And almost all dogs love me.

the food all looked lusciously appealing, and the prices were probably higher.

Geli picked up a large onion. "Put that down, Fräulein," commanded the toothless woman in charge of the stall.

"I was just admiring its size," Geli retorted.

"You can buy it first and admire it later."

"Well, I was going to buy five kilos for the birthday dinner we have tonight," Geli huffed. "Now I'll have to look elsewhere." With that, she turned on her heel. "Come on, Karl."

I suppressed a grin and trotted after her. When we had ducked around to the next row of stalls, she burst out laughing. "You see, Karl, I know how to shop without spending any money. You don't have to worry about me."

"You can play tricks on a peasant woman, but don't try stunts like that in the stores here."

"Want to bet?"

I realized where this could be leading and backed off. "All right, I believe you. Come on, there are some really beautiful churches to see."

"Churches? I told you, I want to see the shops."

"Don't you have plenty of shops in Vienna?"

"What kind of question is that? Of course we do. But people recognize me there. Here nobody knows me."

"What difference does that make?"

"Be patient."

Reluctantly, I agreed to take her to a street with fancy shops—Maximilianstrasse, back in the direction from which we had come. Geli gaped at the displays in the windows: the gowns, the coats, the hats, the jewelry. "Let's go in there," she said, pointing to a haberdasher's shop.

Before I could say anything, she was inside.

A middle-aged saleswoman dressed in a well-tailored long skirt and jacket was accepting payment from an elderly man who was buying a present. When she had finished with him, she glanced skeptically in Geli's direction and asked haughtily, "What can I do for you?"

That's why I can't shake the feeling of, 'How could this have happened to me?'"

Otto, it turned out, had once trained guard dogs. And one of the first lessons a trainer learned was how to put a dog down if he got out of control. "A dog has pressure points just like people," he explained. "Once you know where they are, you can immobilize him or, if need be, kill him by cutting off the flow of blood to the heart. But first you have to reach those pressure points—and the only way to do that is to occupy his jaw with one hand while going for a point with the other. That's why I hit him with my left fist; he went for it, and then my right hand was free and out of his range."

"Good God, I never would have believed it. I owe you a big thanks."

Leo nuzzled Otto, who absent-mindedly stroked his back. "I wouldn't have done it—kill the dog, that is—if I hadn't seen him before. When I was here a few months ago, the dog attacked my Rex. The owner—that tall guy—managed to pull his dog away, but just barely, at the last minute. I warned him never to allow such a close call again, but he didn't seem to care. Told me that if my dog couldn't defend himself that it was his problem. I almost went after him then. I should have; maybe that would have prevented what happened today."

In the morning, I thanked Otto again as I prepared to catch the train back to Munich.

"I told you, you don't need to thank me," he said, waving his bandaged hand in a dismissive gesture. "But I hope you'll still think about joining Gregor and me, about helping us."

"How?"

Otto proposed that I take on two basic assignments. First, I could continue to provide a link between Munich and him and, through him, to Gregor. He knew that not only did Hitler and his aides trust me, but I had struck up a friendship with Emil. "That's good," he said. "It can be very useful. You continue to be our eyes and ears down there. We need to know about even the smallest things that are happening within the party." Second, I could help distribute the Strassers' publications among the Bavarian members of the party. "Our ideas can't prevail unless all members are exposed to them."

"You once talked about my coming to Berlin to work for you directly," I reminded him.

"The time for that may come if you're still with us. Just wait. But right now you can help us more where you are. You may have to travel back and forth some, but your base still should be Munich. What do you say?"

He hardly needed to ask. His program sounded noble and fair to me, even if others would later dismiss it as a ridiculous hodgepodge of unworkable political concepts. And when measured against cleaning and painting houses, his offer was infinitely more attractive. It wasn't even close, although I hesitated for another moment as I thought about how Sabine would see this. But then the image of Otto stepping in to face the enraged rottweiler with nothing but his bare hands flashed through my mind, and I knew I couldn't refuse him.

"I'm with you."

Chapter Ten

*Bruno the Jewish swindler had kept his distance, but one day he caught
me off guard with a bizarre question as I was taking my daily walk in
the exercise yard. "What do you do with maggots, vermin, lice?"*

I looked up, startled. "What?"

"What do you do with—"

*"I heard you the first time. You try to get rid of them, you exterminate
them if you can. Why ask a question with such an obvious answer?"*

*Bruno's dark eyes shone with an intensity I found unsettling. "Because
that's what Hitler called Jews like me. We're spiders sucking the blood
out of the people's pores. That's straight out of* Mein Kampf. *"*

"And?" I asked impatiently.

"And that's what he had in mind for us—extermination."

*"That's crazy," I muttered, not caring if he heard me or not as I tried
to shake him off with a faster stride. Since his limp slowed him down, it
wasn't hard to do. But as I left him behind, he kept sputtering: "Maggots, vermin, lice, spiders. Who was crazy?" He emitted a wild laugh.
"Crazy, crazy, crazy. The whole world is crazy."*

When we came through the door, Sabine dropped to her knees to
stroke Leo's head as soon as she saw his bandaged neck. "Oh
my God, what happened to you?"

"He's all right, really. It's nothing serious," I assured her.

She saw my hand, also bandaged.

"I'm all right, too."

She rose to her feet, still leaning over to continue stroking the dog, who was reveling in her attention. I saw the flicker of suspicion in her eyes before her next question, asked in a distinctly chillier tone: "Karl, did you drag Leo into one of your Nazi brawls? Are you and Otto responsible for this?"

"If you only knew," I said, feeling the anger welling up inside me. I sat down at the tiny kitchen table and gave it a whack with the palm of my hand. "Sure, we're to blame, you've figured it all out."

Sabine was watching me carefully. "Knew what?"

I didn't say anything for a long moment; then it all spilled out of me. How I had been merely walking Leo in the sleepy town of Landshut, listening to Otto's latest political theories, when the rottweiler had attacked; how everything had happened so quickly, and how Leo looked doomed; how Otto had performed his incredible rescue, dispatching both the aggressor and his master. I took a breath. "Otto saved Leo—and me. That was one vicious dog and one terrible owner."

"I'm sorry, I just didn't know. I didn't know Otto saved him. I thought with his and your politics—"

"I know, you think it's always the politics to blame. But there's plenty of cruelty and viciousness in this world, with or without politics."

A memory resurfaced that I'd almost forgotten, and I found myself describing it to her. I was probably only about five or six when my father took Gerhard and me out on a boat on the Wannsee. It was a beautiful, hot, sunny day, and he had either borrowed or rented a rowboat, promising us a swim. We rowed out toward the middle of the lake, but our father insisted that we get closer to shore before we jumped in the water. We couldn't actually pull up at one of the beaches, since they were almost all private, so he lifted the oars when we were relatively close to shore. "All right, jump, boys," he commanded, and we gleefully obeyed.

Gerhard, who was older and a much better swimmer than I was, raced up and down the shore with a powerful stroke I could only admire as I splashed around closer to the boat. He slowed at one point, put his legs down to see if he could touch bottom and suddenly screamed. "It hurts, it hurts," he shouted in a high-pitched voice.

My father ordered me to hold on, and he rowed the boat quickly toward Gerhard, pulling him on board and me immediately afterward. I was horrified to see my brother's right foot covered in blood. As tears washed down his face, our father pulled out pieces of glass. "Easy, easy, I'm almost done," Father reassured him. While he wrapped the foot as tightly as he could in a towel, he kept muttering, "Those bastards."

"You see, some of those lovely rich folks on the lake were so intent on preventing anyone else from trespassing on their beaches that they put down broken glass in the water, at the edge of what was legally their property," I explained to Sabine. "We weren't bothering anyone—no one else was there, but they still did this. See what people are like, especially rich people?"

She shook her head and gently took my bandaged hand. "That's horrible."

I pressed my advantage, telling her that I had agreed to keep working for Otto—since I continued to believe in him, since he and Gregor would keep the party committed to fighting for the rights of ordinary Germans. They'd make sure Hitler wouldn't steer the party in the wrong direction.

"Does that mean you'll still be playing soldier, like my grandmother said?" she asked, but softly, without any sting.

"I won't be playing anything, just helping any way I can."

Sabine dropped the subject. As much as she wanted me to abandon what I was doing, she saw that my allegiance to Otto now transcended politics. And she sensed that this wasn't the moment to push me to reconsider, at least not very hard. I'm sure she hoped there would be a more propitious moment; or, even better, that I'd arrive at her conclusion on my own.

Emil told me that Hitler was writing the second volume of *Mein Kampf* on his frequent retreats to Obersalzberg, his hideaway in the Bavarian Alps. I felt more and more that the future of the movement lay in the north. From Otto's letters and reports, I knew that the Strassers were forging ahead. As a Reichstag deputy, Gregor made full use of his free train pass, traveling all over the north and even the Rhineland to deliver speeches and recruit members. By the end of 1925, he had more than tripled the number of party branches in northern Germany, from 71 before the putsch to 262. Otto launched a newspaper, the *Arbeitsblatt,* and, with the help of Goebbels, published the fortnightly *Nationalsozialistische Briefe.* They were making good on Otto's promise to spread the message of Strasserism far and wide.

Emil and Hitler knew of my ties to Otto. They were happy to have me serve as a conduit for messages, seeing me as a useful go-between. I worked hard to make sure that the Bavarian leaders, from Hitler on down, received copies of the Strassers' publications and regular reports about their progress. Otto frequently asked me in his letters whether Hitler betrayed any signs of nervousness about their success, and I could honestly report that I didn't think so. Since he had been banned from public speaking, Hitler seemed less combative. Although he insisted that only *he* could make the major decisions, he allowed Gregor Strasser to become the voice of the party in the north.

But how far would this take him, I wondered. The big issue of the day was what to do with the houses and property of German royalty. Or former German royalty, since the Weimar Republic did not recognize royal titles. There was never any doubt where the Strassers stood on this issue. As Otto had explained to me, those properties should be expropriated. It was a popular position, since workers were eager to see this happen. I couldn't have agreed more with this socialist part of our agenda.

I knew also that Hitler was likely to feel differently. I had relayed to Otto the rumors that he was receiving fifteen hundred marks a month from the divorced duchess of Saxony-Anhalt. He also regularly courted other members of the old families and rich industrialists. He never appeared short of funds, although he had no visible means of support. Word spread that Hitler was denouncing the pressure for land expropriation as "a Jewish plot," and I kept the Strassers fully informed about what looked to me like a looming confrontation.

To my surprise, Otto betrayed little anxiety about this prospect. "It's time to clear the air," he wrote me from Berlin. "And we plan on doing so very soon."

Later I learned the details of Gregor and Otto's strategy. Gregor calculated that if he could line up all the north's Nazi *Gauleiters*, district leaders, behind his call for expropriation, Hitler would be forced to follow their lead. The goal was to get Hitler to abandon his flirtation with the "reactionary" ideas of his financial backers in Munich and to commit the party to a program based on Otto's principles. Gregor asked Goebbels to help him draft the formal program that would then be presented at a meeting of the northern *Gauleiters,* to be held in Hanover in late January 1926.

Otto instructed me to formally notify Hitler's aides, since word would get out anyway. But the northerners were taken aback when Hitler dispatched Gottfried Feder, one of the early theoreticians of the movement, as his personal representative. "No spies in our midst!" Goebbels exclaimed, siding with those who wanted to bar Feder. Gregor argued that Feder's presence might have its benefits: He'd see first-hand how unified the party leaders were on the major issues, and that Hitler needed to accept the new direction. A narrow majority of the delegates voted to admit Feder as a guest.

As Otto recounted to me in a long letter he wrote immediately afterward, the meeting turned into an angry battle. The northerners voted to accept the Strasser program point by point, including the call for expropriation of property owned by the royals and the rich. Feder protested every decision. "Neither Hitler nor I will accept this program," he declared.

That came close to inciting a revolt against Hitler. "In these circumstances, I demand that the petty bourgeois Adolf Hitler be expelled from the National Socialist Party," Goebbels yelled. More calmly, Bernhard Rust, the local *Gauleiter* in Hanover, declared:

"Hitler can act as he likes, but we shall act according to our conscience."

"It was a magnificent moment," Otto concluded in his letter. "We had turned the party around, the result of only a year's work, and Gregor is convinced that Hitler won't have any choice but to shift his politics to the left. He says we still need Hitler, since he's a natural leader. But if Hitler doesn't follow our lead, I say, the party will march off to its future without him."

I saw the new big black six-seater Mercedes parked on Maximilianstrasse, and something made me stop and turn my face toward the window of a shoe shop, pretending to examine the kind of soft leather shoes I'd never be able to afford. When I glanced to my left, I could see the back of Emil's head in the driver's seat. But there was no sign of the person I assumed he was waiting for. I had no reason to hide from Emil or from Hitler, if he really was somewhere near, but I held back, waiting to see what the boss was doing. If it seemed natural to do so, I'd approach and greet them.

For several minutes, nothing happened. Hitler finally emerged from a shop between the car and my position, awkwardly carrying a hatbox. Emil must have seen his boss in the rearview mirror, because he was instantly out on the sidewalk, rushing to meet him and take the box. They exchanged a few words, with Hitler nodding briefly toward the shop, looking at his watch, shrugging and smiling. It was an apologetic series of gestures, a confession of his inability to hurry things up. In any case, I hadn't seen anything like it from Hitler before. I kept my face in the shadow of the shoe store's awning. Emil smiled as he took the box to the car. Hitler returned to stand in front of the hat store, looking in.

Several more minutes passed. Hitler was trying to look casual, self-consciously so. An occasional passerby greeted him, and he'd nod curtly in response. I was impatient to know who would keep Hitler hovering for so long. A woman, I had to assume, since this was a woman's hat shop.

Then I saw Hitler's face light up, and a familiar head of brown wavy hair. I stepped forward and stopped. It was Geli, more mature than a year ago, her face less puffy, now accented by strong cheekbones, but with the playful smile I remembered. Hitler seemed to be admonishing her, but she disarmed him as she handed him a second box. Once again Emil materialized to take the box, nodding at a command and returning to the car. Hitler and Geli stood on the sidewalk talking, and he appeared less charmed than earlier. He talked to her rapidly, gesturing toward the car. She shook her head, pecked his cheek and turned around to walk in my direction. I ducked into the doorway of the shoe store.

Geli walked past, her eyes straight ahead. I peeked around the corner to my right and, seeing that the black Mercedes was gone, turned left and fell in step behind her. "Fräulein, would you prefer mink or sable?" I asked just loudly enough for her to hear.

Geli whirled around, her face looking both startled and suspicious. "It's you," she said, her features softening. "Are you spying on me, Karl?"

"You think I don't have better things to do? I was just walking home and saw your uncle in front of the store, and your little exchange with him, so I backed off. I didn't want to interfere in what looked to me like a family tiff."

Geli fiddled with the top button of her coat. "It wasn't anything of the sort. He wanted to drop me off at my place, but I have other things to do first."

"Your place? What are you doing here, anyway?"

She threw her head back proudly and extended her hand for me to shake. "Meet Geli Raubal, the medical student." She laughed, putting her left hand up to her mouth as our right hands remained joined. "Come on," she added, dropping my hand, somewhat to my disappointment. "Walk me a ways, and I'll tell you about me and you tell me about you."

After graduating from high school, she had gone to Obersalzberg to help her mother keep house at Hitler's alpine retreat. She cooked and cleaned, and Hitler sometimes took her on rides in the country, but she grew restless. "My mother is satisfied with that kind of a life, but I'm not," she declared. "Besides, Uncle Alf likes my company, and he'll be spending more time here from now on." She turned to me. "So here I am in Munich and loving it."

Hitler had set her up in a rented room on Königinstrasse, on the west side of the English Gardens, and she had just started classes.

"You're sure you plan on studying?" I asked.

"Why not?"

"Well, I saw you with a lot of hats, but I haven't seen any books."

"You know how I like to play those games."

"But they're for real now."

"What do you mean?"

"You're really buying now. Or your uncle is."

"Not really, not much," she said, tapping me lightly on the arm. "In fact, I bought only a couple of hats today, because Uncle Alf gets so embarrassed when I spend a lot of time trying things on and don't buy anything. He's not like you."

I smiled at the compliment.

"And it's still just a game."

"And your studies?"

"No, no, they're serious. At least I think so."

"Sounds very serious," I said teasingly. "I'm sure you're running off from your uncle to bury yourself in your books."

"Well, not exactly. There's this boy I met when I was registering. He asked me for a coffee, but Uncle Alf doesn't want to hear about such things."

"Oh, I see."

Geli shot me an amused look. "Do I detect a note of disapproval? Or maybe jealousy?"

We had reached a busy corner and stood waiting for a tram to rattle by before we could cross. I looked away, and we crossed the street.

"And what about your girlfriend—are you still with her?"

"We're married."

Geli seemed not to hear. Her eyes were focused on the window of the café in front of us, and I saw them light up as they locked on to a lanky young man with a scrawny beard who looked up expectantly. "Congratulations," she said, distractedly kissing me on the cheek.

I already felt forgotten, but she must have sensed my mood. She turned back at the door to the café. "Thanks for walking with me, Karl." She kissed me on the cheek again, this time letting her lips linger. "And remember," she whispered as she did so, "married men shouldn't be jealous of other women." She drew back, looked me over and added with a gleam in her eye: "You didn't wait long, did you? I'm the one who should be jealous."

I picked up more than just political gossip about Hitler. As a local celebrity and a bachelor in his mid-thirties, he naturally attracted the attention of women. In the case of older, rich women, he seemed to know exactly how to make them open their purses for him. But with other women, he was awkward. Emil told me about his appearance at the New Year's party thrown by Heinrich Hoffmann, the photographer. Several of Hoffmann's young models took an interest in the man they had heard so much about, who looked intriguing in his cutaway coat with his small mustache. "And those were some women," Emil told me, relishing the memory. "Gorgeous, beautiful bodies . . ."

As Emil told it, one of the models, who was wearing silk stockings and a clinging gold-fringed dress, winked at her friends and crossed the room toward Hitler. She marched over in a way that made him take a step back, which placed him directly under the mistletoe. Then, without any preliminaries, she kissed him on the lips—not a quick peck but a long, inviting kiss. "Me, I would have known what to do," Emil boasted. "But with the boss, it wasn't just embarrassing but painful. He stood there like a mummy, not kissing her back. He'd gone completely cold. The poor girl stepped back, not knowing what to say, and it was totally silent in the room for a moment." The girl scurried away, with Hitler looking after her as if she had committed some unbelievable crime.

Hoffmann tried to lighten the mood. "You've always had luck with the ladies, Herr Hitler," he declared. Hitler didn't say anything. He put on his mackintosh and left. "I had hoped to spend the rest of the evening feasting my eyes on those women, maybe even getting one of them to agree to meet me later, and instead I had to scramble after him," Emil complained.

There were other stories that Hitler, who went to Vienna as a young man in the hopes of studying art, had dragged a friend along on a late-night walk up and down the Spittelberggasse, where the small houses were lit up so men could see the prostitutes available inside. Hitler had ranted half the night about the repulsive evil of the sex trade, conjuring up images of blond women subjected to the most sordid humiliations by long-nosed Jews. His fantasy life extended in other directions as well. He reportedly told a friend during that period of his so-called romances with several "proper" women. When his friend questioned him, it turned out that Hitler had seen these women only from afar, never daring to try and meet them. According to one story, he was still angry with one of these women for marrying someone else.

Once when I was delivering the Berlin publications to Hitler's room on the Thierschstrasse, I saw a young girl on the way out. She carefully averted her eyes as we crossed paths on the stairs, but my glimpse was enough to see that they were filled with tears that she was barely holding back. She looked no more than about fifteen, a schoolgirl rushing away from a secret rendezvous. "She's sixteen," Emil assured me later. "Her name is Maria, and the boss met her walking his dog in Obersalzberg."

"So he does like women?"

"Yes, in his own way. When they're young and in awe of him."

"What does that mean?" I asked. "Maria didn't look very happy. Some sort of quarrel?"

Emil looked away, and I could sense that he regretted having said this much.

"It's not important," I assured him.

But I didn't need Emil to pick up some of the other hints about

Hitler's views on women. Even in mixed company, he talked about the malleability of young women, how a man should put his mark on them. He quoted Nietzsche: "You are going to see a woman? Do not forget your whip." Women, he said frequently, should be "cuddly and stupid."

Otto liked it when I sprinkled such gossip in with my political reports. He savored every tidbit and seemed to have other sources as well. "He has a perverse imagination," he mused in one of his letters. "And whatever relationships he has with women, I'd bet, are perverse, too. Pity the women who ever cross his path."

Otto soon had more important matters to worry about. Hitler didn't take news of the Hanover meeting lightly. In mid-February, just three weeks later, he convened his own meeting of party leaders in the Franconian town of Bamberg. I sent an urgent message telling Otto that Hitler had summoned the southern leaders and their deputies, who all had been recently placed on the party payroll to ensure their loyalty. Most of the northern leaders still made their own living, and many of them couldn't afford to break away from their jobs and pay for the trip to Bamberg. Gregor, of course, made the trip with his free railway pass, and he took Joseph Goebbels along for support. My SA unit was called up and ordered to Bamberg as well.

I hadn't spent much time with my unit. First, it had been formally disbanded after the failed putsch. Once it was activated again, I kept my distance most of the time, and the officers assumed I was busy with other party assignments. But Hitler wanted to mount a convincing display of his command. We were told to guard the hall but that there shouldn't be any need for force. I felt uneasy in a role that once had felt natural to me. I wondered what I would do if there was some sort of confrontation. Otto assured me that he didn't expect anything of the sort. He was convinced that Gregor could talk the delegates into endorsing the decisions made at Hanover and that Hitler, recognizing his miscalculation, would fall into line.

I was part of the security detail in front of the building where the officially secret meeting was to take place. I watched nervously as a fleet of expensive cars deposited Hitler's top men. When Emil emerged from Hitler's Mercedes and opened the door for his boss, he looked unusually stern. He nodded in my direction before stepping back into the car, but there was no hint of merriment. The boss had obviously been in a somber mood on the ride up. I caught a glimpse of Gregor Strasser and Goebbels walking in from the station. Goebbels looked admiringly—and, I thought, enviously—at the cars pulling up with the southern leaders.

My unit was ordered into the building, and I took up a position near the door of the meeting hall, which allowed me to hear some of the proceedings. I had a sudden urge to relieve myself. If fighting broke out, I thought, my bladder wouldn't hold. Pissing in my pants when the fighting started, what a way for a brownshirt to act.

Hitler took the floor and held forth for a good two hours. He talked about the need for Germany to avoid any alliance with Russia, which would lead to the country's "Bolshevization." And Bolshevism, he warned again and again, was the supreme Jewish plot to destroy the German nation and seek world domination. Germany's future had to be secured by colonizing land to its east: in other words, through a direct confrontation with Russia.

Hitler launched his assault on the decisions in Hanover to support the expropriation of royal land. "For us today, there are no princes, only Germans," he declared to the enthusiastic applause of the southern leaders. The party "will not give a Jewish system of exploitation a legal pretext for the complete plundering of the people."

I saw Goebbels rise as soon as Hitler sat down. Here goes the first volley of the other side, I thought. "Herr Adolf Hitler is right," Goebbels announced. I saw surprise and anger cross Gregor's face. Hitler betrayed only the slightest trace of a smile. "His arguments are so convincing that there is no disgrace in admitting our mistakes and rejoining him," Goebbels added.

I couldn't hold out any longer. With no officer in sight, I risked deserting my post to bolt for a toilet. I let loose as fast as I could, alarmed but relieved by the stream that didn't let up for what seemed like an eternity. I hurried back, grateful that no one had noticed.

Gregor was speaking, although now I was too far back to catch much. I heard Hitler intervening, but he was even harder to hear. Once Hitler stepped up to Strasser, and I tensed. But Hitler put his arm around him and whispered something. By the end of the meeting, I heard everyone pledging their loyalty to Hitler.

I left Bamberg dispirited and confused. Otto explained in a letter. Hitler, he conceded, had made a "brilliant" defense of the princes, making it sound like he was standing up for German interests. He had stacked the meeting in his favor more than Gregor had realized, but he had been conciliatory. At the moment when he put his arm around him, he told him: "Strasser, you really mustn't go on living like a wretched official. Sell your pharmacy, draw on the party funds and set yourself up properly as a man of your worth should."

Otto was shaken, but he tried to remain optimistic. "We had to reach a compromise," he wrote. Its essence: The Strassers would continue to run their expanding publishing operations in Berlin, but they had to renounce their Hanover program and accept Hitler's original party platform. Otto hinted that he had warned Gregor against taking funds from Hitler, since that would enslave him. "We have to maintain our independence at all costs," he wrote. "But Gregor argues—and I'm willing to accept his argument for now—that we need Hitler and that Hitler needs us. Therefore, this compromise should work. We can still use our newspapers and periodicals to steer the party in a more socialist direction, although I admit that it may prove more difficult than I originally thought."

If Otto was willing to continue working with Hitler, he was furious about Goebbels's sudden switch. Hitler, it turned out, had been quietly courting him even before the Bamberg meeting and afterward invited him for get-togethers with the southern party leaders, making sure that an official car was put at his disposal and that he was treated like a major dignitary. "Goebbels has the character of a dog," Otto wrote contemptuously. "He'll go with whatever master pampers him more, and then do anything to please him."

Hitler, however, didn't ignore his chief internal rival. When Gregor Strasser was injured in a car accident shortly after the Bamberg showdown, Hitler paid him a surprise visit in Landshut, where he was recovering. By the end of 1926, Hitler announced two major changes within the leadership of the party. He appointed Goebbels *Gauleiter* in Berlin, effectively displacing Gregor as the top party leader in the north; and named Gregor the party's propaganda chief. Otto was nervous about the changes, but Gregor assured his brother that the position would allow him to inject their message more effectively. And that was the tone of the messages Otto sent to me. "We must be patient," he wrote. "And we have to redouble our publishing efforts in Berlin. Which means I may need you here sooner than I thought."

Chapter Eleven

I was relieved to receive Otto's summons to Berlin. The distribution
of the Strassers' publications in Bavaria was extremely limited, so it
didn't occupy much of my time. And I was too lowly a party figure to
provide much on Hitler's thinking. Gregor was spending more and
more time in Munich, meeting with Hitler and the other top party
leaders often. I'm sure he provided more information than I did—although Otto always claimed he found my reports helpful. Did I consider myself a spy? Not then. I believed I was working to keep the lines
of communication open between the Strassers and Hitler, ensuring a
coordinated national strategy to combine the Strassers' socialism with
Hitler's popular appeal.

I occasionally participated in SA exercises, although the brownshirts were themselves pulled in different directions depending on the
loyalties of their leaders. And I helped organize activities for one of the
branches of the newly founded Hitler Youth Movement. An occasional
camping trip, picnic, that sort of thing. But even when I wasn't busy, I
pretended to be so that Sabine wouldn't start pushing me again to look
for other work. Besides, there were times when I wanted to escape the
confines of our small apartment; when, as much as I loved Sabine, I felt
restless in her company, unable to share her sense of contentment that
we were constantly together.

Emerging from the Anhalter Station, I hesitated. Sabine had eventually made me admit that I didn't visit my mother on my last trip,
and left no doubt that she wouldn't forgive me if I failed again. She

didn't mind my traveling to Berlin, she said, but only under this condition. I had made her a solemn promise.

The S-Bahn would take me north toward the center of town. The U-Bahn would take me south to my old neighborhood of Neukölln. As I stood there, a group of foreigners approached, arguing loudly in what I assumed was Russian, since I had heard the city was full of Russians lately. A short, square man with a wispy mustache was shouting at his tall companion, who looked on with disdain while delivering a terse reply. They passed on either side of me. For a moment, I thought they would come to blows and I'd get it from both sides, but the only thing I got was a glob of spit from the mustached man's mouth as he started yelling again. Before I could react, they had moved past me to the S-Bahn entrance, continuing their argument. Wiping my cheek in disgust, I turned in the other direction.

In the U-Bahn, I wondered what I would say to my mother.

It felt odd to follow the streets from the subway station to our building. I walked past the bar, bakery and tobacco shop that I remembered. Back then they had loomed, imposing; now, they looked cramped and seedy. An old woman behind the bakery counter used to slip me an occasional roll or cookie. My father had been furious when he caught me taking her handout. "I won't have my child begging," he informed me after he dragged me home. And then, as so many times, he made me hold out my hand and delivered several stinging whacks with his ruler. As I passed the bakery, I glanced inside and saw a young woman behind the counter.

Our building was diagonally across the street, a battered, dirty gray six-story structure leaving no doubt that its inhabitants were not among the privileged. I pushed on the main door, which, as always, creaked loudly as it gave way to the courtyard, where a woman was methodically beating a rug thrown over the lowest branch of the single tree. Clouds of dust burst into the air each time she whacked the rug with a broom, and two small children jumped away laughing, only to sneak up on the rug and retreat from the billowing dust again. "Get out of here, you nasty little brats," she shouted. It was hard to believe that Gerhard and I had once raced around the same way, playing the same game as our mother had performed the same exercise. Yes, that was one nice memory, I thought, but it came with the pang that I felt whenever I remembered Gerhard. Which was not very often, I had to admit. My return was triggering thoughts I hadn't had for a long time.

I directed my steps past the garbage bins, which were as filthy as ever, to the third entrance. A familiar dank smell invaded my nostrils as I started up the stairs to the second-floor landing. It was a mix of piss from the stairwell and cabbage cooking inside one of the apartments. I paused in front of the big brown door I knew so well and knocked lightly. There was silence. I knocked again, this time louder.

The door was flung open by an unshaven middle-aged man who obviously had been drinking. "What the hell do you want?"

I stood there speechless.

"Can't talk?" he growled, slurring his words.

"Is Frau Naumann here?" I asked.

He laughed. "That's a good one—I hope not."

I grabbed his tattered shirt and shouted at him. "What do you mean, you hope not? Who are you?"

He put his hands up. "Hey, don't do anything to me. I don't have anything worth stealing."

"What are you doing here? Where's Frau Naumann?"

"I don't know," he protested, trying to squirm away. "I just live here. I never met the lady. She died before I moved in."

I must have released him, because he quickly stepped back and started to slam the door. I stuck out my arm to block it.

"I'll call the police," he yelled.

"Please," I said. "Please, are you sure she died?"

"Ask the neighbors if you don't believe me."

"When?"

He looked at me curiously, no longer with fear. "What's it to you?"

"She was my mother."

"Two years ago. Didn't you know?"

I shook my head.

"Kids nowadays," he muttered. "Never do think about their parents. I don't have any idea where my girl is. She could be a hooker for all I know."

He eased the door shut, and I didn't try to stop him. I sat down on the stairs, not crying but sinking into oblivion, no longer noticing much of anything. When I finally got up and walked through the courtyard, it was getting dark. The woman who had been beating her rug was nowhere to be seen; there was no trace of her two kids, either.

I don't remember the journey across town. I assume I took the U-Bahn again, but I might have taken a tram or even walked. It was dark when I reached Otto's neighborhood. My first recollection of that evening is of standing under a lamppost, realizing where I was and trying to decide if I really wanted to meet with Otto, or with anyone, for that matter. The next thing I remember is facing three young men, one of whom was screaming that I had walked right into him. Before I could do or say anything, he punched me in the face, but I instinctively pulled away, and the blow didn't feel that bad. I struck back, landing a hard punch to his midsection, but then his companions were all over me. Within seconds I was on the ground, trying to curl up and protect myself. It must have hurt, but I felt detached. "That should teach you a lesson, you piece of shit," I heard one say. And then they were gone.

I got up, shaken, and walked the few steps to Otto's building. I climbed the stairs and knocked on his door.

Otto pulled me out of the dimly lit hallway into his apartment. "My God," he said. "You're a mess. They worked you over well."

"It's not that bad."

"Not bad?" He led me to a washbasin and pointed to the small wall mirror. I saw a black eye forming, and blood smeared under my nose and dribbling from my mouth.

Otto sat me down on a wooden stool and filled the washbasin with water. He dipped a rag into it. "Here," he said. "Clean yourself up, and we'll see how much damage there really is. If it's very bad, I'll get the doctor we use in such cases."

I followed his instructions, then looked in the mirror again. "Nothing broken?" he asked.

"I don't think so."

"Good, you were lucky. Not like some of the others."

"What others?"

"You're not the first. People who work for our press operation or who visit me often get a welcoming committee."

"You mean this wasn't an accident? One of those guys said I bumped into him."

"They always make some phony excuse. They're your buddies, brownshirts. Except these are Goebbels's brownshirts. He's trying to push us out of town so he can be the only party publisher here. That's why I called you. I've made a report on his actions that I want you to deliver to Hitler. Only he can stop this, if he wants to."

I had heard that Goebbels had started his own daily in Berlin, *Der Angriff*, in competition with the Strassers' *Arbeitsblatt*. It had seemed to me a strange situation, but Otto was convinced there was nothing unusual about it. "Goebbels is trying to run us out of business, so that only his publications are read by party members," he told me. "He keeps the times of party meetings secret from us so we can't publish them, while of course he makes sure that *Der Angriff* does. Party members have to buy his paper to find them."

Otto paced the cramped room, which still overflowed with the leaflets, newspapers and propaganda I remembered from my last visit. He lit a cigarette.

"Haven't you complained to Goebbels about this?"

"Sure I have. And you know what he told me? Those must be communists who are attacking our people. He said I should get the SA to protect us." Otto waved the hand holding the cigarette, sending a few loops of smoke floating in my direction. "Can you believe the audacity? He wants us to take the SA, his SA spies, into our organization. The same guys who have been beating our people up. He'd like that, he sure would."

"And you think Hitler will order Goebbels to leave you alone?"

Otto shrugged. "I'd like to believe that, which is why I'm sending this report. But will Hitler do anything? I have doubts. Goebbels is his man, and he follows Hitler's line, which is friendly, much too friendly, to the big industrialists. Our publications are against them. We are keeping the commitment to socialism. Gregor thinks Hitler will listen." He paused and took a deep drag on his cigarette. "But I worry that we have a Dr. Caligari on our hands. You remember the movie?"

I had seen the movie, but I wasn't sure I was keeping up with Otto's train of thought.

"Caligari, the madman, remember? The guy who travels in a carnival and sends out his assistant, Cesare, to kill anyone he doesn't like. And when the friend of one of his victims tracks Caligari down to an insane asylum, he turns out to be the director instead of an inmate."

"Hitler as Caligari?"

"Maybe, maybe not. But I have no doubt Goebbels would be happy to play the role of Cesare."

First the news about my mother. Then the beating. And now Otto was suggesting that our leader might be a deranged monster.

"I'll deliver the report. But you'll see, Hitler will stop Goebbels. He's no Caligari."

"I hope you're right," he said. "But I'm beginning to believe that I have to prepare for the possibility that you and Gregor are wrong."

I was to meet Emil at a Munich café that he had suggested, just off Marienplatz. The ban on Hitler's public speaking had been lifted. The boss, Emil explained, was busy preparing his next round of meetings and didn't want to be disturbed. Emil assured me that he would deliver Otto's letter directly to Hitler, and I had no doubt he would keep his promise.

Emil's choice of café surprised me. I knew he liked the beer halls better, and this establishment was the kind that attracted its fair share of old ladies along with the young, well-groomed men and women who made me feel scruffy. I took in the rows of polished wood tabletops and the molded white ceiling with pale pink designs that matched the pink curtains. I felt out of place. Sabine had been angry when I returned the previous evening with my black eye and swollen lip: further evidence that I should abandon politics for a normal life. We would have quarreled if not for the news about my mother's death, which made her wipe away tears that I hadn't expected to shed. I fell asleep in her arms, and in the morning she kissed me gently before going off to work.

I didn't see Emil. I picked out a table in the back where I'd be inconspicuous. A waiter asked for my order. I decided on tea, figuring it would be the cheapest thing. When the waiter returned with a translucent blue cup and saucer and silver spoon, his expression said: Don't think you're kidding anyone. This isn't a place for deadbeats like you.

Emil arrived a few minutes later. "Sorry I'm late," he started—and then stopped. "What happened to you?"

"Nothing much, a little run-in with some boys in Berlin."

"What boys?"

"I don't know. Maybe they were our boys, brownshirts. Maybe they weren't." I handed him the letter. "That's what Otto is writing to Hitler about."

I explained Otto's theory that this was Goebbels's doing.

"You know I'm close to the boss, but I often don't know what's going on," he confessed. "Somehow it all seemed simpler earlier."

The waiter came to take Emil's order. "The usual, Herr Maurice?"

Emil nodded. "That'll be fine." And bring a piece of that strudel for my friend here, so he doesn't go away hungry.

"Certainly, sir."

"The usual?"

"I know this isn't the kind of place we usually hang out. But the boss likes to come here. So they've gotten to know me." He leaned forward. "And Geli likes it here."

"You and Geli?"

"Surprised? Don't tell me you hadn't noticed her Viennese charm."

I confessed that I had.

"And didn't you notice her *occhi parlanti?*"

"Her what?"

"That's Italian for eyes that speak."

"Well, excuse me. I forgot what a man of the world you are. Viennese charm, Italian eyes. I'm just a simple German, you know, and I can't identify these things by their nationality."

"So you did notice her eyes?"

"They're hard to miss."

"Well, don't let them carry you away, my friend. She's already taken, or soon will be." He laughed. "Anyway, you're a happily married man."

The waiter returned with a Turkish coffee for Emil and two pieces of strudel. I took a bite of mine. "Delicious. But what about the boss—how does he feel about you and Geli?"

Emil scanned the room. "You know, I have a confession to make: I arranged to see you here because I'm to meet Geli. She's always late."

"And what does he say?"

I saw something like anxiety in Emil's face. "I don't know—I mean, he doesn't know yet. Geli and I haven't made any big decisions so far. But he's very possessive of her, sometimes too much so. Geli doesn't tell me much, but I see plenty. And she did tell me about this one incident." Emil looked like he was about to continue but stopped.

"Well?" I asked. "What incident?"

He had a bite of strudel and sipped his coffee. "It may not mean anything."

Geli and Hitler had been sitting in the same café a week or so earlier, and Hitler had asked her what kind of a man appealed to her, how such a man would look. Geli laughed, saying that she had to see a man to know, since there was no ideal type. Hitler quickly pulled out a pen and a drawing pad and proceeded to sketch the outlines of a face.

"Someone like this?" he asked.

Geli said no.

He sketched another face, and then another. Each time Geli shook her head, even when Hitler outlined a face like his own.

"I want the man I fall in love with to be a surprise. A total surprise, even in the way he looks."

Hitler had not been pleased, although he tried not to show it. He paid the bill and rushed off, claiming an important appointment. Normally when he was with Geli, Emil noted, he acted as if he had all the time in the world.

"You know Geli," Emil added, draining his coffee. "She just thought it was terribly funny that Hitler would want her to fall in love with someone who looked like him. I'm not sure it was really so funny. What does he want from her?"

"She's his niece. You don't mean—"

"I don't know what I mean," he cut me off and stood. He had spotted Geli at the door. She looked at the front tables, then saw us in the back. She rushed over, her cheeks red and damp from the wind and rain, her hair curling more than usual.

"What are you doing hidden back here?" She embraced Emil and held out her hand to me.

"I think our friend is less than at home here. He chose the table."

"Oh, Karl, we must instill a bit of sophistication in you. And if I were your wife, I'd make sure to keep you away from those beer-hall brawls."

"If I were your husband, I'd ask why you're hanging around fancy cafés instead of studying medicine like you're supposed to."

"And I'd say it's none of your business why I dropped out of medical school."

"I didn't know, honestly I didn't," I protested. "I'm sorry—I was just joking."

Geli patted my hand on the table. "No offense taken," she said, smiling again. "Besides, I'm taking singing lessons now. Uncle Alf feels that's a better occupation for a woman than medical studies."

The conversation steered into more neutral territory. When Geli learned that I was involved with the Hitler Youth Movement, she wanted to know about the activities. I told her about the camping trips, the bonfires, the games we played.

Her face lit up, and she turned to Emil. "Why don't you drive Uncle Alf to one of those outings and I'll come along? It sounds like so much fun."

"If you talk him into it. You know I can't tell him what to do, and you can talk him into anything."

I thought I detected a trace of resentment in his voice. Geli hadn't noticed. Or if she had, she pretended not to and smiled at me. "Oh, I'll do that, all right. He should see how good a job Karl is doing with recruiting young people."

"Thanks," I said, preparing to leave. I began reaching into my pocket for money.

"Forget it, Karl," Emil ordered. "My treat. You'll buy me a beer next time."

I shook hands with them both.

"Don't be a stranger," Geli said, giving my hand a light squeeze. "Be sure to tell Emil when your next outing is so I can get Uncle Alf to go there."

As I gathered up my coat, she persisted: "Promise you won't forget?"

"Of course not." I avoided Emil's eyes. "You can count on me."

As I left, I was sure they were looking at me. But when I turned at the door, I saw I couldn't have been more wrong. Geli was regaling Emil with a story, her laughter echoing across the room, their eyes never leaving the other's.

Chapter Twelve

You're stupid to be thinking about her, I told myself. I felt foolish and excited about the way she teased me. She tantalized me. So did the life she led, the afternoons spent at elegant cafés, the rumors I had heard that Hitler took her to dinners and concerts. I knew it was crazy to think that way about Hitler's niece, to believe that there could be more between us than an occasional flirtation, that I could somehow become part of her glamorous world. But what I knew and what I felt couldn't have been further apart.

In early spring, as the weather improved I organized the Hitler Youth Movement's first outing of the season. And I was quick to tell Emil of our plans so he could let Geli know. She was supposed to talk Hitler into seeing his young followers in action. I spent the night with my group beside a campfire I had located to be visible from the road. As we sang songs and roasted sausages, I kept glancing toward the road, hoping for the headlights of Hitler's Mercedes.

A few days later, back in the city, I made sure I ran into Emil.

"Hey, what happened the other night?" I asked. "It was a great evening, but you never showed."

"The boss was busy: He and Geli went to the opera."

I feigned indifference. "In case he's interested, I've scheduled different groups in the same place for the next three Friday nights."

He promised to pass along the information. On the next outing, I was again disappointed. The following Friday I resisted the impulse to keep looking at the road. They're not coming, I told myself.

The weather was perfect for our final outing, a warm, sunny day that sprouted fresh leaves from the trees and brought dandelions seemingly from nowhere. My teenage charges were bursting with energy as well, chasing one another around and between the trees and, I couldn't help noting, disappearing in couples for a few moments, the girls often reappearing with flushed faces, the boys trying to both hide and trumpet their sense of triumph. When Monika, one of my favorites, emerged holding Klaus's hand with a guiltily happy look, I called the group to order. We prepared the bonfire, with a few more couples slipping off as they supposedly gathered wood, but I kept Monika near me cutting up the sausages, and I assigned Klaus the job of collecting and sharpening the sticks we'd use for roasting. "Herr Naumann, can Monika help me with the sticks?" he asked. Monika blushed and looked at me expectantly. "No, she's busy here," I replied more gruffly than I intended.

I looked in the direction of the road a couple of times, without any real anticipation. "This isn't how you hold the knife when you cut sausages, Monika," I said, reaching around her and grasping her hand, supposedly to show her a different technique. She had a long blond braid that brushed against my face as I stood behind her, and she turned to shoot me a questioning look, knowing full well that she hadn't done anything wrong. I stepped back, feeling silly, and retreated to the bonfire, where I issued orders to two boys to light it. I sat down, wondering why I was behaving so stupidly. I felt more awkward than the kids.

The bonfire sent up showers of sparks when a log slipped down through the large pile. As twilight set in, the teenagers settled into singing songs and roasting sausages with only minimal direction from me. I found myself watching as the couples, including Monika and Klaus, sidled closer together and leaned or pressed against each other. Monika cast one or two abashed looks my way, but when I didn't react, she stopped paying attention and turned back to Klaus.

The dry logs burned quickly, and the bonfire diminished. The logs now emitted low flames that licked around their sides. Manfred, one of the most athletic boys in the group, grabbed a girl's hand and yanked her up. "Let's jump," he said. It was a game we had played before, usually when the bonfire had burned down a bit more. When I didn't object, Manfred and the girl backed up far enough to get a running start and leap over the flames; they made it but not by much. The others cheered, and Klaus jumped up with Monika. I considered stopping them but thought better of it. As the leaping began in earnest and the couples became more and more excited, I remained glumly perched on a log, wondering what I was doing there.

Someone tapped me on the shoulder. I turned around and bolted at the sight of Geli, in her simple plaid dress, brown shoes and white socks, her eyes alive with excitement. Behind her on the road, I could see the black Mercedes, with Emil standing beside it. He gave me a short wave. I waved back.

"You made it—I didn't think you would."

"I said I would, didn't I?"

"And your uncle?" I asked, glancing at the car. It wasn't dark yet, but I couldn't see inside.

"He's there."

"Shouldn't I go greet him?"

"Not yet. He said he wanted to watch and for everything to continue the way it is. Maybe he'll come out later." She paused, plopped down on the log where I had been sitting and swiftly pulled off her shoes and socks. She reached out her hand for me to pull her up. "Let's go. I haven't done this for I don't know how long."

"Jump over the fire?"

"What do you think I mean?"

The others must have been watching us, but I had been too absorbed to notice. As I stood hand in hand with Geli, the kids cheered us on. I saw Monika and Klaus laughing as they joined in.

A log tumbled, and a flame briefly shot up from the dying fire.

"You sure?"

"Yes."

Geli broke into a run, pulling me forward with her. We didn't have much running room, and I wasn't sure we'd clear the fire, but she wasn't about to stop. I accelerated as much as I could, and we flew through the air, feeling the heat of the low flames lick the bottom of our feet. Geli stumbled as we hit the ground on the other side, and I tightened my grip on her hand to prevent her from falling.

"My knight, my hero," she said, offering a mock curtsy. The kids applauded.

"May I present Fräulein Raubal," I said to the group with a sweeping gesture. "She's a friend who wanted to see what kind of activities we have on these outings."

The teenagers looked at one another uncertainly. Geli leaned over and whispered in my ear, "They think I'm your girlfriend."

"This young lady is related to someone who is very important for all of us," I said. "But I'll explain this later. Let's continue before it gets too dark out. So, more songs or a game?"

They wanted a game, and we decided on hide-and-seek with two teams. One team had to tag the members of the other team before they reached the bonfire, but they couldn't guard it. Everyone was supposed to spread out and find hiding places.

Geli and I were on the team that had to hide. She took my hand again. "Let's go," she urged, and we ran to the nearby trees.

"This way," I ordered, pulling her to the left, where I knew the trees and bushes were dense and provided good cover. We had to sprint across an open field before we reached the better hiding places, and we could be caught on our way. We crouched for a moment, and then I whispered that we had to run for it. I glimpsed one of the boys from the other team at the edge of the field, starting to run in our direction, but we sped up and plunged into the thicker woods on the other side before he came close.

"Farther, farther," I said, pulling Geli on until we reached a line of trees with broad trunks. She was panting and laughing as we rushed behind one of them. I leaned against the tree, and she abruptly pinned me against it, putting her arms around my waist. "Shhh," she whispered. "We have to be quiet. If you hold me tight, we'll be invisible."

My arms enveloped her, and I felt every part of her body pressing against me, her lips searching mine and her mouth opening with a hunger I couldn't recall ever feeling from Sabine, even before we were married. I no longer cared who might be near and pulled her even tighter, so she couldn't escape feeling the full force of my arousal.

She withdrew slightly and gave me a bemused look. "It's all part of the game, Karl. You're the group leader, we have to make sure you don't get caught first. In anything."

Her face was flushed as I stroked her cheek with my right hand and let it descend to her neck, wanting desperately to let it wander farther down, to where she had once pressed it. I encountered a gold swastika necklace.

"Where did you get that?"

"Uncle Alf gave it to me. Don't you think it's pretty?"

I pushed myself away, but Geli still had her arms around my waist and tightened them. "You don't approve."

"No, it's none of my business."

Geli dropped her arms, and we stood facing each other. "Maybe you're right, Karl, maybe I shouldn't accept his gifts."

"I didn't say that."

"But he's nice to me, at least most of the time."

"What about the other times?"

"It doesn't matter. He's good to me, he takes me to the opera, to concerts, to cafés. All the girls envy me."

There was a rustling nearby and a shout: "There they are!"

"Come on, Karl," Geli said, grabbing my hand again. "Let's run for it."

We sprinted, with our pursuers—two girls and two boys from the other team—right behind us. We nearly made it, but this time I stumbled and fell, dragging Geli down with me. We were tagged only a few steps from the bonfire.

We were both laughing as we struggled back to our feet, and it was then that we noticed the rest of my charges lined up at attention in front of Hitler. He was wearing lederhosen and holding a riding crop behind his back as he inspected the kids.

"*Heil* Hitler!" I saluted.

He nodded. "It's not good for a leader to lose," he said sternly. Then he smiled. "This time I'll make an allowance for it, since I'm impressed with your young people here. They look healthy, physically strong." Turning back to them, he added: "Strong bodies as well as sound views will be crucial for our movement in the struggle ahead."

He paused and took his hands from behind his back. He hit his left open hand with the riding crop, making a stinging thwack. "We must be strong, always strong. Remember that. Carry on, all."

I caught up with Hitler as he made for his car, where Emil was opening the door for him. "I really appreciate your visit, sir. I'm sure it means so much for these young people. And I apologize if all this looked a bit disorganized."

"You're doing very well, Naumann," Hitler responded. "You can see it by the young people you've attracted. Good German stock, all. But I meant what I said about the games. You're the leader, and you should win. I know it isn't possible to win always, which is why I don't play any sports or games. I can't afford to lose, ever." He got into the car. Emil was still holding the door open. "You can afford to lose once in a while." He paused, then added: "But only once in a while. Don't let it become a habit."

I saluted.

"It's time for Geli to come," Emil ordered me.

I looked back across the field to the last embers of the bonfire. "I'll get her."

Geli was walking toward the car with her shoes and socks on again. We fell into step. "Karl, come visit me," she said softly, still out of Emil's hearing range. "Soon. I'm living on Thierschstrasse now, just two doors down from Uncle Alf."

I looked at her.

"He wanted me closer to him," she said. "Just come, please."

Emil inspected Geli. "A little messy, I see, after playing with those children."

"Bye, Karl. See you soon, I hope." She settled into the backseat beside her uncle.

Emil closed the car door and sighed. "That's one wonderful girl."

"Sure is."

"And you know what, Karl?"

"What?"

"We're getting married soon."

I tried not to look startled. "You've asked her?"

He drew himself up, making sure the passengers couldn't see us. "I
have, and she's agreed."

It was as if a dense fog had seeped into my head. "Congratulations."

"Don't tell anyone else yet. The boss doesn't know. We still have to
tell him. As Geli said, see you soon—at the wedding."

He slapped me lightly on the back and got into the car. I stood on
the country road, watching until the Mercedes disappeared from view,
and then turned slowly back to my young charges. The news I had
heard lingered in my head, and the rich, pungent taste of Geli lingered
in my mouth.

The letter must have been hand-delivered by someone from Berlin. It
showed up in our mailbox without a stamp, and I retreated into our
apartment; Sabine was at work. The sender's name wasn't on the envelope, but I recognized the handwriting.

Karl,

I have to confide in someone, and Gregor is still too mesmerized by
Hitler to listen to me, or at least to accept what I have to say. You
may feel the same way, but I'll take that risk. Besides, I feel I owe it
to you to be honest, since it was because of me that you went to Munich in the first place and hooked up with Hitler. You'll have to
make your own choices about what to do next, and I'm not saying
that I've decided completely myself on that score. But I feel that we
are reaching a decisive moment, and I no longer can rule out the

possibility that the current conflicts and tensions will lead to an open break. You, like Gregor and the others, will have to decide which side you're on. Maybe our disagreements can still be worked out, but my doubts are growing. This letter is to tell you why.

As you know, I wrote to Hitler protesting what is happening here, how Goebbels is trying to intimidate us and supplant our newspaper with his own. Gregor backed me up on this point, since he also feels committed to our paper and hates what Goebbels is doing. It took a long time for Hitler to respond to my letter, but when he did, he wrote: "Your paper is certainly the official party organ in Berlin, but I can't stop Goebbels from running a private sheet of his own." The audacity of that reply! Does he take us for fools who could really believe that Goebbels is just a free agent, not his agent?

I was furious and didn't respond to what I considered a provocation. And then the most extraordinary thing happened. I was sitting in my office one morning, examining the layout of the next issue, when who should show up unannounced but Hitler himself. I hadn't known he was in Berlin.

He simply walked in, didn't even bother to say good morning and sat down opposite me. All he said by way of greeting was: "This can't go on."

"What can't go on, Herr Hitler?" I asked him.

Hitler accused me of quarreling with all his people. He named Streicher and Rosenberg and asked what I had against them. I told him that Streicher's paper in Munich is nothing more than pornography, filled with rantings about how Jews deflower German women. As for Rosenberg, I told him, his so-called ideology is nothing more than paganism. It has nothing to do with Christianity and can only bring us into conflict with Rome.

Hitler defended both men. He called Streicher an important racial theorist, and he called Rosenberg's ideas about the superiority of the German soul, and why it should be unfettered by the rules of lesser beings, "an integral part of national socialism." I reminded him that the party hadn't declared war on the Catholic Church, as far as I knew, or on any of the other Christian churches, and that such a step would be suicidal. "I may not be particularly religious; for me, socialism is my most important ideal," I told him. "But I know better than to think a party that goes to war with a nation's core beliefs can succeed."

It was a point that I felt any reasonable politician would concede. But Hitler, while admitting that Christianity was included in the party program "for the moment," called Rosenberg a prophet. "His theories are the expression of the German soul," he told me. "A true German cannot condemn them."

I didn't know what to say; it all seemed so outrageous and beyond any rational discourse. But Hitler waved his arm as if to indicate that we should forget this quarrel, perhaps forget what he had just said. "It's the Goebbels business that I've come about," he said. "I tell you again, this can't go on."

My response was simple: He should tell that to Goebbels. I pointed out that Goebbels had come to Berlin after I did, and that I had founded my paper earlier than his. I was in the right here, I insisted. There was no ambiguity about the sequence of events.

"It's not a question of right but of might," Hitler said. "What will you do when Herr Goebbels's storm troopers attack you in your office?"

I was not ready for such a brazen threat, but I felt oddly calm. I pulled out the big revolver from my drawer and put it on my desk. I told Hitler that the revolver had eight bullets and that if such an attack were mounted, there'd be eight dead storm troopers.

Hitler became angry. "I know you're mad enough to shoot," he said. "But you can't kill my storm troopers."

I asked him whether they were his storm troopers or Goebbels's. If they were his, I said, he'd be better off not sending them. And if they were Goebbels's, he should make sure they weren't sent. "I will shoot anyone who attacks me," I told him. "No one can frighten me into surrender."

He used my Christian name for the first time. "Otto, be reasonable," he said, his voice trembling and his eyes suddenly misty. "Think it over—for your brother's sake."

There didn't seem anything more to say, but I told him I'd think everything over if he'd do the same. He left as abruptly as he had come.

I still can't quite get over this meeting. I think it tells you quite a lot about our leader. I told Gregor what happened just as I'm telling you, but he claimed I shouldn't get too excited. He pointed to the Reichstag elections where the party only won 2.6 percent of the vote—this in May 1928, after several years of hard work—as evidence that we needed to keep working with Hitler, since he's the only one who can draw the big crowds. I conceded this point but argued that our dismal performance in those elections showed the party was on the wrong path no matter how good a performer Hitler is. I reminded Gregor that Hitler was making deals with the capitalists, and that we had always backed the workers. And that his other ideas were increasingly dangerous, particularly his scorn for Christianity, which I saw during our confrontation.

Gregor wouldn't budge. "I will tame him," he insisted. "I won't allow myself to be unhorsed."

I warned him that he had lost control of the reins a long time ago, and that he may get entangled in and dragged by those reins if the horse runs wild. Gregor wasn't convinced; he stuck to his position. So—and not because Hitler told me to—I will stay in the party for now because of my brother. But I told Gregor he should be ready to jump free of this horse. I certainly will if I feel I can't do anything else. And I think you may have to consider doing the same. That's why I've written you this long letter. I felt I had to prepare you for what may be a critical decision ahead.

Yours in the struggle,
Otto

I relied on Otto's judgment. Maybe it was his bluntness, the trust he placed in me by confiding his thoughts even as we both ostensibly continued to work for Hitler and his party, that kept up my own trust in him. Maybe it was our old Berlin ties and his fierce dedication. And, of course, there were the ties forged by his courage in Landshut. In any case, I never thought of him as a potential traitor, which, I realize in retrospect, Hitler was already doing.

But if I wasn't about to question Otto's judgment or motives, I was oddly calm about his letter. I simply figured that Otto was saying we should all continue what we were doing until he indicated otherwise. I was perfectly willing to do so—in effect, leaving the difficult decisions, if there were to be any, to him. When Sabine ventured a question about Hitler and the party, implying but never directly saying that I should abandon them, I changed the subject. I wasn't sure what I thought.

That didn't make life easy at home. Sabine resented my evasiveness. And I felt she might reproach me for contributing so little. We survived on her pay, much as I hated to admit it. She never reproached me for that; nor did she remind me about the abortion even when she raised the possibility of having a baby and I hastily agreed. But when she failed to get pregnant, I sensed—and resented—a silent reproach.

When we made love, it was not as it was in the beginning, and I found myself imagining that I was in bed with Geli, only then feeling a moment of true excitement. The first time I felt guilty about it. Then I became immersed in my fantasy and almost wanted to shout out Geli's name.

"What are you thinking?" Sabine would ask me. "You aren't here."

She was imagining things, I said.

"I'm not blind, you know. Something is wrong, something is making you distant. What is it?"

"I'm a bit preoccupied."

She propped her chin on her fists in a gesture I had once found endearing. "But you won't tell me with what."

"All right, some of it has to do with the party."

"And the rest?"

"No, I guess all of it is about the party."

When I didn't say anything else, she allowed the silence to lengthen between us. Her voice dropping so low that I had to strain to hear, she finally said: "Karl, I once felt I knew you, everything about you. That seems like ages ago." She reached out and ran her hand over my face, then all the way down the front of my body until she cupped me in her hand. "Come back to me, Karl."

My body responded to her touch even as my mind continued along its own trajectory.

"I'm here," I assured her.

I didn't see Geli for a long time, but I heard about her frequently from party members, catching veiled references to Hitler's preoccupation with her. They were constantly out together. There were plays, operas, dinners at his favorite Italian restaurant, the Osteria Bavaria, where he ate the same spaghetti dish each time he took his seat at a corner table that was permanently reserved for him in one of the two back rooms.

At parties, I heard, Hitler would come in and introduce her with a curt but proud "My niece, Fräulein Raubal."

Emil still drove them out of the city for picnics and other outings, and I detected grumbling among some party leaders that Hitler was spending too much time and party funds squiring her around. I passed on this gossip to Otto, who assured me I was providing valuable information. I didn't feel any of his satisfaction about such news, only a growing sense that I must have been an idiot to imagine Geli could have been interested in me. She was floating in a different world.

Persuading myself that I was doing Otto's bidding, I caught up with Emil, whom I hadn't seen since he drove Hitler and Geli to my outing. I saw him dropping off the boss one evening at Thierschstrasse. I had lingered there on several occasions, hoping to catch a glimpse of Geli. Emil parked the car around the corner, away from the tram tracks. I hurried to catch up.

"Emil, it's been a while," I called. He looked up and smiled, but it was perfunctory.

He shook my hand. "Too busy to see old friends?" he asked with only a trace of the old mockery.

"It's you who's always busy."

"The boss keeps me busy, what can I say?"

"And Geli?"

"Not as busy on that front as I'd like to be."

"At least until the wedding, I guess."

"The wedding is postponed."

"Why?"

"Hitler told Geli that he had no objections to the marriage, but that she's very young and she should give it some time."

"How much time? She's what, twenty now?"

Emil nodded glumly. "Almost twenty-one. He said two years."

"Two years?"

"Yes, two years."

"And you and Geli, you'll wait that long?"

"Geli says I should be patient. She won't disobey her uncle."

I proposed going for a beer—more for lack of anything better to say than out of a real desire to prolong the conversation.

"Thanks, but I have some errands to run," Emil said.

Relieved, I turned and crossed Thierschstrasse, not sure what to do next. I had my head down, trying to sort out this news, when I stopped short just before colliding with someone. It was Geli, standing defiantly in front of me on the sidewalk, her arms crossed and her upper lip curled up in a familiar grin.

"What does it take for you to notice a girl?" she demanded. "You would have walked right by me without seeing anything. Why can't I ever get your attention?"

"Geli, you're not serious."

"I'm deadly serious." She raised her hand to her face as if wiping away a tear, then slyly looked at me to measure the effect. I laughed, and so did she. "So why haven't you visited me? I've missed you, I really have."

"I've heard you're always busy."

"Not too busy to see you."

She cast a quick glance over my shoulder. I turned and realized she was checking the window of Hitler's apartment, which I recognized by the statue of the Virgin mounted into a recess alongside. No one was at the window.

Geli leaned forward, close enough for me to feel the warmth of her breath, offering a hint of the taste that I remembered so well. "I'm going inside; it's number forty-three, the third floor on the right. Follow me in a minute or two."

Before I could respond, she was off, crossing the tram tracks to the other side of the street.

I walked back to the corner I had just come from and strode briskly toward the same door, not looking to my right or left as I pushed it open.

It was late afternoon, and the hallway was nearly dark. I found the stairs and tried to force myself to climb them slowly, but when I heard a door slam behind me as I passed the first-floor landing, I took the remaining steps two at a time and knocked quickly on her door.

Geli opened it immediately, grabbed my hand and led me through a small common room to her room. The other rooms leading from the living room were closed, but I sensed that the other tenants were around and she wanted to be sure we didn't run into them.

As soon as she had closed her door behind us, she laughed and put her arms around me as she had when we were behind the tree, burying her head in my chest. A small candle provided the only light. "You're panting, Karl. Too much excitement for you?"

"We'll see," I managed.

She looked up and slowly raised her lips to mine. I tried to respond as gently, but in a moment I had my arms firmly against her back and, then reaching down lower, pressed her against me.

"Wait," she said, but it was only to step back and pull me toward her narrow cot. Our bodies joined and detonated even before we had managed to struggle free of our clothes, before I had managed to unbutton more than the lower part of her blouse and reach up under it. After the first time, we stripped off everything and I held her tight, stroking and exploring all the places I had dreamed of. We started over, less frantically than before.

"God, I wanted to do this," I murmured. "I want you, love you."

She ran her hands through my hair and pulled my head down between her breasts. "Be quiet, Karl, don't spoil anything. Quiet."

I was content to lie like that forever. Or at least until our bodies began their rhythmic movement again, this time ever so languidly until I felt a slow, aching release. We didn't speak a word or move apart.

The next thing I remember was Geli shaking me awake. "Karl, you've got to get up. It's two o'clock. You really do have to go." She put her forefinger on my lips. "And don't make any noise."

"When can I come back?"

She kissed me once more, this time stroking me where I felt blissfully sore. As she felt me responding, she squeezed me almost harshly, then pushed me away. "Is tomorrow soon enough?" she asked.

Chapter Thirteen

And so began the strangest and happiest interlude of my life. I didn't recognize it as an interlude then. I thought it was the beginning of something that would last forever, more powerful than all the obstacles and logic arrayed against it. Doesn't everyone experience something like that at least once in their lifetime? If not, I can only pity them.

Geli set the rules, and I was happy to follow them. If she had said that I should walk over hot coals before returning to her several times a week, I wouldn't have hesitated. But all she demanded was that we meet in complete secrecy, that I keep to the rest of my private and public routine as if nothing had changed and that I shouldn't ask too many questions. Or talk about the future.

Sometimes we met at her place when she gave the signal—a repositioning of the potted plant on her windowsill. These encounters were in the very late evenings, her room was almost always only lit by a single candle, and she insisted that I never linger afterward. More often than not, we met for an hour or so during the day in the room of one of her friends who was conveniently out when Geli gave the other signal, a red ribbon tied around the right curtain, indicating we could meet that afternoon. I could count on getting either signal or none by noon, which made it easy for me to check while Sabine was at work.

I stumbled through my life with Sabine then. It probably helped that I had been distracted and unresponsive before, so Sabine saw it as a continuation of my earlier behavior. But, at Geli's insistence, I tried to maintain the pretense that nothing had changed. I did make love to

Sabine on some of the nights when I hadn't been able to be with Geli. Sometimes I did so with an intensity that astonished and pleased her, at least briefly, but she must have sensed that in those moments I was in another world. Still, she clung to me afterward, sometimes with tears in her eyes. We talked less and less. She didn't press me to tell her the truth. If she had, I'm not sure I could have kept my promise to Geli.

Now I recognize the odd parallel between Sabine's willingness not to ask questions and my own to put most questions aside when I was with Geli. I drank her in, I savored her, I couldn't get enough of her, and if the price was skirting so many obvious topics, I was willing to pay it. That is, so long as I could keep seeing Geli, so long as I was convinced she was as hungry for me as I was for her.

And I was completely convinced of that even when our meetings became less frequent, when I had to pass her building repeatedly before I saw the signal I was waiting for. After a few days of absence, we devoured each other; there was no holding back. Whatever doubts I had felt dissipated. She was mine then, all mine. That was all that mattered.

I would wait, I told myself, however long she wanted me to before we would and could align our lives with that central reality.

Of course I should have realized that I was living only a dream. And reality was already beginning to cast a lengthening shadow.

I casually mentioned to Geli that I'd seen the young girl Maria whom I had once spotted leaving Hitler's apartment. It was in a bakery near the center of town. She was buying rolls and a couple of pastries, and at first I hadn't recognized her. She no longer looked as young as I remembered, although it was obvious she was only a teenager. But her eyes had a frightened look, and she moved in an odd way, slowly for someone her age. The left side of her face looked slightly swollen, as if she had just come from the dentist.

Geli turned pale and wanted to know everything. Was Maria still visiting Hitler? Had I seen her going in or out of his apartment? What was she wearing? I hadn't paid particular attention to what she had on, so I couldn't answer even the last question. "You must know more than you're saying," Geli insisted.

"You know that the only girl I really notice is you."

It was as if Geli hadn't heard my lame attempt to lighten the mood. She turned her back to me. When she finally spoke, it was so softly that I wasn't sure I heard her right. "I'm frightened."

I asked her of what, but she didn't respond.

Another time she started on her own. She had pulled me to the bed as soon as I came in, which was nothing unusual, but there was a rough edge to her lovemaking, a fury, that astonished me. It also kept me aroused longer than ever, turning the situation around. I was now in control in a way I never remembered before, feeling a boundless power to drive out whatever it was that tormented her. She came again and again until I finally let go, with both of us collapsing. She kissed my neck and held me, then caught me off guard. "I saw her myself this time."

"Who?"

"I saw her, and I knew right away what she had been doing."

"Who?"

"Maria, who else? Are you saying there are others?"

"I'm not saying anything—I'm just trying to understand what you're saying."

"Ignore me, Karl, please. I didn't mean anything. It's not important."

"You know I can't ignore you. What is it that's bothering you about this girl?"

"It's not her, it's him."

"What about him?"

"I don't know what he wants from us—Maria, me, anyone else I don't know about. He can be so charming, and then he gives you this look that . . ."

"That what?"

"Scares me, scares me so much."

She wouldn't say anything more, and I tried to reassure her that she was imagining things. Yes, I tried to reassure her about her uncle. When I look back at that period, that's what makes me feel most ashamed. Instinctively sensing but not admitting that something was changing already, I just wanted everything to continue the way it was: with my rushing to her whenever she repositioned the flowerpot or tied a red ribbon around the right curtain. With my mind already envisaging her by the light of a single candle, incandescent, irresistible.

Now that I wasn't living in the barracks and had other duties, I wasn't fighting street battles, but I still heard about them. They took place from time to time, less organized, more random. I had seen the broken windows of storefronts afterward and heard the boasting of brownshirts that they had taught someone a lesson, usually a communist someone. The communists were still the enemy, and they still fought back, sometimes furiously.

When I was summoned to my unit one afternoon, I found several of the men badly bruised and battered. Some were bandaged, and a couple had their arms in slings. The mood was sullen.

"Private, we need you today," an officer with a black eye announced to me with no preliminaries. "We're calling anyone we can. Quite a few of the regulars are out of action for a while."

I saluted but didn't feel the enthusiasm I tried to show. It had been a long time since I had drawn this kind of duty.

The brownshirts weren't supposed to be operating in the open, but small groups felt free to attack targets of opportunity. From what I could gather through brief snippets of conversation before our unit prepared for action, the target this time was a printing shop where they had fought and lost a battle a few days earlier.

"What kind of a printing shop?" I whispered to Erich, one of the few from our original Berlin group who was still on assignment. The only difference was that now he was a sergeant. And his face appeared frozen in a permanent scowl. I no longer felt any connection with the young man who had arrived with me in Munich ages ago.

"What do you think?" he snarled. "A commie printing shop. Commie Jews who outnumbered us last time and caught us by surprise. We thought there'd only be a few of them. It's a small place, but they were ready for us, the bastards."

We moved out, not in formation but infiltrating the target zone in groups of two or three.

As darkness fell, we had the place surrounded, although whoever was in the printing shop probably hadn't detected anything unusual yet. Erich, who was calling the shots on the ground, had ordered everyone deployed out of sight until he gave the signal. I found myself in a back alley wishing I were anyplace else. My churning stomach reminded me of the fear that accompanied me during my first battles, and I felt I was spinning backward in time. Except it wasn't exactly like before. Then I hadn't any doubts about the need for what I was doing. Now I wasn't sure. Otto's admonition that I had to keep the party's trust now felt like a burden I wasn't sure I wanted to shoulder anymore.

I heard Erich's whistle, and then there was no more time for thinking. In a way, I guess I was relieved. We must have been an intimidating sight, rushing the shop, breaking down the door, shattering the windows and flailing away with our truncheons. I felt my head clearing and my body kicking into gear as I swung away at the handful of defenders until they became a blur of blood, mangled limbs and screaming faces. It was them or us at that point, and I was as determined as any of my comrades to emerge victorious. They didn't run until we had mauled them completely. Once they escaped out the back door, we really got down to work, smashing the presses and every piece of equipment in sight. I bashed as energetically as the rest of them.

But when I paused to catch my breath, I felt drained. I was empty. The adrenaline rush that usually kept me pumped up for hours after such a battle wasn't there.

As the others finished the destruction, I drifted to the back of the shop, near the door where the communists had fled. My eyes focused on the pamphlets and posters strewn across the floor. There were hammers and sickles, caricatures of capitalists smoking big cigars as workers in chains served them. There was a swastika emblazoned with a skull, and I felt the old anger against the reds return. Then I noticed the words splashed across some of the covers—"Power to the Proletariat," "Nationalization," "Where Workers Rule." My mind flashed back to the pamphlets I had seen on Otto's worktable.

There was a sudden commotion, and the door behind me burst open. Several brownshirts intercepted the young woman, and her arms flailed briefly as she took several blows from her welcoming committee.

I pushed my way forward and saw her lying on the ground, blood trickling from her mouth. Her blouse was torn, and one of the men ripped it further, exposing a shoulder and breast. Someone laughed. "Who the hell are you?" Erich demanded.

She was shaking, but her eyes blazed defiantly. "My husband, the printer," she whispered, then caught her breath and continued. "Don't hurt him."

Momentary silence. Then a shout. "He's here, all right." A brownshirt next to me pulled a small man wearing a grease-stained apron from under a table that had remained standing.

The woman strained to get up. "Don't hurt him, please," she repeated. Erich pushed her back down.

Her husband lurched forward, but I seized him by the shoulders. Just then the brownshirt who had found him punched him hard in the face. His blood splattered onto my shirt and face as I released him and he dropped to the floor.

But he wasn't ready to be silenced. "Let us go," he said, managing to pull himself onto all fours. "I'm just a printer, and she hasn't done anything."

Erich stepped toward him and kicked him hard in the stomach. "Just a printer, right?"

"Erich, let him go, let both of them go," I heard myself saying. "We've taught him a lesson—a lesson he won't forget. Let's get out of here."

He rounded on me. "Have you gone crazy now that you can't be bothered with doing the real work around here? Just a printer, just a Jewish commie printer." He wheeled and pointed at the woman. "And she's a Jewish commie printer's whore." He spat in her direction. "You want us to let them go. Sure, we'll send them home, back to their warm bed. Let's give them a proper send-off, men."

The printer and his wife were lifted to their feet, the rest of the woman's blouse and most of her skirt torn off in the process, and they were both shoved out the door.

"Satisfied?" Erich asked.

I turned away.

Somehow I didn't get into serious trouble, although it wasn't for a lack of trying on Erich's part. The captain who had dispatched us heard both of us out and decided I was guilty of irresponsibly questioning the NCO, but then I had backed off. Erich was still furious, but the story among the men was that I didn't have what it took anymore, so it was probably just as well that I wasn't on regular duty.

I wasn't sure what to think. Maybe the men were right after all. I had fought the communists in numerous battles before, and these were still the same bastards. I knew they were working against us Germans, for the Russians, for the Jews. Why had I wanted Erich and the others to stop? Why had this victory felt so empty? Perhaps it had something to do with the fact that in Berlin the Erichs of the movement were attacking Otto's printing operations, that they were acting as if he, we, were the real enemies.

But when I described everything in a letter to Otto, he seemed less troubled than I was. He said that I should stay the course so long as we remained part of the same movement. But it didn't take much reading between the lines to understand he was thinking this might not be the case for long.

I couldn't talk to Sabine about any of this. But when, after a much longer interval than usual, I saw Geli's signal, I realized I wanted more from her this time than lovemaking, although I desperately wanted that. I wanted to know what she thought about the world around her, around us.

We met at her Thierschstrasse apartment. Once again it was up the stairs two steps at a time, Geli opening up the door as soon as I lightly knocked and quickly leading me to her room, the solitary candle lit as always.

"Geli, I—"

"Later," she whispered. Whatever resolve I had to ask the questions that I had suppressed for so long dissipated as her eyes focused on mine. She teasingly ran her tongue over my lips, and we collapsed onto the bed.

Afterward, as she lay in my arms, Geli murmured, "Karl, I'll be moving soon."

"Where?"

"Not all that far. Prinzregentenplatz."

"You've got to be kidding. Only rich people live there."

"Maybe so, but Uncle Alf is getting a big apartment, and he's asked me to move in with him."

"You can't be serious."

Now she was up on one elbow, leaning over me. "I'm just moving in with my uncle."

"My God, what are you doing?"

She kissed me lightly on the lips. "Don't be angry with me, Karl, please."

"I'm not," I said, and at that moment I realized I couldn't be, not with her so close, not when I was still breathing her in. "But I just don't understand anything."

"What is it that you want me to explain?"

"About you, your uncle, Emil." I hesitated. "About me."

"I'm not sure I can. I loved Emil, at least I thought I did, and maybe I still do, but he agreed so easily to Uncle Alf's terms. To wait for two years, for God's sake."

"I wouldn't," I blurted out, immediately feeling disloyal to my friend, all the more so because I obviously hadn't during all the previous times I was with Geli, when we had both avoided mentioning him.

"You're different, Karl," she said. "I don't just like you, I'm crazy about you. But you have someone else, and who knows what will happen in my life. We're friends, very special friends—whatever happens. None of this means I can't love you forever."

"Like you love a friend? That's all?"

"I don't know what to call it. Friendship, forbidden love—does it make a difference?"

"To me it does."

"We can argue about it, but to me it isn't a mistake."

"It isn't for me, either." I reached out my arm and pulled her toward me. When she dipped her chin, I kissed her forehead. But I wasn't ready to let it go at that. "What about your uncle? I don't know what to think of him anymore."

She didn't respond at first, and I was about to talk about the attack on the printing shop, the woman there, my confused feelings. But she spoke up first. "He's both nice to me and jealous. Sometimes I feel wonderful with him, sometimes horrible—especially when he tells me what I can or can't do, like with Emil."

"So why are you moving into the same apartment with him, where he can control you more? Why don't you tell him you can't do it?"

"Say no to him? Leave him? Karl, you have no idea what he'd do." She was silent for a moment. "Or what he does."

"What?"

She stopped me before I could ask anything more, nudged me gently but firmly out of the bed. "It's getting late," she said. Reluctantly, I picked up my clothes, scattered around the floor, and dressed. She watched me from under the covers.

As I buttoned my shirt, I asked the question I had asked the first time and wasn't supposed to ask again. "When can I come back?"

"I'll let you know."

"Then it's not tomorrow?"

She stood up, not bothering to reach for anything to cover herself.

She put her arms around me, and I greedily ran my hands over her one more time. "We'll find a way to see each other soon," she murmured.

"Promise?"

She nodded, standing on her toes to kiss me again but at the same time pushing my hands away. "Don't make this more difficult than it is—it's so hard to let you go."

Chapter Fourteen

She avoided me. At first I thought that she wasn't able to spring loose to see me and was only waiting for the right occasion, arranging for another seemingly casual encounter. I made sure I passed by Thierschstrasse often, but the potted plant remained firmly rooted, and no red ribbon appeared. I had to be careful not to be seen by her uncle or, more likely—since Hitler was usually absorbed in his own thoughts when he went in and out of his building—Emil.

I also lingered near her favorite cafés and did spot her on a couple of occasions—with Hitler. I hovered far in the background. Most of the time she looked as animated as ever, and every time I saw her laugh and her eyes sparkle, I felt longing. But sometimes I'd catch her in a moment when Hitler's attention was turned elsewhere, and she'd have an unfocused, self-absorbed look that I couldn't decipher. Her eyes never seemed to see me, even when I tried to position myself carefully in her line of vision. It was as if I were invisible. I finally realized she didn't want to see me, which made me even more jealous. I couldn't understand.

I decided to confront her. Late one evening I retraced the steps into her building and up to her door. I stopped on the dark landing and listened for sounds. I thought I heard something from inside but wasn't sure. I knocked softly. Nothing. I knocked again, this time a bit louder. Nothing again, except the creak of the door on the opposite side of the landing. I bolted down the stairs.

The next day I saw her going into a café with Hitler. I tried to catch her eye, with no luck as usual. Feeling foolish and sorry for myself, I started walking away.

"Karl, stop."

I turned around and there she was, standing on the sidewalk just outside the café, without her coat despite the cool weather. Her face was flushed, and her eyes bore into mine with not a hint of their usual flirtatiousness. "What do you think you're doing?"

"I'm not doing anything. I just want to see you."

"So knocking on my door at night—"

"You said you'd let me know when we could see each other again."

"I have to get back inside before he starts wondering what I'm doing. But I want you to stop this. Don't follow me, don't knock on my door at night."

I could find no trace of sympathy in her determined expression. "Whatever you say," I muttered.

She took my hand, and her face softened. "There are some things you don't understand, Karl."

"I understand that I want to see you again."

She dropped my hand. "If you keep acting like this, we won't see each other at all anymore."

She reached for the café's door, then hesitated. "Oh, Karl, I'd like to see you, too—and we will see each other. But nothing is ever as simple as it seems." And then she was gone.

It was simple enough to see that she was ensnared again in Hitler's world, where she could play the princess, I thought bitterly. Where she could ignore me, act as if I didn't exist, do whatever she did with her uncle, whatever it was that she didn't want to talk about. Where she could be the escort of the man everybody in Munich, and increasingly all over Germany, was talking about.

For, I had to admit, Hitler was reenergizing the party, which for so long had appeared to lapse into a low level of activity and support. It wasn't an accident, I realized later, that this was happening precisely when the German economy, which had looked almost stable for several years, was once again falling apart. Farmers had been protesting against deteriorating conditions for quite some time, but in 1929 everything began to unravel. There were the world crisis and the Wall Street crash, and in Germany we suddenly had more than four million unemployed, factories closing and wages dropping.

I couldn't stop thinking about Geli, but I found myself busier than I had been in years. Hitler was determined to take advantage of the new situation, and the party mounted strong campaigns everywhere it could. Otto was redoubling his efforts in the north, saying this wasn't the time to dwell on whatever internal differences we had with Hitler. Our job, he insisted, was winning converts, and foot soldiers like me could get the message out. I received instructions to take my Hitler Youth Movement members on trips to the areas where local elections were scheduled that fall: the state of Baden, the city of Lübeck and Thuringia.

These trips were a far cry from my outings with the SA, from the displays of muscle and violent clashes. My charges and I were assigned much easier tasks. We'd paint swastikas all over the towns and villages we visited, and we'd hand out our party pamphlets. The leftists still taunted us, and occasionally we'd scuffle with their supporters, but usually we went about our jobs unimpeded. True, we painted a lot of the swastikas at night, when no one was looking, but we found more and more people willingly taking our propaganda.

It helped that my kids had that clean-cut healthy look, and it helped that so many people felt so desperate. They had thought their lives were getting better, and now they were threatened once more with losing everything, which only made them angrier. The war had ended over a decade earlier, but here they were confronting impoverishment again. As we handed out the pamphlets, people would say: "Anything to get rid of the bastards who are doing this to us," and "I'll vote for anyone who can get us out of this mess."

Our results were still modest, but they showed that the party was winning supporters. In the Baden state elections, we won 7 percent of the vote; in Lübeck's city elections, it was over 8 percent; and in Thuringia, it was an impressive 11.3 percent, the first occasion we broke into double digits. We didn't do as well in the Berlin city elections. The party won 5.8 percent, but that still represented a big gain over the year before. I jokingly told my kids that maybe the party would have done better in my home city if we had gone there as well. We hadn't been given that assignment. Somewhat to my surprise, I felt a genuine pride, which they shared, that we had contributed to some of the results.

In Munich I heard encouraging bits of news. By the end of the year, the number of party members had risen to a hundred twenty thousand or more. I felt my old enthusiasm returning, my doubts receding. Maybe, I thought, this movement could really transform Germany. As ambivalent as my feelings were about Hitler, particularly when I thought about him with Geli, or about his followers like Erich, I found myself again impressed by his ability to move the crowds he attracted, by the sense he conveyed that he knew how to set things right.

And there was something intriguing in all his talk about restoring the glory of the German nation, especially when I knew from people within the party that he still hadn't succeeded in becoming a German himself. Legally, he remained an Austrian, unable to get the citizenship papers he craved despite his heroic service in the kaiser's army.

At home, Sabine was far from pleased by my renewed enthusiasm for my party work. She was upset when I traveled, and upset when, back in Munich one evening, I showed her some of the leaflets we had been distributing. "You can't believe that your Hitler will suddenly find a miracle solution for all our problems," she asked as she fried eggs for our dinner.

"Maybe not, but he can't do worse than the current crowd. At least he'll restore German pride."

"Pride—or hate?"

"We really shouldn't talk about this, you know."

Sabine brought our plates to the table, sat down wearily and didn't say anything. Finally she asked, "Karl, is there something else we should talk about?"

"Like what?"

"It's not just that we disagree about politics; there's something more—something that must explain why you avoid me, why things aren't working between us."

"I'm not avoiding you, I'm just busy."

She listlessly mopped up her egg yolk with a piece of bread. "We both know it's more than that."

I reached across the table, running my fingers over her face and across her lips. "Honestly, there's nothing more."

She pushed my hand away. "I don't believe you, Karl. You're hiding something from me. Who is it?"

"What? Who? Are you crazy?"

Sabine stood up, knocking her chair over. I rose to pick it up, but she stood in my way. "Look, until you want to be honest about it, until you show you care something about us, you'd better sleep in Grandma's bed."

"Sabine, believe me, there's no one." My indignation felt genuine, since at that moment there technically wasn't.

I saw a flicker of hesitation in her eyes, but then it vanished. "I wish I could believe you. But I don't."

For the first time we slept in separate beds. Even on the nights when I returned from Geli, I had slipped in under the same blanket, wrapping Sabine in my arms, pretending that all was well between us. It wasn't just a matter of pretending, I abruptly realized; I didn't want to lose her or Geli. I wanted them both.

As I dozed off, the thought occurred to me that maybe I was like Geli, who wanted it all—whatever it was that she had with her uncle, Emil and me. Should I be angry with her for refusing to make a choice?

Otto's arrival in Munich signaled that the brief suspension of hostilities within the party was already over.

I'd heard that Hitler had summoned Otto for a personal meeting, so I wasn't surprised to hear from him. We met in one of the grimier beer halls, nothing like the cafés that Hitler frequented. Otto was as animated as ever, bringing news from Berlin that Goebbels was now propaganda chief, having replaced Gregor, whose new job put him in charge of organizational affairs within the party.

The struggle for power was reaching its decisive moment, Otto told me. The deteriorating economic situation meant that the workers couldn't endure their conditions much longer, and big strikes were inevitable. "This will be the real test of Hitler and the party. If the party is going to live up to the socialist part of its name, it has to back the workers," he said. But he hadn't been able to get Hitler's assurance that it would do so. "You know why Hitler called me here?" he asked, grabbing my forearm and gripping it tightly.

I shook my head.

"He wanted me to sell him the *Kampfverlag*. He wasn't interested in talking about the workers or the strikes, only about getting hold of our publishing operation in Berlin. You know what that means? He wants everyone and everything to be under his control. He's furious that our *Arbeitsblatt* criticizes some of the party leaders in the south. He won't accept criticism of any kind. He told me directly: 'What I'm doing can't be wrong because it is the will of history.' Can you believe that?" Otto didn't pause for an answer. "Well, I'll only stay in the party as long as I have a weapon, our press, to fight for what I believe in."

Otto sat back and drank his beer, looking at me. "And what about you, Karl? Will you fight for what you believe in, for the workers?"

"Of course I will," I said, trying to summon more conviction than I felt. I no longer was sure what I thought, although I still liked and admired Otto.

"Good," he said. "I'll need every supporter I can get. It won't be easy." And he added softly, almost to himself: "I wish Gregor wasn't so blinded that I could count on him also. But I can't, not at all. We'll be on our own, completely on our own."

.   .   .

I heard the knocking dimly through my sleep. Sabine must have left for work much earlier, but I had remained in bed—still in Grandma's bed. When the knocking continued, I pulled myself up. "All right, I'm coming."

I opened the door a crack and saw Emil. He pushed it open the rest of the way. "The bourgeois life, as usual, I see," he said, examining my bedraggled appearance and flashing his familiar grin. "The wife's out working while the man sleeps."

"Not anymore, thanks to you," I shot back, but I couldn't help smiling. "What's going on?"

"Orders from the boss, what else. He told me to bring you to his apartment when I come to pick him up. Apparently he's got an assignment for you."

"What kind of assignment?" I asked, reaching for my clothes and splashing my face with cold water.

"He didn't say."

I was ready within a few minutes and found myself sitting in the backseat of the black Mercedes for the first and only time. I wasn't sure what to say to Emil, since I had no idea whether he suspected anything between Geli and me. Or whether he still was engaged to her. I inquired about our destination because I knew Hitler had moved out of his small room on Thierschstrasse. "Is the new place as big as they say?"

"Bigger. It's nine huge rooms, at least I think so. It's so big it's hard to keep track."

"And he lives there alone?" I couldn't resist asking.

"No," he replied evenly, his eyes facing straight ahead as we swung left on Prinzregentenstrasse, a busy street that ran along the southern edge of the English Gardens. We crossed the Isar and swept by the gilded Angel of Peace on the other side. It was only as we glided between Prinzregentenplatz's elegant buildings that he added, "Geli lives there, and he has people who cook and clean."

I couldn't tell from his studiously neutral expression what that meant for their relationship. Emil parked the car in front of a cream-colored five-story building, Prinzregentenplatz 16. It wasn't as fancy as some of the neighboring buildings with more dramatic curves and arches, but it was imposing enough. Emil pointed to the front windows situated in the middle of the building, above two lions' heads carved into the facade. "That's it, on the second floor. Go on in."

"You're not coming?"

"My job is to wait here. The boss will be leaving right away. I have to be ready for him, today especially—we have things to talk about."

I climbed the broad stairs, which conveyed a sense of the luxury of the building. Unlike most buildings I knew, there were no dark corners, no steep, narrow climbs through the dark.

A woman wearing an apron opened the front door of Hitler's apartment. "He's through there," she said, pointing down the corridor that ran between rooms on both sides. "The second room on the left."

I smelled fresh pastries from the kitchen on the opposite side of the corridor as I stepped into the designated room. I looked around and didn't see anyone, only the tall windows that looked across Prinzregentenplatz to the buildings on the other side.

"In here." The command came from my left, and I saw another room that hadn't been visible from the hallway. I stepped inside. Hitler was standing behind his desk, his back to a set of bay windows that offered an even more impressive view.

"*Heil* Hitler!"

"I don't have much time: I have to leave in a moment," Hitler replied, his eyes briefly taking me in and focusing back on his desk. It was only then that I noticed the gun. He caught my glance following his. "You know what kind of pistol this is?"

"A Walther 6.35 caliber."

"Very good. I know you're a responsible lad, well trained and good with young people. I have a job for you. My niece lives in a politician's house, which means she needs to know how to protect herself." He picked up the gun and handed it to me. "Politics can be dangerous, as you know. I want you to take her to the shooting range today and teach her how to use this."

I kept my eyes on the gun in my hand, hoping I hadn't colored when he mentioned Geli. "Yes, sir."

He gave me a curt nod, gathered up his briefcase and left. A moment later, I heard low voices in the corridor and the front door close. I remained standing in the study, uncertain what to do next.

Geli appeared in the doorway, dressed in a brown skirt and a white blouse that she hadn't tucked in. Her hair was still tousled from bed, and she was barefoot. I felt an almost irresistible desire to grab her, to pull her to me, to let my hands disappear under her loose clothing, but I only stood there. "I see I have a new teacher today," she said, casting a bemused look in my direction. "Leave it to Uncle Alf to come up with surprises."

I recovered enough to offer a slight bow. "At your service, Fräulein."

She put her hands on her head, trying to cover her unruly hair. "God, I must look like a witch. Go get some coffee or whatever you want in the kitchen. I'll be ready in a couple of minutes."

It's funny about that day. I remember only fragments and emotions, elation one moment, despair the next. I recall a long tram ride, but only because at a certain point so many passengers had crowded on that we were pressed together, not for long, but long enough to make me feel that everything was possible again, until she stepped back without saying or doing anything to acknowledge what had happened. When I saw her distracted look, I realized that the moment had meant nothing to her. It wasn't that she seemed angry, as she had been in front of the café. Her mind was elsewhere.

At the range, showing her how to aim the gun, I let my hands grasp hers to steady the weapon. Just for a moment she looked straight at me. "Sorry, this must be so boring for you," she said, resorting to the teasing tone that I so desperately missed. I didn't let go of her hands when I should have. She casually shook them off and fired. "Another miss—see what you made me do?" she scolded me.

But in the next instant, she was as distracted as before, talking about "Uncle Alf" and "that monkey girl." When I asked what girl, she launched into a disjointed account of how the photographer Hoffmann and a girl called Eva had appeared at a café where she and Hitler were the night before. "He tried to make it look like they just happened to stop by while we were there, but I know that they'd planned it all out. Can you imagine: She wore this coat with fur hanging from the sleeves and collar—it looked ridiculous. I told Uncle Alf it looked like a monkey coat, and he was furious with me. What can he see in a girl like that?"

I wanted to ask why she was so upset, what difference it made to her, but I didn't. I taught her to shoot as best I could, and I listened. I no longer remember most of what she said, but there were snipes at other girls who took an interest in Hitler. And I recall when I finally asked her about Emil.

"Oh, Emil. You know the marriage is off—it's been off for a long time."

I went through the rest of the day in a happy haze, convinced that whatever happened, I was in a better position than I'd thought. True, she hadn't indicated that she was interested in me the way she was before. But when I hesitantly asked her whether I could see her again, she allowed that if I knew Hitler was out, I could drop by at some point, even if she didn't make it sound like much of an invitation. At least she wasn't rejecting me. And Emil was out of the picture.

But when I returned to Prinzregentenplatz with Geli in the afternoon, he was leaning over the front seat of the Mercedes looking for something.

"What have you lost?" I asked.

"Nothing that can't be replaced."

Geli kept walking, not saying a word. She asked me for the gun. "I'll take it up." She paused. "Thanks for the lesson."

When she had shut the front door behind her, I turned to Emil, who was now standing beside the car. "Give me a lift back?"

He shook his head. "I'm not driving anymore."

"So where do you keep the car at night—right here in front?"

"That's not my problem. I'm done."

I looked at him uncomprehendingly.

"I'm done with both of them," he said stonily. "With Geli, with her darling uncle. If you want my advice, you should do the same."

"You're leaving Hitler? Just like that?"

"Yes."

"Why?"

Emil started walking away from the car and the building, and I followed. He didn't reply at first, but then he said: "I guess I can tell you about it now."

"About what?"

He was staring straight ahead, his jaw set and his eyes cold as he kept walking. "I have pictures."

"What kind of pictures?"

"The kind that made it possible for Hitler and me to reach, let's say, an amicable parting of the ways. The kind that didn't allow him to cheat me out of my back pay. The kind that guarantee he'll never touch me, never dare to harm me. The kind that make me sick to think I worked for him for so long and that I actually planned on marrying Geli. I've had it with both of them; they can play their games alone now, or with anybody else Geli wants to trap. She's already got her eyes on some medical student."

I was waiting for him to explain more, and he knew it. We stopped at a corner. "I'm going left here, and you're going straight, so I guess it's good-bye for now."

"Come on, Emil. What kind of pictures?"

"You don't want to know."

"Yes, I do."

"All right, they're sketches," he said. "His sketches."

"Sketches of?"

"Geli. At least *I* know they're of her."

I waited again, not daring to ask.

He held out his hand, and I shook it. "Figure out the rest yourself," he said curtly.

He started down the street, but then he looked back at me and stopped. "Oh, all right. If you have to have this spelled out, they're pictures of Geli, from the bottom up as it were." He tried to summon a smile, but his face twisted into a grimace. "We'll grab a beer sometime."

"From the bottom up?"

"Yes, Karl, how much do I have to explain? If you want to see a woman—I mean, really *see* a woman, you'd lie down on the floor and look straight up between her legs. Not many of us would think of doing something like that, and I can't think of anyone who would see this as an artistic opportunity. Except for . . ."

He shook his head and walked off.

It was one of those strange dreams when I knew I was dreaming but everything was so vivid that, even as I was struggling awake, I couldn't shake the feeling that it was really happening.

I had been walking along the shore of a lake when Geli surfaced from under the water not far ahead of me. Her wet body shimmered in the fading sunlight as she emerged fully naked, and although she wasn't looking at me yet, I knew that the excited anticipation in her eyes was only for me. I rushed forward excitedly to greet her, knowing that we would soon be making love on the grass. But in that instant, I saw a figure on the grass already—a familiar face dominated by a short cropped mustache. Holding a whip and dressed in a suit and tie, he was lying back, propped on his elbows, a terrifying smile on his face as his eyes locked on Geli, who saw only him. She was oblivious to my presence. Hitler motioned her forward with his whip, and she began to step over him, planting her legs on either side as he leaned back further. From her moist triangle, a few drops of water dripped onto his forehead, nose and mouth, which was contorted in an euphoric grin. I tried to yell at her to run away, but I couldn't get the sound out. I woke up in a cold sweat, my blanket scrunched up at my feet.

I stood at the washbasin, looking into Sabine's small mirror at the sorry reflection. What was going on? I sat back down on the bed, trying to banish the dream and succeeding only in conjuring it. It was then that something caught my attention at the door, and I noticed the envelope lying there. It must have been delivered by hand, since there was no stamp. I tore open the envelope and unfolded the single sheet of paper: "I'm sorry about yesterday." It was signed "Geli."

Snapped out of my lethargy, I dressed and rushed back to Prinzregentenplatz. I approached cautiously, checking first if there was any sign of the black Mercedes. As I drew nearer, I saw the woman who had greeted me the day before open the door and, basket in hand, step outside. I pulled back so she wouldn't see me. Once she was gone, I entered the building and ran up the stairs. I caught my breath and knocked, preparing an explanation for whoever opened the door about finishing up the shooting lesson with a few final instructions.

The door swung open almost immediately, and I was facing Geli.

"I wanted to see you," I said.

She looked at me quizzically and motioned for me to be quiet, pulling me by the hand to her room. It was brighter than Hitler's study next door, and her belongings were strewn about. On a small desk, I could see a letter she must have been writing as I knocked.

She closed the door and looked me up and down. I wanted to step forward and pull her to me, but I didn't even try. Something in her expression stopped me cold.

"Aren't you glad to see me?" I asked and immediately felt foolish. I must have flinched, because she abruptly laughed.

"You don't have to be scared of me." She leaned forward and kissed me on the mouth, a short kiss, making me eager for more. But when I reached out, she deftly eluded my grasp.

"No," she insisted with a coquettish grin. "Well?"

"I got your note."

"Yes?"

"I thought you might want to see me."

She sat down on the edge of her bed. "Last night after you left, I wanted to talk to you. I guess that's why I sent you the note. But now . . ."

"But now what?"

She shook her head and didn't respond.

I looked around and spotted a familiar watercolor landscape. "Wasn't that in your uncle's room on Thierschstrasse?"

Her voice dropped to a low whisper, and she dropped her head. "Yes, it's something he painted."

I stepped forward and knelt in front of her, cupping her face in my hands and drawing it up so she couldn't avert her eyes. "What is it, Geli?"

"Nothing."

"I don't believe you."

Her eyes filled with tears. I sat down beside her and put my arm around her, meeting no resistance as I eased her head onto my shoulder. "Help me, Karl, help me."

"I will," I promised. "Just tell me how. What's the matter?"

She looked up and smiled, wiping away the tears. "Oh, Karl, you're such a sweetheart. I know I can count on you, but there's nothing to worry about. I just felt a little down for some reason. You've cheered me up. Thanks."

I never knew where I stood with her.

"Don't look at me that way." She laughed. "Don't you know women are strange?" This time she was the one who embraced me, and I eagerly rushed in, tasting her mouth and running my hand over her breast. She matched my hunger with hers but then pulled back. "Slow down, Karl, please. I don't know how long he'll be out. He could come back at any moment."

"Why are you so scared?"

"Oh, it's nothing. He just can be so demanding at times. He wants to know where I go, who I'm with. I need a bit of breathing room. But he's wonderful in so many other ways."

"You're afraid of him, aren't you?"

"Aren't you, Karl?"

"No."

"Oh, really? If he walked in right now, what would you say?"

"I don't know."

"You see, you help him, you admire him, but you also aren't sure what to think of him. We're not all that different."

"Maybe not, but I don't live in his apartment." I hesitated before adding: "And what about, you know . . ."

Geli's eyes met mine with an unwavering gaze, and no remaining trace of tears. "What?"

I couldn't summon the courage to respond honestly.

"Did Emil tell you something yesterday before he quit?"

"No."

She stood up. "If he did, don't believe anything. He has some strange ideas. Because he's still jealous, I suppose." She paused. "It's a good thing Uncle Alf didn't let me marry him when I wanted to."

"Look, I just wanted to know that you're all right. I want to help you."

Geli moved toward me, running her hand across my cheek. "You don't have to worry. I'm fine. But if I ever need your help, I know I can count on you."

"Is that all you want from me?"

"Oh, Karl." She kissed me again, allowing me to press her against me before lightly pushing me away. "You're almost like a brother to me."

"You certainly have some odd ideas about family relationships."

"I think you should go," she said frostily, starting to turn away.

"Geli, I'm sorry. I just think about you all the time, and I worry about you. It makes me think and say stupid things at times."

She relented slightly, turning back toward me. "Why do you keep saying you're worried about me?"

"When I watch you with your uncle, you have this strange look sometimes."

"Oh, Karl, as if you're the cheerful one, always laughing. Can't a girl be lost in thought?"

"It's something else, too."

"Yes?"

"I had this dream about you last night."

"What kind of dream?"

"Look, you're right: I'd better be going."

But she took my hands in hers and stood blocking the door. "You can tell me, really you can. Whatever it was, I won't mind."

"You sure?"

"Yes, absolutely."

So I blurted it all out, not sparing any details.

"You did talk to Emil, and you believed him." Her fists struck my chest. "You bastard, what kind of a girl do you think I am? Who do you think you are?"

"Geli, I didn't say I believed the dream," I said, backing away from her blows. "I didn't even want to tell you. You were the one who made me."

"Get out!" She yanked the door of her room open and shoved me through it. "Don't come back again. Never, I warn you."

"Geli, please, listen to me."

At that moment, we both heard the front door opening. Hitler entered. I stood there paralyzed, but Geli was already in front of me, rushing to greet him. "Uncle Alf, can we go for a drive today?" she asked in a cheerful voice.

"You know I can't today," he replied, but his gaze rested on me. I tried not to show my discomfort; I was convinced that I was failing miserably.

"That's too bad, the weather is so beautiful. You remember Karl—Private Naumann?" She didn't wait for an answer. "He left his cap here before we went out shooting yesterday and came to pick it up. He also was kind enough to ask whether I'd like another lesson."

"Would you?"

"No, I learned all I needed." She laughed. "Besides, a girl can only do so much with a gun."

"I'll be going now," I added. "Sorry I forgot my cap." I nodded to Hitler, who didn't respond.

Geli held open the door. "Bye-bye," she said in the same cheery voice that she had used to greet Hitler. "Thanks again for the lesson."

As she closed the door behind me, I heard her pattering on in the same voice, though I couldn't catch the words. I walked down the stairs, out of the building and, I was convinced, out of her life.

Chapter Fifteen

"Do you feel any remorse?" the prosecutor asked.

I knew what my answer should be. "No, none at all."

My lawyer looked away, dismayed. But I felt a rare moment of elation. It felt liberating to speak the truth, nothing but the truth.

In Sabine's tiny apartment, it was impossible to stay apart for long. When I came home late one evening after she had already gone to bed, Leo barked, and she whispered, "Come here." I gratefully accepted the invitation. But as much as I wanted her, and wanted to make amends, I never fooled myself into believing that I regretted Geli. As much as I tried to push her out of my mind, she was always there—an alluring, maddening presence that hovered in Sabine's apartment as well.

On a sunny Saturday morning, I slipped out of bed early. By the time Sabine awoke, I was back, emptying my bag on the table as Leo sniffed the contents. "Wine," I announced. "Bread, sausage. Everything we need for a hike in the woods on a beautiful spring day."

Sabine stretched and responded with a luminous smile. "I'll be ready in a few minutes." She looked at Leo, who was watching us expectantly. "You'll go, too."

We caught a ride out of the city, ending up not far from the area I had taken my Hitler Youth groups. We made our way through fields covered with blossoming wildflowers, some of which I picked for Sabine, who put them in her hair, and then we entered the woods.

Leo bounded ahead of us most of the time, and it was when we were in an area of heavy foliage and older trees that I abruptly signaled Sabine to halt. "Leo, Leo," I called out quietly.

"What's the matter?" Sabine asked, mystified but keeping her voice low.

I pointed past Leo to a group of trees.

"I don't see anything." Then she looked again. "Oh, my God," she added, dropping her voice and gripping my arm tightly. "I've never seen one before."

Blending perfectly into its surroundings with its gray-brown colors, a wild boar was standing impassively, watching to see if Leo would approach.

I called Leo again in a soft but insistent voice. At first he ignored me, but then he backed off, giving the boar a wide berth. "Come on," I said to Sabine. "Just keep walking."

When we were clear of the animal, Sabine let out an audible sigh. "How dangerous are they?"

"Usually not dangerous at all. But if you run into a mother with a baby, forget it. And often you don't see the baby. I've heard that a boar can throw a big dog—much bigger than Leo—right over her, breaking its back."

Sabine let that sink in. "I'm glad I'm with you."

We picked a spot for our picnic and settled onto our blanket. I poured the wine into two small glasses I had wrapped carefully in a rag before putting them into my knapsack. I reached for Sabine's hand and kissed it. "To us," I said, raising my glass.

She smiled and took a sip. "Yes, to us."

It was after I had offered the bread and sausage and we had eaten our fill that she reached for my hand. Leo crouched nearby, waiting for the scraps he knew would come his way.

"Did you mean it?" she asked.

"What?"

"The toast."

"Of course I did. Sabine, I love you. I really do."

She met my gaze and squeezed my hand tighter. "And what about her?"

I wanted to deny it, but I couldn't get the words out.

"Who is she?" Sabine persisted.

"All right, but the question should be: Who *was* she?"

I didn't give a name, and I didn't tell anything like the whole story. But I admitted that I had flirted with a young girl who was related to one of the Nazi officials.

"Just flirted?"

"Yes, that's it. I swear."

"So it was nothing?"

I explained that it was no more than a brief infatuation when Sabine and I had been drifting apart.

"But you made love to her?"

"No," I insisted, shaking my head. "What did I just say? It was nothing, no."

Sabine dropped my hand, tucked her head down between her arms with her elbows propped on her knees, and didn't respond. I tried to approach her, but she held up her hand. When she finally raised her head, she was biting her lower lip, but there was nothing indecisive in her voice. "Tell me this, and answer me honestly this time: Is it over for good?"

"Yes, absolutely. Whatever it was—and it wasn't much—it's over. I only want to be with you."

This time when I reached out for her, she didn't stop me.

Our peace lasted for several weeks, until I heard from Otto again. "The moment we talked about has arrived," he wrote. "I need you in Berlin—as soon as possible."

Sabine erupted when I told her that I was going on party business to Berlin, and that I didn't know how long I'd be away. "It's always your crazy politics that matters, your Hitler—not us, not me," she told me. I tried to assure her that Otto was probably summoning me to prepare for the break with Hitler. She didn't believe me. "You've said that so many times, but you're still in the party, still wasting your life, still playing your games."

"Fine. You know, I'm glad I'm leaving."

"Good, just go," she said. "Maybe you're going with her, or to see her."

"Sabine, stop it. This is about politics, nothing else, I swear."

"I don't know if that makes it better or worse."

I was tossing a few belongings into my knapsack, and I didn't reply, letting my self-pity wash over me.

"Karl . . ." she murmured.

"What?" I snapped.

She looked at me carefully for a moment, evidently searching—but not finding—whatever she hoped to see there. "Nothing."

I could see the tears in her eyes, but I ignored them. We slept in the same bed that night but perched uncomfortably at the opposite edges. The next morning I left without saying another word.

On the train ride up to Berlin, I felt angry and sorry for myself. Angry with all of them—Sabine, Geli, Hitler. Yes, I had tried to banish Geli from my thoughts, I had tried to prove to myself as much as to Sabine that I was forgetting her. But I wasn't. Once Sabine had startled me by lighting a candle as we sat down for dinner. Instead of enjoying a romantic evening, I had withdrawn into myself.

Hitler had to have some hold over Geli, I reasoned, something that explained why she was still in his apartment, why she was attracted to others—Emil, me—and then cast them off. I realize now, as I look back, that my fight with Geli only made me more ready than ever to side with Otto in his looming showdown with Hitler. I didn't have to think anymore about which side I'd be on.

The May afternoon was unusually warm as I began my trek from the railroad station to Otto's place. I caught a tram and, through a window, saw a girl with short blond hair standing on one of the chairs of an outdoor café, cranking the awning shut. With her face flushed red, she wasn't particularly beautiful, but something about her compact body, her sturdy legs and determined expression, reminded me of Geli. And triggered a momentary vision of our bodies intertwined, the girl hungrily taking me in. Enough, I told myself. But I kept looking back through the window until she disappeared from view.

Otto offered me a cot in the back of his small apartment for the first couple of nights, promising to arrange something better later. As always, his desk was awash in papers—manuscripts, leaflets and books. Almost as soon as I arrived, he picked up one sheet from the pile. "You know what this is?" he asked.

I shook my head.

"An order from the Reich Party executive signed by Hitler himself. It forbids—mind you, *forbids*—any party member from backing the strikes in Saxony. Not that it's going to stop us. We're continuing to support the strikes in our publications. But look what we've come to."

He sat back, letting the sheet float back into the pile, and lit a cigarette. "I don't like all this cabaret fare in Berlin," he added. "It's mostly degenerate and defeatist. But I have to tell you, I think Brecht is really on to something."

He must have seen the blank look in my eyes. "Brecht, Bertolt Brecht," he repeated. "The playwright. I forgot, you're from Munich —maybe not everyone knows him there the way they do here. Anyway, he does have a gift for lyrics, the kind that capture a feeling, a moment. Listen to this: 'Do everything tonight that is forbidden. When the hurricane comes, it'll do exactly the same.'" He paused. "It does feel like a hurricane, but we have to make sure it blows in the right direction."

He flicked his ashes in the general vicinity of the overflowing ashtray, oblivious to those that landed on the desk among the papers. "Your timing is very good: We'll know soon enough which way things are blowing. I'm about to see Hitler—to continue our friendly chat, I'm sure," he said, chuckling sardonically. "He's in Berlin, and right before you came, I was summoned for another meeting. It should be interesting."

·   ·   ·

I wasn't there when Otto had his final showdown with Hitler, but I felt I almost was. Hess had called Otto to set up the "urgent" meeting at the Hotel Sanssouci. Hitler hated the city, was always much more comfortable in Munich, but he admired grand old hotels like the Sanssouci and the Kaiserhof, holding court there for hours on end. In Otto's case, it was for most of a day. I know what happened, or a lot of it, because Otto asked me to help write up a report on their meeting. He was determined to have his own version of events on record to counter the attacks he knew would come from Goebbels and others.

Hitler met Otto in the lounge of the hotel, offered him a seat and started off in a conciliatory tone. He was most impressed with the reports he had received about Otto's publishing house, the *Kampfverlag*. So impressed that he was ready to pay 180,000 marks for it, enough to allow Otto to live very comfortably for a long time. Otto flatly turned it down.

Hitler immediately abandoned any pretense of civility. Otto's publications, he charged, were "a public disgrace," "an insult to the party program," and they contained articles that "infringe the elementary laws of discipline." "The *Kampfverlag* will go into voluntary liquidation," he announced. "If you refuse your consent, I shall proceed against you with all the means in my power."

"Herr Hitler," Otto responded, "I am quite prepared to talk things over, but I refuse to accept an ultimatum."

Hitler backtracked, claiming he didn't want to lose a valuable party member like Otto and that it was simply a matter of discussing their disagreements. "Surely," he said, "we can come to an accommodation—for the good of the party." He tried flattery: Otto was a gifted young man, the kind the party needed. He could become press chief, he suggested—so long as they settled their differences.

The ensuing conversation touched on almost every possible subject, but Hitler kept steering it back to one theme: race. Even when the subject was art. Hitler insisted that Otto had no understanding of art.

He argued that there was only one kind of art—Greco-Nordic art, he called it—and that nothing else could be considered art at all.

"How do Egyptian and Chinese art fit that theory?" asked Otto.

Hitler conceded that the Egyptians and Chinese had produced some masterpieces. "But that doesn't prove there was such a thing as Egyptian or Chinese art, since they hadn't been produced by a homogeneous race," he lectured as if explaining the obvious. "Their bodies were those of inferior races. It was the Nordic heads on them that were responsible for all their masterpieces."

It was race that explained everything, Hitler argued over and over as they meandered through philosophy, religion and other subjects. The guiding principle of Germany's foreign policy, he said, should be the Nordic race's right to dominate the world. When Otto objected that Germany must seek allies that served its interests, Hitler was appalled. "Never with Russia—a Slav-Tartar body with a Jewish head," he insisted. Instead Germany would take over Europe, leaving the seas to England. And in Germany a "master class of men" would rule, knowing they were entitled because of their superiority over all others.

Otto warned Hitler that his ideas were "a flagrant contradiction of the great mission of national socialism," and that they would destroy the German people if implemented. But Hitler was contemptuous of Otto's "liberalism." "All revolutions have been racial," he said. "I know because I have studied them all."

In an attempt to steer the discussion back to the economic issues he cared most about, Otto argued that he was opposed to both Marxism and capitalism, but he couldn't see that Hitler was equally committed to the battle against capitalism.

"Tell me, what do you propose—nationalization?" Hitler scoffed.

"Exactly," Otto replied. "Major industries must be nationalized, as we spelled out in the party program in Hanover."

"The party immediately refuted that program," Hitler reminded him. "That would be pure Bolshevism and would destroy the German economy. You'd destroy all human progress."

Otto pointed out that Hitler's own program contained a mention of nationalizing property, but Hitler made a dismissive gesture.

"What would you do about Krupp? Would you nationalize it or leave it alone?" Otto persisted.

"Of course I'd leave it alone," Hitler responded without hesitation. To do anything else, he maintained, would trigger the destruction of Germany's powerful industries. Without companies like Krupp, the country would never be able to rebuild its economic and military might. Only industries that didn't serve the German nation would be nationalized. "Loyal German industries should have, and will have, nothing to fear from us."

"How can you call yourself a socialist?" Otto protested.

"How can you call yourself a patriot when you want to destroy German industries to uphold Bolshevik ideas? Don't you realize Strasserism is dead? Your brother realized this, although he, too, is a Strasser. He understands there can be only one führer. Why can't you learn the same lesson?"

Both men fell silent. Hitler stood up and began pacing back and forth, lost in his thoughts. Then he stopped before Otto's chair. "Party members don't decide anything," he said. "I won't have anything to do with a debased form of democracy and all its cant about equality. The führer is the embodiment of our idea, he defines national socialism and he must be obeyed." He looked straight down at Otto, who remained seated. "I must be obeyed. Do you, as a party member, swear to obey the führer?"

Otto drew himself up, and Hitler involuntarily took a half step back—but their faces were still only a small distance apart. "No, I do not," Otto replied. "It's up to each party member to decide whether the führer and the idea are one."

Hitler sank back into his chair and rubbed his knees in a strange, almost frenetic circular motion. When he spoke, it was more like a public pronouncement than a conversation with Otto. "Discipline is everything in any organization, in any country, and your ideas would mean an end to all discipline. No crazy scribbler will destroy the party. Here you are, a man who could have become press chief for the whole Reich anytime you wanted, and instead you've decided to throw everything away." His voice dropped almost to a whisper. "Everything, absolutely everything." Without saying anything more, he stood and walked out.

There was no public announcement about the confrontation between Hitler and Otto, and no immediate word from Hitler as to what the consequences might be. Otto and I half expected a swift attack on the publishing house, and he put me in charge of a group of guards who kept watch twenty-four hours a day. We had little to do at first, though Otto's publications kept up their support for the strikers and lashed out at Hitler for his alliance with the industrialists.

But Hitler hadn't forgotten his threats. Over the next few weeks, several of the contributors to Otto's publications were expelled from the party. As usual, it was Goebbels who did the dirty work, allowing Hitler to keep his distance. "There's only one way to deal with this: to confront Goebbels directly at a party meeting and win the others over to our side," Otto told me. But when he tried to attend a meeting of Berlin party officials in early July to debate Goebbels, SS blackshirts blocked his entry. Inside, a few of his allies tried to speak, but each was cut off with a warning that they were the subjects of a party inquiry. Several of the delegates left the hall in protest.

"No more pretense, no more games," Otto told me that evening. "I'm leaving the party. There's no possibility of reaching any agreement with that man."

I helped make copies of the telegram Otto sent Hitler in early July: "Herr Goebbels has expelled certain of my colleagues from the party. At yesterday's meeting, on the flimsiest of pretexts, he deprived others of the right to speak. If these measures are not revoked within the next twenty-four hours, I shall consider myself and my friends to have broken with the party."

I considered myself one of those friends. When Otto told me this meant splitting with his brother, who was staying in the party, I was disappointed in Gregor, not Otto. That feeling was reinforced when word got back to us that Gregor was calling Otto's fight against Hitler "pure madness."

"We'll see who's mad," Otto declared.

"Who's Caligari, right?"

He offered a wan smile. "So you've figured that out."

When Hitler didn't respond to his telegram, Otto and the rest of us formally broke ranks. The headline of our paper, which Otto wrote himself, announced on July 4, 1930: SOCIALISTS LEAVE THE NAZI PARTY.

There weren't many of us. Otto valiantly proclaimed the formation of a fighting unit of "revolutionary national socialists" whom he named "the Black Front." But many of the people he had counted on —the members of the Strasser faction—saw Gregor's decision to stick with Hitler as justification for them to stay on as well. Besides, as Otto bitterly noted, Hitler was now rolling in money from his industrial backers. As a result, he had no problems paying his followers and the SA and SS troopers who also remained on his side.

In the September Reichstag elections, the Nazis abruptly emerged as the country's second largest party. With 18 percent of the vote, they had garnered 107 seats—up from the mere 12 seats they won two years earlier. The party had clearly reaped the benefits of the worsening economic crisis. At the first session of the new Reichstag on October 13, the Nazi MPs marched in wearing brown shirts, and each answered the roll call with: "Present, *Heil* Hitler!" Gregor Strasser announced that the party was willing to abide by the rules of the Weimar Republic "as long as it suits us." On the same day I saw SA troopers, out of uniform but several of whom I recognized, smashing the windows of Jewish shops.

Otto explained that this anger was misdirected: It needed to be focused on the big capitalist bosses who were really responsible for exploiting the German workers' desperate situation. That was the message he continued to espouse in his publications that I was both guarding and distributing. Although our circulation was smaller than it had been before the break, Hitler and Goebbels still treated us like dangerous enemies—which only convinced us that we should fight harder and that we might yet succeed in bringing more party members over to our side. Hitler denounced Otto as a Bolshevik, and Goebbels even claimed that he was working for Moscow.

If the Black Front didn't succeed in recruiting many more members from Hitler's party, it did begin to attract some younger men who shared our hatred of the Weimar Republic and capitalism but had always remained suspicious of the Nazis. We were patriots, we insisted, dedicated to our country, not one man. Instead of "*Heil* Hitler," we greeted one another at meetings with "*Heil* Deutschland!" I may have envied the Nazis their growing success and recognition, but I felt part of a new fraternity and didn't regret my decision to remain at Otto's side.

Not even when we were attacked. Otto and I were returning one evening to his apartment from a Black Front meeting when we were surrounded by a group of young men. Someone threw pepper into my eyes, blinding me. I took several punches to the stomach and face, and I felt the sharp edge of a knife graze my arm, which I had been flailing about. "The first man who moves is dead," I heard Otto shout.

The punching stopped. I managed to open one eye and saw Otto crouched with his Browning pistol pointed at our attackers. One of them brandished a club and another a knife, but they had no guns. They ran. Otto fired a shot in the air and came over to me. "They won't get rid of us so easily," he declared, still pointing the Browning in their direction. "Not so long as I'm carrying this. From now on we should be armed at all times."

After that incident, Hitler and Goebbels continued to attack us in their publications, but remarkably, we weren't assaulted physically. My life began to feel almost normal—back to the routine of standing guard, distributing publications and attending Black Front meetings. I can't quite explain what happened, even now. Maybe Hitler had decided that, at a time when he was seeking to present a more respectable image, he didn't want to be associated with violence as before. Maybe he didn't consider us as much of a threat, since our group remained small and fairly isolated. Whatever the case, I sometimes felt like a soldier without a real war.

"Here's something for you," Otto said, handing me a letter. "It came to my address: Maybe your wife has decided she wants you back." I looked at the handwriting; it was familiar, but it wasn't Sabine's. I retreated into a corner and tore it open.

Dear Karl,
I don't know if this note will reach you, since I don't have your new address, and no one here wants to talk about you. But I know that you're together with Otto Strasser in some sort of party that opposes my uncle, and it wasn't difficult finding out where Otto is.

I can't write much here. But I want to talk to you, if that's possible, if you can ever come to Munich. I'm sorry about the way we parted. I can't stand the thought of your thinking badly of me. If you do come, don't come to the apartment. Go see my friend Renate, who lives where I lived before—on Thierschstrasse. She can be trusted.

Yours, Geli

"So she wants you back?" Otto asked.
"Maybe—I'm not really sure."
I read the letter again, and then once more. When I finally looked up, I felt that my face was flushed. Otto was smiling. "There's only one way to find out, you know. Go to Munich and talk to her. We'll manage without you for a couple of days—and maybe she'll decide to move here with you. You didn't take a vow of celibacy when you joined the Black Front."

"Thanks." I nodded, feeling less than honest about what I was doing. I doubted Otto would care if he knew the letter wasn't from Sabine, but I couldn't imagine that he'd react the same way if he knew it was from Hitler's niece.

Chapter Sixteen

*I heard so many of Hitler's speeches, so many of his declarations and ex-
hortations. But the one that stuck in my mind was "There is no higher
justice, only the right that man himself creates." I had felt inspired by
this proclamation at first. But then I began to recognize that Hitler was
replacing the concept of "man" with himself, and that he was using this
credo to justify destroying anyone who tried to stand in his way. Now I
can only wonder why it took me so long to catch on.*

I rushed back to the small room Otto had rented for me, stuffed a few
belongings into my knapsack—along with my Browning, which I
wrapped carefully in a shirt—and caught an overnight train from the
Anhalter Station.

By the time the train arrived in Munich the next morning, I must
have reread the letter a hundred times, especially "I'm sorry about the
way we parted. I can't stand the thought of your thinking badly of
me." Was she saying she wanted me back? Or that, as she had written,
she just wanted to talk to me? It had to be the former, I decided. She
wouldn't otherwise have risked a letter to a known opponent of her uncle. And if that was the case, was she free of her uncle's spell?

I made my way through Munich's familiar streets to Thierschstrasse, barely noticing my surroundings, although I remained vaguely
alert to the possibility that I might run into Sabine. But I didn't see
anyone I recognized, and I quickly entered Geli's old building and
took two steps at a time up to the third floor.

I knocked and waited. There was no response. I knocked again, louder, and heard a shuffling behind the door. A bleary-eyed, tall young woman in a brown robe opened it partway, keeping her right hand firmly on it. "Who are you?" she asked. "Do you know what time it is?"

I suddenly realized it wasn't even seven yet. In my rush from the train, I hadn't considered the time. "My apologies," I said. "But if you're Renate, I had instructions to contact you. I'm Karl Naumann."

"What instructions? From whom?"

"Geli."

The woman opened the door the rest of the way and stepped back, revealing the bed I remembered so well. "Come in. I wasn't prepared for company at this hour, but you're more than welcome." She smiled for the first time. "You'll just have to examine the wall for a few minutes while I get dressed."

I happily did so, already envisaging Geli coming to meet me.

"You can turn around," Renate said. Now sporting a dark skirt and a loose cream-colored blouse, she looked strikingly attractive as she reached for a brush and began stroking her long dark hair. "I'll be out of your way in just a couple of minutes. I'm going off to work, but I'll let Geli know you've arrived. You'll wait here?"

"Of course I will."

She looked at me with amusement, still brushing her hair. "Of course you will. For Geli, who wouldn't?"

When she left, I walked around the small room, peering repeatedly out its window, watching the trams rattle along Thierschstrasse at regular intervals. I strained to see as far up and down the street as I could, figuring that I would spot Geli as she approached.

I lay down on the bed, trying to keep my imagination in check. Nothing worked. I kept imagining Geli rushing in and throwing herself on me, and in a moment I was back at the window, disappointed that there was no sign of her.

One hour went by, then two, then three, and I began to wonder if I'd see her at all that day. Maybe she'd had second thoughts; maybe she hadn't meant what she wrote in her letter, or had written it as a lark. Maybe Hitler had somehow found out I was here and was arranging for his thugs to take care of me. What if she had lured me into a trap?

In the middle of the afternoon I reluctantly opened the door and peered down the stairs. I closed it again and paced back and forth in the narrow space between the bed and the wall, telling myself that she wasn't coming but still delaying in the hope that she would. Just then I heard the door open and spun around. There stood Geli, with her keys still in her right hand and a harried look on her face that was instantly replaced by a flirtatious grin. "So you really came. Was it just for me?"

I nodded and opened my arms, but she only pecked me on the cheek. "You're so good to do this."

"Why are you so late?"

"I know, I'm sorry. But I couldn't get away sooner, you know how it is." She looked around the room with a distracted air. "You must be starving: Did you have anything to eat?"

I reached for her shoulders and made her face me directly. "I don't care about that—I came to see you."

I tried to pull her close, but she took my hands off her shoulders, drew them together and put her lips to them. "Karl, wait."

I wasn't listening. I cupped my hands on her face and kissed her, pulling her tightly to me. She tried to push back, but I wasn't going to be stopped. I kept my arms around her, kissing her harder than before; her mouth remained semiclosed for a moment, then yielded fully and filled mine with the pungent taste I associated with the woods where we had played hide-and-seek. She didn't resist when I maneuvered her onto the bed, where our bodies fused as explosively as the first time and the dream I had been dreaming ever since I had boarded the train to Munich became reality.

Geli rested her head on my chest. "Karl, Karl, Karl," she murmured. "It's been so long."

I would have stayed that way, just basking in the warm afterglow. But she rolled to her side and, before I could pull her back to me, spoke up in a very different tone, soft but insistent. "Karl, I need to talk to you."

"Talk. I'm here."

"You said before that you weren't scared of my uncle, or not much anyway. What about now—now that you've broken with him?"

Something in her voice shattered whatever was left of the spell. "No, not scared, but careful," I replied, now fully alert.

"Careful in what way?"

"I help guard our facilities. We don't take anything for granted."

"Have his people tried to hurt you?"

"Once they did. But we defended ourselves, and since then they haven't tried anything."

She was lying back on the bed, her arm tucked under her head as she stared up at the ceiling. I wanted to reach for her but thought better of it. "Geli, what's bothering you—what's happening between you and your uncle?"

"I'm planning to leave him, to leave Munich," she said softly. "To go back to Vienna. It's about time."

"Have you told him yet?"

She shook her head. "When he isn't giving speeches, he's busy with that Eva," she said irritably. "I saw a letter from her two days ago, thanking him for a lovely evening at the opera. Can you believe that— he took her to the opera instead of me?"

I hesitantly ran my finger over the blanket covering the contours of her body, but she didn't seem to notice. "Isn't it better that he's think-ing about other girls? Maybe now he'll leave you alone."

She abruptly buried her head in my chest. I let my right hand move down her back, across her buttocks and lower. I felt her tongue flicking across my chest and her hand reaching down until it found what it was looking for. I wanted to slide under her, but she abruptly pushed her-self away from me and slipped off the bed. "Come," she said and turned to the wall, planting her hands against it. I was up in a second and roughly thrusting myself into her. "Hey, slow down, gently."

I obeyed, momentarily. But then she was the one who pushed back, and her body arched again and again until we both couldn't hold it anymore. She pressed herself against the wall, and I slipped my hands in to cup her breasts, kissing her neck and shoulders. She turned, took my hands and pulled me back to the bed, where we dropped, facing each other.

She stroked my face, and when the words came out, I barely heard them. "I can't stand it anymore."

"Stand what?"

She didn't respond.

"What do you want to tell me?"

"I don't know."

"What does he do to you—is it what we quarreled about last time?"

"Yes, no, I mean, it's not what you think."

"Is it better or worse?"

Her eyes darted away from mine. "Worse than you can imagine. He makes me do these things . . ." She stopped and shook her head impatiently. "I don't want to talk about them."

"Are you sure?"

"I don't know." She was on the verge of tears, and I took her hand, kissing her fingers as she continued talking. "I hate those things, but they aren't what bothers me the most. It's just that he's always trying to prevent me from doing what I want, from seeing other people. He can do anything with me, with that Eva, with anyone else he feels like. And that Maria earlier, but she's disappeared."

"How disappeared?"

"Vanished, gone. I don't know what's happened to her, but there are rumors I don't want to even think about."

"What kind of rumors?"

She ignored my question. "I've had enough. You and those others broke with him; I can, too." She turned toward me with pleading eyes. "Isn't that right?"

"Of course it is," I assured her.

"Will you help me? I don't know anyone else who has stood up to my uncle."

"I'll help you, Geli."

She snuggled against me, and we lay still for a long time. When she began speaking again, I tried not to move, but I had to strain to hear her. "You remember your dream, the one we quarreled about last time?"

"Yes."

"Well, imagine the dream continuing. He commands the girl standing over him to crouch lower and lower, until he can see every detail—every detail that he'll then be able to draw. But before he gets to that stage, he wants more than just water to splash all over him. 'Let yourself go,' he begs the girl, and his face looks more and more contorted, twisted—I can't describe it. He is thrashing below the girl, holding himself and waiting desperately for the girl to obey. 'Hurry, hurry,' he shouts. The girl wants to escape but can't. She knows the only way she can get out of there is to follow his orders. When she hesitates, he reaches for his whip and—"

She tensed. "He doesn't have to use it, never has, as far as I know. It's enough that he reaches for it. And so she releases the stream he has been waiting for, and the happier he is when she does so, the more she hates herself, the more she dreams of being anywhere else." Geli drew a sharp breath, and a shudder worked its way through her entire body, which trembled even after it was gone. "That's her dream within the dream."

I held her until her breathing steadied. "You can escape, Geli."

"You really believe that?"

"Yes. I'll help you—I'll go with you wherever you want." She smiled and put her finger on my lips, as if trying to silence me, but I continued. "I can't stand the thought of your uncle being anywhere near you. I'll keep him away from you, I'll protect you, I won't leave you. Nothing else matters to me."

She sat all the way up in bed, the blanket falling into her lap. She looked more desirable than ever. "Oh, Karl, I didn't mean that. You shouldn't take anything I say too literally."

"What?"

She sighed. "You're so kind, and I do like the idea of your helping me if I need it. But I'll manage, we'll manage."

I looked at her, still uncomprehending.

"I have plans. You see, Josef and I are going to get married in Vienna."

"Josef?"

"Yes, Josef. He's a medical student, and he loves me. We have it all worked out." She picked up my hand, but if that gesture would have excited me a minute before, it did nothing now. I felt dead inside.

"Does this Josef have a beard?"

"Yes, how did you know?"

"I walked you to the café where you met him, shortly after you moved to Munich," I said, not hiding the bitterness I felt. "I suppose you were already making your plans back then."

"Karl, please, don't be like this. I'm really happy that I'll finally be able to lead a normal life. You have to understand that. It's normal for people to marry. You're married, remember?"

"But my dream is to be with you."

She stood up and started grabbing her clothes. "You don't believe in dreams, do you?"

I stood up, too. "Shouldn't I believe your dream?"

Her face betrayed a moment of hesitation. "Look, I get carried away at times. The only part you should believe is that I want to leave my uncle, that I want a normal life."

"A life without me?" I said, unable to keep the petulance out of my voice. "Why did you write to me?"

Geli was buttoning her blouse. "I'm sorry. I thought you could help me, as a friend. Which you did. You helped me make up my mind. I'll leave him."

I stood there glumly, not knowing what else to say.

Her face softened. "And it means so much to me that I know I can turn to you for help again if I need it." She paused. "Can't I?"

"Of course you can. But I—"

She put her fingers up to my lips. "I know."

I kissed her fingers once more, desperately wanting to find a way to hold on to her.

She stepped back. "We're friends, remember, special friends. My getting married won't change that. It never will."

She kissed me quickly, and as much as I hoped against hope that I was wrong, I knew it was for the last time.

Chapter Seventeen

Once upon a time, I believed in something. Once upon a time, I felt a part of something larger than myself. And once upon a time, I thought a single life had little or no meaning. Now I know better, and how does this knowledge help me? Not at all.

The train ride was interminable, although it was a shorter route to Vienna than the others, which went via Breslau or Passau. I watched the stations go by on the way to Prague—Elsterwerda, Dresden, Bodenbach, Bad Schandau and Aussig. I couldn't read anything but the station signs, and I didn't eat much except for a couple of rolls with cheese that I had brought along. I wasn't interested in food, drink or anything else. All I could do was stare out of the window, oblivious to the landscape rolling by, vaguely aware that we were following the Elbe and climbing higher as we approached the border with Czechoslovakia. Someone told me many years later that this was a ride not to be missed for its beauty, but I didn't see any of it that day. After Prague, I ticked off the rest of the stops—Tabor, Böhmisch Wieland, Gmünd, Schwarzenau, Siegmundsherberg—but they seemed to crawl by even more slowly until finally I saw that we were entering a large city that could only be Vienna.

It was many months after my visit to Geli in Munich. Curiously enough, it was a visit that had ended in my reconciliation with Sabine, just as Otto had expected it would. After I had left the Thierschstrasse apartment, I realized that I didn't have the strength to catch a train back to Berlin. And I didn't have any place to stay in Munich. I ended up in front of Sabine's building, the building I had called home for so long. I stared at it and then marched up the stairs without any consideration to what I would say or do if she was at home. Or what I would do if she wasn't, since I hadn't thought to bring my key with me.

But she opened the door after my first knock, and we stood facing each other, neither of us knowing what to do. Luckily, Leo didn't have any of our inhibitions, and he jumped all over me, keeping me busy petting him as his tail excitedly swished back and forth. "Come in, Karl," she said finally.

I can't say what she must have been feeling then, nor did I particularly try to figure it out. My thoughts were still back there on Thierschstrasse.

"You look pale and tired," she said, examining my face. "Have you had anything to eat?"

I shook my head.

She had been frying potato pancakes and, within a few minutes, put them on a plate in front of me.

"What about you?" I asked.

"I'm not hungry—I ate something earlier."

I knew she was lying, but I didn't protest. I was suddenly ravenous and quickly dispatched the potato pancakes.

"Feel better?"

I nodded. "Thanks, I guess I was hungry."

Her lips turned up in a smile, but her eyes still looked at me sadly. There was something so tender, so gentle in her face, something so vulnerable in the way she sat across the small table from me, something so familiar and comfortable in the drab confines of the apartment that I found myself reaching my hand out to grasp hers.

I don't remember what I said to her then, how I explained myself or my behavior. There must have been an apology somewhere, probably a bumbling one, but something in it touched her, sweeping away the barriers that had grown up between us. All I recall from that point on is a sense of relief as I settled into her arms, and then how flustered I became when nothing happened, how I tried to explain to her that I was exhausted and how she reassured me that there was nothing to explain and nothing to worry about. During the early morning hours, I awoke aroused and ready, and she straddled me as she had done the very first time, simultaneously weeping and laughing, and all I could think was why had we been apart for so long. I told myself that Geli was the past, and Sabine was both a longer part of my past and my present and future.

It was truly amazing, the trust Sabine could still have in me. Within a couple of weeks, she gave up the apartment in Munich, quit her job in the doctor's office—an almost insane decision, it seemed, at a time when unemployment was huge and still rising—and joined me in the tiny one-room quarters that Otto had arranged for me in Berlin. She brushed aside my apologies about the meager living conditions. "It'll be better later, I'm sure," she insisted. "What matters now is that we're together." She also refused to become discouraged by the lack of jobs, maintaining that doctors always needed nurses. And sure enough, after weeks of searching, she convinced a doctor to hire her, although he paid her less than half of what she had been making in Munich.

During those early days with Sabine in Berlin, I still dreamed of Geli almost every time we made love—although I tried not to, since now it did make me feel guilty. Sabine was the one who, I'm still not sure why, wanted to be with me, and I told myself that Geli clearly never imagined doing the same, so it made no sense to keep brooding about her. We were poorer than we had been, but Sabine was regaining her old glow, her humor, her self-confidence, and I felt I was back with the woman I had fallen in love with a long time ago. Sometimes I succeeded in banishing Geli from my mind altogether.

But this period didn't last. I'm not sure when I sensed the old tensions returning. Maybe it was the night when we treated ourselves to a rare movie, and Sabine suggested we see *All Quiet on the Western Front.* I knew only that it was about the war, nothing about what kind of a movie it was. When the theater lights went on, I felt confused and angry. This couldn't have been a true depiction of how my brother fought and died, I told her bitterly. It made the war look senseless, like mindless destruction. Her eyes were still watery as she replied softly: "Isn't that true of any war?" "No," I snapped back. "You've got it all wrong."

As we emerged from the theater, there was shouting and shoving. I couldn't tell what was happening at first, but then someone beside us muttered, "Those brownshirts again—we'd better get out of here."

I saw them up ahead—a group of young men attacking the moviegoers in front of us. I pulled Sabine down as a rock crashed through the window of the theater behind us. I felt her shaking. "Run," I commanded, yanking her up again and rushing forward. One of the men tried to block our way, but I punched him hard, and he reeled away, providing us with an opening to escape. We ran across the street and down an alleyway, stopping only when we were alone. Sabine was gasping for breath, and I pulled her to me. I could still hear shouting and more crashing of glass. "Thank God you got us out of there," she said, clinging tightly to me.

We didn't speak more about the movie then. We spent that night wrapped in each other's arms, with Sabine drawing me into her again and again at the least sign of my arousal, even when I could no longer manage any more than a few weak thrusts before slipping out.

But the movie had restarted some of our old arguments, I realized later. After attacking theaters across the country, the Nazis managed to pressure the government into banning the film altogether, and I found myself in agreement with that decision. "You know I'm not with Hitler anymore, but he's right about that movie—it's a disgrace," I told Sabine.

"How can you say that? Was it right when they attacked us?"

"That's not the point."

We couldn't agree, and it wasn't only about the movie. Although I had told Sabine I was involved with Otto and his party, she had focused on my break with Hitler. When she began to realize that my life still revolved around politics, she again began to pressure me to do something else.

"We had these same discussions in Munich."

"I know," she responded. "And I thought you had changed."

"I have—I don't have anything to do with Hitler's party anymore. I'm no longer a brownshirt, you know that."

"Instead you're fighting them."

"Isn't that what you wanted?"

She shook her head. "I just wanted you out of all this. I just wanted you—and us—to lead a normal life." I heard the eerie echo of Geli's words, which only made me more reluctant to heed them.

Since those discussions went nowhere, we'd both try to change the subject. But Goebbels and his thugs weren't about to let us forget them. They began hunting Otto's supporters all over Berlin, and I was attacked on the street—this time taking much more of a beating before I managed to fight my way out. Two other members of the Black Front weren't so lucky and were beaten unconscious. At a crisis meeting, Otto instructed me and several other well-known members to leave Berlin and scatter for at least a few days to other cities, to drum up support and, above all, to get out of harm's way. He would use a hiding place in Potsdam, just outside of Berlin, during that time.

I told Sabine that evening that I had to leave right away, without telling her why. But she didn't need an explanation: She knew from my bruised face and from seeing me wrap up my Browning. "Karl, think about what you're doing," she pleaded. "How long can this go on?"

I said little beyond a terse good-bye. If I sensed she was right, I wasn't about to admit it. Besides, I couldn't disassociate myself from Otto and his party at that point even if I'd wanted to. Our enemies knew who we were.

My destination was Nuremberg. I wasn't known there, and we had received inquiries from a few men who also were disaffected Nazis. My mission was to contact them and see if they could organize anything on our behalf in a city where we had no real organization yet.

I knew the route well. It was the same train I had taken several times between Berlin and Munich; I'd just be getting off earlier. But this meant that the train carried passengers to and from Munich, which was why, when I reached down out of boredom for a newspaper that must have been dropped by someone traveling in the other direction, I came up with the *Münchener Post*. It was a paper I had scorned as a leftist rag that always attacked Hitler, but now that no longer mattered. In fact, I realized, I'd probably agree with most of what they'd have to say about the threat he represented. As far as I was concerned, they didn't know the half of it, and the saner half at that.

I almost grinned when I saw what I was holding, thinking about how much my situation had changed. Then a headline stopped me short. A MYSTERIOUS AFFAIR: SUICIDE OF HITLER'S NIECE, it read.

God no, I thought. No, this can't be . . . no. In a daze, I began reading:

In a flat on Prinzregentenplatz, a 23-year-old music student, a niece of Hitler's, has shot herself. For two years the girl had been living in a furnished room in a flat on the same floor on which Hitler's flat was situated. What drove the student to kill herself is still unknown. She was Angela Raubal, the daughter of Hitler's half sister. On Friday September 18 there was once again a violent quarrel between Herr Hitler and his niece. What was the reason? The vivacious 23-year-old music student, Geli, wanted to go to Vienna, she wanted to become engaged. Hitler was strongly opposed to this. The two of them had recurrent disagreements about it. After a violent scene, Hitler left his flat on the second floor of 16 Prinzregentenplatz. On Saturday September 19 it was reported that Fräulein Geli had been found shot in the flat with Hitler's gun in her hand. The dead woman's nose was broken, and there were other serious injuries on the body . . .

My eyes were swimming, and my head was pounding. I couldn't make out the words for a while, then I reread them. As my mind began to focus, I caught an obvious error. Geli didn't live in a flat on the same floor as Hitler's, she lived in the same flat. A small detail, I told myself, but didn't that mean some of the bigger things were wrong, too, that other things hadn't been falsified to avoid admitting embarrassing truths? I tried to convince myself that Geli might be alive, but then I had to admit that this wasn't something even a newspaper that hated Hitler could fake. But what about the suicide—was it suicide? How could they be sure? Where did the broken nose and other injuries come from? Geli had wanted to leave Hitler; had he tried to stop her with force or, realizing he couldn't keep her prisoner there, killed her himself?

My first impulse was to stay on the train all the way to Munich, to find out what had happened. And I might have done so if I hadn't had time to think it over. The pounding in my head gave way to a dull pressure. By the time the train arrived in Nuremberg, I had come up with a better plan. I'd be too easily spotted in Munich, and no telling what would happen then. The war between Hitler and Otto was deadly serious now. So instead, I stuck to my plan to get out in Nuremberg and meet up with the disaffected Nazis who were eager to prove that they could help our cause. I'll give them a way to prove themselves, I thought, a real-life test right away.

This was how I ended up sending one of them on that very same day to Munich, explaining that since he wasn't known there, he could safely carry out the mission. His assignment: to find Emil Maurice, the one person who might know the truth of what had happened, give him a message from me and then await a response. Otto would want to know the truth about Geli as much as I did, I told myself, so I wasn't acting purely out of selfish interests. Even if my concern was personal.

The fidgety young man, who hardly inspired confidence, performed better than I expected. The next day he was back, a big smile on his face. "The reply," he said, saluting and handing over a letter.

I hastily tore it open and read:

Tuesday, September 22, 1931

Dear Karl,

I know how shaken you must be by the news about Geli. I knew you were taken with her, although I'm not sure how involved you were.

If I had my suspicions earlier and resented you at times, I'm way beyond that now. Geli was too much of a free spirit to be satisfied with
just one man. Which, I suppose, may have ultimately been the reason she died.

You ask how she died. I don't know for sure. As best as I can tell,
Hitler really wasn't there at the time. They quarreled, as the papers
reported, and then he left. Or so go both the official and unofficial
versions of events circulating here. There are some rumors that she
may have been pregnant. I don't know about that, or who the father
would be if that were true. But it is true that she was planning to
leave for Vienna, and that she seemed happy about it. She had been
writing a letter to a girlfriend about her plans, and the letter was in-
terrupted in midsentence with no sign of trouble. Hitler's people are
spreading the story that she was to have some kind of musical debut
as a singer, and that she may have been frightened that she'd fail.
But there's no evidence to support that. And you know Geli—she
wasn't ever serious about any of her studies. I think they're just trying to cover up the real reasons, whatever they were.

All I know for sure is that she died from a bullet fired from
Hitler's Walther 6.35, the same one you taught her how to shoot. I
also know that there are plans to bury her in Vienna, at the Central
Cemetery. Her body was sent to Vienna yesterday, and I believe the
funeral will be held soon.

I wish we had managed to have that beer together before you disappeared. But I understand why you can't come here now. I'm still
safe; none of Hitler's people will dare touch me. They know I have
too much evidence that could be used against him, especially now.
But I doubt we'll ever know exactly what happened to Geli. God
rest her soul.

Yours, Emil

I read and reread the letter. First I focused on the pregnancy rumor
but then dismissed it. She had been happy, writing a letter to a girlfriend, breaking off in midsentence. Someone who is thinking about

suicide doesn't do that, I thought. And the talk about a musical debut was nonsense, as Emil pointed out. They were lying about everything. Hitler was lying.

I had slumped back against the wall of the room where I had met the messenger-recruit, and I realized that he was still standing there, looking at me strangely. I tried to pull myself together. "Good job," I said. "You've performed your first assignment very well. Now I have to return to Berlin."

"Already? I thought you said you'd be here for at least a few days."

"This changes everything. It's important information that our leaders need to have as soon as possible."

In reality, I hadn't decided what to do or where to go at that point. I just needed to get away, to be alone. I also needed to learn more. I wouldn't be able to do that, hiding in Munich, and it slowly dawned on me that going back to see Otto in Potsdam might be the most promising course of action. After all, Otto and Gregor, although now in opposing camps, were still brothers. I knew they hadn't cut off all contact with each other. Maybe Otto would know something. But it was too late to catch a train that evening; I had to wait another day.

It wasn't until two days later that I reached Otto in our safe house— an attic, really, in a dilapidated house owned by an elderly couple delighted to collect rent and rarely be bothered by tenants.

"Who is it?" Otto asked gruffly when I knocked.

He opened the trapdoor of the attic enough for me to see that he was holding a gun. When he saw I was alone, he opened it all the way so I could climb up. "Why are you back so soon?" he demanded.

I explained what had happened on my trip to Nuremberg, how I had learned about Geli. I showed him the letter from Emil, which he read and handed back to me. "You realize that you're thinking more about her than about your instructions? How well did you know her?"

I didn't reply, and Otto chose not to press further. "I heard the news, too. It wasn't just in the Munich papers, although that's where it got the biggest play."

"And what else do you know?" I asked.

"The same from the papers that you do. I did hear from Gregor, who says it's true Hitler had left the apartment and was on his way north to start another political speaking tour. When he heard the news, he was in Nuremberg, at the Hotel Deutscher Hof. Hess called him there, but the phone connection was bad, and he wasn't sure if Geli was alive or dead. Hitler rushed back to Munich, where he was too late to do anything but answer a few questions from the police. And then issue denials to the newspapers that he and Geli had quarreled."

"I don't believe him," I said stonily.

"Sure, he's probably lying. Especially about the quarrel, since his servants even testified about that. But who knows?" Otto shrugged. "At the very least, this should make people think twice about him."

"What else do you know?"

"The funeral has already taken place in Vienna." He looked at me carefully and appeared to be making up his mind about something before he continued. "I received an interesting tidbit, not from Gregor, mind you. I still have a few other sources in Munich."

"Yes?"

"Hitler is speaking today in Hamburg, but then he's arranging a secret visit to Vienna. He'll have to go quietly, without his usual full escort of heavies, since the Austrians don't want any incidents. He wants to go to the grave."

I reached for the trapdoor.

"Where are you going?" Otto demanded.

"I don't know," I lied as I began climbing down from the attic. Over my shoulder, I added, "I need a bit of time to think all this over."

But I already knew exactly where I was going. Which was why on early Saturday morning, September 26, I was on the train pulling into Vienna.

Chapter Eighteen

Intimidated by the majestic buildings and elegant boulevards of Vienna, I summoned the courage to stop an old man and ask him for directions to the Central Cemetery. He directed me to a square between the Kärtner Ring and the Schubertring, where I found the tram that he had instructed me to take. It headed straight away from the city center, skirting the Belvedere Palace and its imposing gardens, then propelled me along the Simmeringer Hauptstrasse past smaller buildings, factories and poorer-looking shops that proved this city also had its ordinary sections.

If my mind registered these impressions on one level, on another it was preoccupied with a different reckoning. If Otto's information was correct, I'd soon see not only Geli's grave but also Hitler. Unless he had somehow arrived faster than I believed possible, or had abandoned his plans to pay his last respects.

Last respects—the very notion that he would think in those terms made me tremble with anger. I had gone over everything I had heard again and again, and I had found little reason to trust his story. The lie about Geli living in a different flat was the least of it. In his letter of reply to the *Münchener Post*, he had denied not just that they had quarreled but also that she was engaged and wanted to marry in Vienna. Instead he insisted on the crazy story that she was "tortured by anxiety whether she really had the talent necessary for a public appearance" and wanted to see a voice specialist in Vienna. Of course, he said, he had raised no objections.

If those lies were so obvious, what about the lack of a precise time of death? The only doctor allowed to examine Geli had declared that she died during the night of September 18 but not at what time. Even if Hitler had left the apartment, as appeared to be the case, couldn't he have returned and shot her? Why would she stop writing a perfectly normal letter in midsentence and then shoot herself? And what about her other injuries?

The high brick wall of the cemetery came into view, stretching as far as I could see. I was confused, not knowing whether I should get off right away or later, since there were obviously several gates. I asked an old woman clutching a bunch of already fading tulips where the main entrance was. I noticed her unkempt hair and the wild look in her eyes only when she responded, and I thought she might give me the wrong directions. But when I followed her instructions and got out at the next stop, I found myself in front of a gate flanked by two large pillars. Immediately inside was the two-story administration building she had mentioned.

Although it was a mild, overcast day, I shivered and drew my jacket closer around with one hand as I continued holding my small bag with the other. I hesitantly approached the main door to the administration building and stepped inside. A man behind a counter barely looked up from his paperwork. "Yes?" he inquired.

"I'm here to find out about the funeral of a cousin of mine," I stammered. "Or where her grave is."

"Well, which is it?" he asked impatiently. "Are you looking for a grave, or do you want to know about a funeral?"

"You see, the funeral was a couple of days ago."

"Talk to Father Johann. He handles most of the funerals around here. You'll probably find him in the chapel."

I went back outside and made for the chapel a short distance away. As I approached, a thin, balding priest came out and started to walk past me. "Father Johann?" I asked, doffing my hat and falling in step beside him.

The priest didn't break his stride. "What can I do for you, my son?"

"I'm here to find the grave of my cousin," I said, clinging to the cover story that I had just concocted. "I missed the funeral because the news reached me late, but I want to pay my last respects."

"What's the name of your cousin?"

"Angela Raubal."

Father Johann stopped and turned to look at me carefully. "You really are her cousin?"

I nodded.

"Well, you did miss the funeral. It was two days ago. But you can find her grave by taking path four to lot twenty-three." He pointed to the right of the entrance where I had come in. "It's the second section beyond the gate. The family has already put up a headstone, so it's easy to find. Besides, I hear you won't be the only visitor this morning."

"Is that right—who else is coming?"

"Apparently her famous relative, too, but I have to respect the privacy of everyone involved, you understand."

"Of course," I said, then hesitated. "May I ask you one more thing?" I felt my throat constrict but managed to get the words out. "Did Geli really commit suicide, as they say?"

Father Johann drew himself up and cast me a cold, dismissive look. "I don't know what church you grew up in, but in our church we don't give funerals to people who commit suicide." His eyes swept across the graves stretching out in all directions. "This is holy ground—it's not for people who don't understand the sanctity of life." Without another word, he marched off.

I stood frozen in place for several minutes. I knew next to nothing about Catholicism, but something in what he said revived an old memory of a beer-hall discussion in Munich. Some of the Berliners had been teasing the Bavarians about having a religion that didn't even allow them to kill themselves. Uwe had made a stupid joke about how you could do a good deed by killing a Catholic who wanted to put himself out of his misery, since otherwise he'd go to hell. I hadn't given it any thought then. Father Johann had said that priests didn't give Catholic funerals to suicides. Which meant Geli hadn't committed suicide. Which could mean only one thing.

What I remember next is standing in front of the fresh grave, feeling hot and slightly ill, with a foul taste in my mouth. My eyes watered, and I blinked several times to clear them enough to read the words:

HERE SLEEPS OUR BELOVED CHILD
GELI
SHE WAS OUR RAY OF SUNSHINE
BORN 4 JUNE 1908 — DIED 18 SEPTEMBER 1931
THE RAUBAL FAMILY

Sleeps, I thought bitterly, repeating the incongruous word to myself several times. This was really Geli, maybe not my Geli, maybe not anybody's Geli, but the Geli who had pressed herself against me under the tree as we hid from the others, the Geli who didn't hold anything back when she decided to love me, at least for a time, who claimed to love me in her own way even when she was planning to be with another.

I dropped to one knee—not to pray, since I didn't know how, but to brace myself. I felt sickened by another thought. What if Hitler had asked me to teach her to shoot so that, as he told the authorities, he could convincingly explain that she had used his weapon before? What if he had used me to prepare his alibi?

I suppose part of me recognized that this didn't make much sense, that it was too far-fetched. But I had taught her to shoot, hadn't I? To shoot the gun that would bring her to this grave. I found myself suddenly on both knees, asking Geli for forgiveness—for teaching her to shoot, for not finding a way to help her escape Hitler and Munich as I had promised to do if she asked, for abandoning her, for not saving her. I suppose I recognized even then that she was the one who had left me, insisting that we couldn't really be together, but it didn't help. Not at that moment, not at her grave.

Shakily, I stood up. At almost the same moment, I saw the figures approaching on the path I had just come on—Hitler walking first, then two burly men whom I didn't recognize. But that was hardly surprising, since I had been out of Hitler's circle for some time now.

I ran in the other direction, dodging among other fresh graves as I moved away and then circled farther back into the cemetery where I could observe his movements from behind. Hitler must have said something to the two bodyguards, because they abruptly stopped as their boss continued forward. I had maneuvered myself back to the other side of path four, crouching behind a large headstone in an older part of the cemetery. From there it would be only one large step to get back on the path that Hitler would have to take when he returned to the main gate.

For some reason, my hands were completely steady as I reached into my bag and felt for the Browning. It was there, all right; its cold metal felt reassuring to my touch. I grasped it in my right hand and thrust it under my jacket, leaving the open bag near the headstone that provided my protection. I looked again in the direction of Geli's grave. The two bodyguards were pacing nervously between me and Hitler, who stood with his back to all of us, almost immobile, in some world of his own. Once or twice I saw his head sway jerkily back and forth, and once his shoulders twitched, but nothing more.

I have no idea how long he stood there. Time meant nothing to me then. All that mattered was my resolve, and I felt its presence every moment as I calmly surveyed my surroundings and plotted my escape route. I'd avoid the main gate, I decided, since that was where they would expect me to go. Instead I'd retreat as far back as I could into the cemetery, skirt the chapel from the far side and then make for the corner of the cemetery where the wall could be first seen from the tram, where there was no gate. The wall, I figured, was about three meters high. I'd find a way to get over it.

A slight but noticeable tensing of the two heavies drew my attention back to them and to Hitler. He had turned from the grave and was walking haltingly toward them, stumbling at one point. One of the bodyguards rushed up to help him, but Hitler brusquely shook him off and muttered a command. The bodyguard's right arm shot out in a familiar salute, and he returned to his companion. The two conferred, and one pointed toward the gate and ran off in that direction, passing close enough for me to hear his labored breathing as I crouched behind the headstone.

I looked back at Hitler and the remaining man, who was now several steps in front, nervously scanning the path. An older couple was up ahead, and he picked up his pace to make sure there would be no problems. Like his colleague, he passed almost close enough for me to reach out and touch him.

"Step back," he ordered the couple.

"Who are you to give me orders?" the man protested.

I was vaguely aware that they were still arguing and that the old man's wife had entered the fray as well when I saw the top of Hitler's head over the headstone. I jumped out in front of him. "*Heil* Hitler!" I whispered, just loud enough for him alone to hear.

His eyes looked uncomprehending, glazed. But as he halted, he saw the gun, and I saw the momentary fear and anger. "You?"

I raised the gun and fired. One shot to the chest, but that must have hit lower, because he clutched his stomach. As he doubled over, I fired again, and the top of his head exploded in blood. He dropped into a heap as if a mysterious giant hand had suddenly clutched him and jerked him down from below.

I ran, faster I'm sure than at any time in my life. I heard the shouts and shots going off behind me, but I followed my plan of plunging deeper into the cemetery, dodging behind the bushes and graves and circling behind the chapel. As I emerged on the other side, I thought I had lost my pursuers and bolted straight down the path running parallel with the brick wall. Suddenly I heard shots again and felt a sharp stinging sensation in my right arm. I simultaneously realized I no longer had my gun and that my arm was covered with blood. But that didn't prevent me from accelerating my final sprint. I saw the wall meeting at right angles before me, at the corner of the cemetery, with a large headstone conveniently situated almost right up against it. "Get him!" I heard someone shout. I vaulted off the headstone and managed

to grasp the top of the wall, almost slipping back as the pain shot through my right arm, but then I reached the top and came crashing down the other side onto the street.

I tried to get up and felt an excruciating pain in my ankle as I tumbled onto the sidewalk. I tried again, but by then two policemen were standing over me with guns drawn. "Just stay on the ground," one of them warned me. "Don't move."

I couldn't anyway.

Postscript

I was lucky, I suppose, that the Austrian police got to me first. If Hitler's men had beaten them to it, I never would have survived. Instead the Austrians arrested his bodyguards, since they had given permission for them to cross the border with Hitler only if they'd come unarmed. They were furious to have been deceived.

I was lucky, too, that the Austrians arranged good security at my trial. When one of Goebbels's thugs stood up and fired a shot in my direction, the police quickly wrestled him to the ground. That incident probably reinforced the judge's lack of sympathy for Hitler. Mind you, he didn't approve of me, either; the Austrians were angry that, as they saw it, German political warfare had spilled across their border. Their immediate assumption was that I was motivated by politics, by Otto's peculiar left wing nationalism. I remember the headlines: SPLINTER GROUP ASSASSIN KILLS HITLER and SOCIALIST REVENGE. I wasn't about to disabuse them, since I had no desire to begin explaining Geli, Hitler and Geli, Geli and me.

And I've probably been lucky to be in prison these seven years, long enough for Goebbels and his cronies to fail in their efforts to keep the Nazi Party alive in the aftermath of Hitler's death. Now that Germany is ruled by a military government, the party has been banned. It's probably safe to go home, where I'll find a job that will make me as inconspicuous as possible to avoid reminding anyone of who I am and what I did. A tram or bus driver, perhaps, since I never learned a trade like fixing automobiles, which I had once envisaged as my future.

But what's home? Sabine isn't waiting anymore. She'd been patient long enough, and after all, I had abandoned her altogether to avenge another woman—a woman I had claimed was no longer a part of my life nor meant anything to me. When I had heard the news about Geli, I could think only of her, abandoning Sabine in my thoughts as well as my deeds.

I've spent these seven years in prison thinking about that other woman, about Geli. And I keep coming back to the same conclusion: Hitler killed her.

Maybe not directly, as I thought at first, as I thought when I pulled the trigger. I only later heard about the speeding ticket his driver received in Ebenhausen on the night of her death, which appeared to corroborate the story that Hitler did hear the news in Nuremberg and then raced back to Munich. But so what? If he didn't kill her directly, he drove her to it.

How? I'm still not sure. "I can't stand it anymore," she told me without ever explaining exactly what "it" was. There was her version of my dream, but she told me I shouldn't take it literally. Then again, maybe there was more to the dream rather than less. Didn't her mood swings, her contradictory statements, her impulse to open up to me and then to push me away prove that she was still withholding so much? Was that what she was trying to tell me?

Whatever he made her do, she was his prisoner. Yes, she had liked her uncle's fame; she had liked the attention focused on her when she was with him; she had liked the nights at the theater, concerts, restaurants and outings. Maybe, in her own way, she both loved and hated her uncle. And yes, people had gossiped about her, calling her flighty, a flirt or worse. But who could blame her for enjoying the reflected glory of a local celebrity, for wanting to enjoy her life? She wanted to live it fully, and yes, she ultimately realized that she had to escape him to do so. She wanted her freedom. That's why, however it happened, she died. He was responsible, he was to blame.

So he deserved to die. He trapped her, and ultimately he killed her. Whatever anybody thought of her, she finally decided she wanted to lead a normal life. I know: not with me. I realized that even when she was still alive. But that doesn't mean I was able to shake her hold on me, and when I learned of her death, I couldn't let it go. She had been so alive, so much more than anyone I had ever met. And now I'm about to be free, but I feel my life is over, too. It died on the day the bullet pierced her heart.

EPILOGUE

In real life . . .

OTTO STRASSER fled the country as Hitler came to power in 1933, first to Austria and later to Canada. In his writings, including his autobiography, he continued to predict that the Germans themselves would overthrow Hitler. He returned to Germany in 1955, tried unsuccessfully to reenter politics and died in 1974.

GREGOR STRASSER remained in the Nazi Party when Otto broke with Hitler, but in 1932 he, too, quarreled with Hitler. Seen as a potential rival who was considered more moderate than his boss, Strasser fell out of favor and was gradually removed from most top decision-making sessions. On December 8, 1932, he announced his resignation from all party posts. In early 1934, with Hitler already in power, Strasser was given a special party award for his early role in the founding of the Nazi movement. But on June 30, 1934, he was among the scores of victims murdered in "the Night of the Long Knives," which would prove a foretaste of Hitler's reign of terror.

EMIL MAURICE, Hitler's former driver, served in the SS after Hitler came to power and later was the president of Munich's Craftsmen's Guild. He died in 1972.

ANGELA RAUBAL, or Geli, wasn't able to find peace in death any more than in life. Hitler brooded for a long time over her death and, after cleaning the blood stains, kept her room just the way she left it, allowing only a servant to clean and bring in fresh flowers once a week. He also commissioned a bronze bust of Geli, a copy of which he kept in the Chancellery after he took power. But he didn't make provisions to maintain her grave at Vienna's Central Cemetery in perpetuity. In 1965 the grave and headstone were removed, and Geli's remains were consigned to an unmarked section of the cemetery. Today there is nothing to indicate where they lie.

A Note on Sources

Although this book is a work of fiction, I drew on many accounts of the period to describe the early years of the Nazi movement, Hitler's actions and the still disputed circumstances surrounding the death of Geli. Karl Naumann is, of course, a product of my imagination, but he moves among real characters and real events. The boundary between fact and fantasy may be readily apparent in some cases and intentionally less so in others. But I want to both acknowledge the sources I used most extensively and, in a few cases, point out what is quoted directly from them.

I read and cherry-picked details from many of the standard Hitler biographies: Alan Bullock's *Hitler: A Study in Tyranny,* John Toland's first volume of *Adolf Hitler* and Ian Kershaw's first volume *Hitler: 1889–1936 Hubris,* to name those I found particularly helpful. The quotes from the report about Hitler by Otto Leybold, the governor of Landsberg prison, are taken from Kershaw's excellent study. Hitler's *Mein Kampf* was a valuable source in and of itself. I also found biographical details about some of the lesser-known figures in the early Nazi movement in more specialized German books like *Biographisches Lexikon zum Dritten Reich* and *Die Braune Elite II: 21 weitere biographische Skizzen.* And Eugene Davidson's *The Making of Adolf Hitler* yielded some information I didn't see elsewhere.

But the single most valuable source for the internal feuding within the Nazi movement was Otto Strasser's autobiography, *Hitler and I,* which was published in 1940 by Houghton Mifflin. In it, he described many of the scenes between him and Hitler that appear in the novel.

While I rendered them as I saw fit, I tried to stay largely with his version of the events, particularly when it came to describing Hitler's actions and words. In several cases, I used parts of conversations, as he conveyed them, intact or only slightly altered to fit my narrative. When they argued over nationalization, for instance, I wanted to adhere as closely as possible to their actual exchange—or at least to remain faithful to the main points of disagreement. I quoted verbatim Strasser's final telegram to Hitler, announcing his plan to break with the party.

Another very useful source was Ronald Hayman's *Hitler + Geli*, which painstakingly examines what is known about this tragic relationship. This is where I found, among other items, the *Münchener Post* report on Geli's death, which I quote directly, and the wording of the inscription on Geli's grave. Many of the details he provides about Geli's personality and behavior also inspired scenes in my book.

Many other books contributed to my feel for the developments and atmosphere of the period I describe. Among them: Otto Friedrich's *Before the Deluge: A Portrait of Berlin in the 1920s,* Anton Gill's *A Dance Between Flames: Berlin Between the Wars* and Christopher Isherwood's *Berlin Stories.* The English translation of Goethe's poem "The Diary" is taken from *Roman Elegies and The Diary,* a bilingual edition from Libris.

I was fortunate to be able to live in Germany when I was starting to write this book. Helped by Benedikt Weyerer's *München 1919–1933: Stadtrundgänge zur politischen Geschichte,* which explains what happened building by building, street by street, during this period, I set out to see what I could of Hitler's Munich. Thanks to the courtesy of the current tenant, on whose door I simply knocked, I was able to see the small room on Thierschstrasse 41 that Hitler lived in when he first came to Munich. When I went to see if I could take a look at the huge luxurious apartment on Prinzregentenplatz where Hitler lived after attracting generous financial support—and where Geli died—I was lucky again. The building was full of workers completely renovating the interior. Dressed in a jacket and tie and armed with a notebook, I was clearly taken as an inspector and didn't disabuse anyone of that notion. I exchanged *Guten Morgen*s with the workers and proceeded to examine Hitler's apartment—which has now been split into several offices—unimpeded.

My other important trip was to Vienna, where I took the tram to the Central Cemetery. Like Karl, I stopped in the administration building, where, after some initial reluctance, one of the bureaucrats confirmed the essential details about the history of Geli's grave—and why it no longer exists. I retraced the steps that Karl would have taken to where it once was, and then imagined everything else.

ANDREW NAGORSKI is a senior editor at *Newsweek International*. He was *Newsweek*'s Berlin bureau chief from 1996 to 1999 and its Bonn bureau chief from 1985 to 1988. The winner of two Overseas Press Club awards, he has also reported for *Newsweek* from Moscow, Warsaw, Washington, Rome and Hong Kong. He is the author of *Reluctant Farewell: An American Reporter's Candid Look Inside the Soviet Union* and *The Birth of Freedom: Shaping Lives and Societies in the New Eastern Europe*. *Last Stop Vienna* is his first novel.